**"MY PEOPLE
THE PI
BROGNOLA SAID.**

"Indian Point and Calvert Cliffs are their biggest and best targets to cause hysteria, even if they fail in the attempt."

"But they pushed up their timetable now that Phoenix Force stopped them in France," the President countered. "And then there's Syria. And when Damascus suffers from their own chemical weapons, the response will be worse than riots. They'll hit everyone who knew about their facilities, which means our people in Iraq and Israel."

The President thought about the pictures of the dead Kurds that had been used in the Fallen's threat video. "Europe's out of control, and America and the Middle East are under threat. If we ever needed a miracle, we need it now."

Price took a deep breath. "Luckily, that's Stony Man's job description. The Impossible missions."

The President nodded in agreement. "Things don't get more impossible than this."

DON PENDLETON'S

STONY

AMERICA'S ULTRA COVERT INTELLIGENCE AGENCY

MAN®

EXTINCTION CRISIS

A GOLD EAGLE BOOK FROM
W☉RLDWIDE®

TORONTO • NEW YORK • LONDON
AMSTERDAM • PARIS • SYDNEY • HAMBURG
STOCKHOLM • ATHENS • TOKYO • MILAN
MADRID • WARSAW • BUDAPEST • AUCKLAND

Recycling programs for this product may not exist in your area.

First edition December 2009

ISBN-13: 978-0-373-61988-7

EXTINCTION CRISIS

Special thanks and acknowledgment to Douglas P. Wojtowicz for his contribution to this work.

EXTINCTION CRISIS

CHAPTER ONE

Carl Lyons stopped at the edge of the wide puddle of blood, attempting to control his rage at the murder of a Department of Energy investigative agent. Mare Hirtenberg had been a beautiful woman, closing in on forty, but nothing pretty remained in her blood-spattered features, hazel eyes bulging out as her mouth was stretched and distorted in agony. The Able Team leader had been assigned to work with Hirtenberg for the past few days, reviewing infiltration attempts at nuclear power plants around the nation.

Hirtenberg had been Lyons's kind of Fed, a no-nonsense woman with a sense of irony and cynicism that appealed to him. But today, he had found her seated at her desk, her throat slashed.

The Able Team commander hit a button on his Smart phone, a speed dial command that would bring a Justice Department evidence team running. There was no hope for Hirtenberg, not with two gallons of blood painting the floor tiles and her desk. Paramedics would only be good for confirming the blatantly obvious fact that she was dead.

Something whirred softly on the other side of Hirtenberg's desk and Lyons drew the Smith & Wesson Military and Police 357 from its shoulder holster. He sidestepped the puddle of blood and saw something move Hirtenberg's lifeless leg along the side of the desk. He was able to notice two small darts embedded in her calf. Whoever had murdered her had utilized a Taser, directed just above ankle level. Theories of the Israeli Negev Nuclear Research Center break-in rushed to Lyons's mind. He briefly considered the possibility of a small trained animal slipping unnoticed through defenses.

Lyons snapped his MP-357 to eye level, brow furrowing as he realized that animals didn't have electromotors. A dull gunmetal-black tendril writhed as it disappeared around the base of Hirtenberg's chair. Not having a clear target, Lyons held his fire.

"Come on, show yourself," Lyons growled, tracking the floor.

Air pistons hissed and Lyons felt an agonizing jolt in his shin. A twenty-thousand-volt current blasted along a pair of fine wires, and the Able Team commander's entire body seized up. The paralyzing charge tightened every muscle in the former cop's body, including the index finger curled around the tuned, 6-pound trigger of the sleek new Smith & Wesson. The high-pressure .357 SIG round cracked loudly, a bark that was nearly as intense a bellow as Lyons's old favored .357 Magnum cartridge, and in a moment, the continuous Taser charge dissipated.

Lyons was physically as powerful as any two men,

but in the wake of a Taser jolt, even his mighty musculature went limp. Only his incredible athletic conditioning kept him from falling unconscious or careening
uncontrollably off the corner of Hirtenberg's desk. He
managed to catch himself on his hands and elbows, the
Smith & Wesson MP clattering from numbed hands.

At floor level, he saw a bulbous, insectlike head
staring at him. Two hexagon-patterned domes formed
eyes reminiscent of a dragonfly, and the only flaw in the
space between them was a smoking .357-inch hole.
Beneath the bullet entry, a rectangular turret dangled,
slender wires dangling from it like drool. The buglike
object writhed, twisted, as if recovering its senses at the
same rate that Lyons did.

"No, you don't, you little bastard," Lyons growled,
pushing off the floor. The metallic worm turned almost
completely over on itself, a nodule rising from a second
bulbous segment just behind the head. The Able Team
leader knew it was another weapon, and he reached
out, fist closing on a wastebasket. It was only a few
pounds, but to his Taser-hammered muscles, it felt more
like a few tons. He swung the metal receptacle in front
of his face before another air-piston hissed and an
electric motor whined to angry life. The wastebasket's
aluminum skin screamed as a deadly cutting wire
whipped at it. There was very little physical push behind
the miniature lash, but a gash appeared in the bottom
of the wastebasket from Lyons's point of view.

Mystery solved—time to get primitive, the former
LAPD cop thought. Lyons lunged, his wastebasket
shield bashing against the side of the metallic caterpil-
lar as its hydraulic whip continued to carve at the
aluminum bucket. The impact jarred the yard-long au-

tomaton, disrupting the slicing cord. The hydraulic whine ended, and Lyons reached around to grab the lethal worm.

The robot's blunt tail whipped around and struck the Taser-stunned warrior in the forearm with enough force to break a lesser man's bones. Lyons grunted, stunned as his limb was jammed into the floor. A second whip-lash of the heavy tail slapped aside the wastebasket and glanced off of Lyons's head. The robot flipped to its upright position, silvery metallic rollers dragging it rapidly toward a battered ventilation duct.

Cursing his weakness and vulnerability, Lyons knew there would be no way to catch up to the escaping automaton.

Hirtenberg's mechanized murderer had gotten away, but the Able Team leader vowed that whoever had built it would not live to celebrate his colleague's demise. If he had to battle to the end of the planet, he would get vengeance.

EHAN FARKAS WAS A TRUE son of Egypt, and as a soldier in the elite Unit 777 of the Egyptian Army, he would fight to the very end, attempting the impossible to protect his nation. In this instance, it was a slightly unusual case. He was stuck in the confines of a Peugeot station wagon with a young woman of obvious Euro-pean descent and two Americans of different ethnic backgrounds. The woman was known only as Atalanta, and she was obviously an agent of the Israeli Mossad. Top-secret joint operations between the two countries' agencies were fraught with intrigue and mistrust.

The two American men had been sent to engage in field training with Unit 777. The agent introduced as

Farrow was a tall, lanky black man, and Rey was a compact, muscular Hispanic. The two U.S. operators were considered friends of the antiterrorism unit, but Farkas had heard rumors from Muslim Brotherhood prisoners about the pair. A few months back, al Aksari and two of his allies had struck a brutal blow against the radical terrorist group as they were operating in Alexandria, supporting a central African militia. The two mystery men working alongside the legendary soldier had similar descriptions to Farrow and Rey.

The timing of this sneak-and-peek operation cemented Farkas's worries. A week ago, Israel had been thrown into a state of high alert by a security breech at the Negev Nuclear Research Center. Cairo had been informed of the "near event" in the reactor core. With a 150-megawatt reactor, reportedly capable of producing enough material for one hundred nuclear warheads, a near event generally meant that the world *almost* ended for several thousand people. Had the reactor gone critical, the effects would have been akin to the nightmare that was Chernobyl, except that the much smaller, more heavily populated nation of Israel would have had a much larger percentage of habitable land turned into an inhospitable radioactive deadland. Both Jews and Arabs would have been sickened or killed, not to mention an area stretching as far north as the West Bank and as far east as Safi would have been rendered unsafe for farming or livestock.

That kind of news left Egypt on edge, and Farkas was fully aware of the proximity of the particular Brotherhood cell they were watching to the Inshas Nuclear Research Center. The Inshas core was only twenty-two megawatts, and was part of a pilot program for Egypt to develop her own nuclear warheads. Still, a meltdown incident would produce carnage and weaken the country's standing in the Mediterranean community. All in all, if Farrow and Rey were the same high caliber of warrior that al Aksari was, then Farkas felt a sense of relief with their presence.

"We have movement," Rafael Encizo said. "They're loading a van." Encizo's cover name for this mission was Rey. His Phoenix Force partner, Calvin James, was using the cover name Farrow.

Farkas rested his fingers on the keys in the ignition. "All right. I'll give them thirty seconds' lead driving time before firing our ride up."

"Good plan," Atalanta said without a hint of irony or condescension.

"That's a strange stack of boxes that they loaded," Calvin James mused. "They don't resemble any weapons storage that I've ever seen."

"That would be too obvious, wouldn't it?" Farkas asked. "Police would know rifle crates if they saw them in the back of a van."

James frowned, his black mustache deepening the gloom of his expression. "But why would they use any kind of boxes to hide rifles? Gymnasium bags or standard luggage would be far more innocuous and just as easily contain assault weapons or grenade launchers."

"Well, what was the nature of the Negev break-in?" Farkas asked.

"This has nothing to do with that," Atalanta lied. Irritation sprawled across the Israeli woman's features.

Farkas rolled his eyes, deepening her annoyance.

"Grow up, Atalanta," Encizo snapped. "Farkas isn't stupid and he's not our enemy."

James nodded in agreement. "Don't let national pride get in the way of an international crisis. Once this is over, Israel and Egypt can go back to their behind-the-scenes pissing contest."

Tanya Kristopoulos, a.k.a. Atalanta, glared at the two American agents. She was a Greek-born Jew who had suffered the loss of family at the hands of jihad terrorists operating in her home country. She'd long ago put aside her anger at Arabs, but her allegiance to the Israeli Mossad had given her a perspective about operational security that bordered on paranoia. "Listen, just because the CIA can't keep a damned secret doesn't mean we have to accommodate your—"

Encizo put his hand up in front of her face to cut her off. "The Mossad doesn't know how the controls to the coolant tanks were sabotaged, except that someone used a 9 mm handgun to shoot up vital components. There were no signs of entry except for minor damage to ventilation duct covers that were too small for even a child to crawl through."

"God damn it, Rey!" Atalanta complained.

"Yell a little louder next time," James sneered. "The pricks loading the van didn't quite hear you."

"So no human could have entered the Negev plant, but somehow a handgun punctured pipes and wrecked electronics-packed consoles?" Farkas asked.

Atalanta's eyes narrowed. "How did you know about the pipes? You just asked about the nature of the security breech."

"There were enough rumors flying about, but very little was substantive enough to quantify or qualify what really happened," Farkas explained. "Rey filled in some holes in the theories that have been flying around Unit 777 and other national security agencies."

"Well, whatever broke in either had a magical invisibility cloak or was shrunk to doll-size," Encizo added.

"Invisibility cloaks are fantasy, not reality, Rey," Atalanta chided dismissively.

"Actually, no, they are real," James countered. "Tokyo University has preliminary technology in development that uses specially reflective beads and camera technology to render solid objects as see-through. That's just technology in the public domain."

Atalanta and Farkas both raised their eyebrows at that particular revelation.

"I doubt that the covert military optical stealth technology was utilized in the Negev break-in, though," Encizo added. "Rear-projection morphic imagery only limits your visibility. It can't phase you through bank vault doors or mask your scent and sound profile to highly trained attack dogs. No stealth fabric that we've encountered works against those particular measures."

Encizo and James had encountered truly remarkable technologies in their journeys around the world. There were few things that they had seen or suspected that could ever surprise them anymore.

Farkas frowned. "'Tis a stranger world than I've ever imagined. Perhaps a trained simian with a gun? I know that bats and dolphins have been trained and used to deliver sabotaging explosives to hard-to-reach areas."

"Any monkey small enough to operate in those particular ducts would have been roasted or frozen to death in various chambers," Kristopoulos reluctantly admitted.

"Plus, it wouldn't have had the intellect to operate a firearm, nor the strength necessary to trigger or handle the recoil of a 9 mm pistol."

Farkas turned his attention back to the suspects. They had just finished loading their van and gotten into the front. "We could just pull over their vehicle…"

"But what would keep them from blowing up their van to eliminate any evidence we'd capture?" Kristopoulos asked. "Remember, the Negev meltdown would have irradiated hundreds of miles, making it impossible to reach minimum safe distance without suffering debilitating, if not lethal, effects."

"Besides, we want to keep an eye on how these guys are doing this," James added. "Those men are only delivery boys, pawns."

"You've got that correct," Farkas agreed. "I know those two from our files. They're errand boys who get handed all manner of shit duty, as you Americans so colorfully put it."

"That's believable," Encizo said. "A lot more than some of the ideas we've been tossing around for the past minute. Okay, start her up."

Farkas fired up their Peugeot and the station wagon pulled out to track the Brotherhood's van as it drove toward the Inshas Nuclear Research Center. He couldn't shake the feeling of dread that filled his gut. Tonight, a twenty-two-megawatt nuclear reactor was going to be assailed by terrorists armed with a form of technology that sliced through high-tech and low-tech defenses like a knife through butter.

Tonight, a radioactive nightmare could conceivably come true.

DAVID MCCARTER LIT another cigarette to give his hands
something to do. The Phoenix Force leader hated to cut
short his vacation with Gary Manning and T. J. Hawkins, even if it was just a working holiday. The remaining members of Phoenix Force were in England to
engage in a little cross training alongside elements of
the SAS, so for McCarter it felt like a homecoming,
despite the bruises and aches he sported from martial
arts sparring with a crew of hardheaded Cockney
recruits who reminded the Eastender of himself as a
man in his twenties.

Still, the news of the French Department of Nuclear
Energy headquarters break-in was a sobering splash on
McCarter's reminiscences. Right now, in the regiment's
guest barracks at Hereford, they were awaiting news
from Barbara Price back at Stony Man Farm for permission to launch their Paris investigation without interference from DCRI, the French version of the FBI or
Homeland Security. As a British citizen, McCarter had
every right to hop on the Channel ferry or to board the
Chunnel train to shoot on over to Paris without much
paperwork, but he would have to undertake such a trip
unarmed and ill-equipped to deal with what had been
reported as a mysterious commando team raiding the
DNE offices with surgical precision.

The European Union's views on firearms ownership
by private citizens, no matter how sterling their prior
military service, was at best intolerant of people with
the determination to defend their lives. Of course, this
meant that McCarter's text message to a friend in Paris
would be what their operation hinged on if they couldn't
get official clearance. McCarter knew people around the

globe, and was able to acquire supplies of reliable weapons from them.

His cell phone burbled with a text message answer to his initial inquiry. What he read soured his mood.

"Can scrounge gear for you and your two friends. No Grand Puissants in inventory, alas."

The Grand Puissant was the French term for a Browning Hi-Power, one of David McCarter's preferred designs and his trusted companion across the globe for his entire professional warrior career. His comfort with the reliable, accurate 9 mm autoloader enabled him to squeeze every ounce of performance out of the classic design. Naturally, his disappointment sparked interest from his younger partner.

Hawkins read McCarter's screen, then checked the look on his commander's face. "Y'all make that sound like we'll be landing in the middle of a nest of ninjas the moment we were within sight of the Eiffel Tower. So what if you have to pack a Glock for a while?"

Gary Manning regarded the youngest member of Phoenix Force with a wry grin. "Once you've acclimated yourself to true perfection, attempting to cope with an egotistical Austrian's proclaimed flawless design is a troubling disappointment."

McCarter chortled. "Besides, I'd be happy to have a row with a troupe of Japanese in black pajamas leaping about with swords and what have you. They're so much fun when you head butt them and get their gobs all messy under those scarves."

The laptop with the teleconference software burbled to life. Stony Man's mission controller, Barbara Price, appeared on the screen, and she wasn't very happy.

"I wonder if she's grumpy over your lack of a Hi-Power, too," Hawkins murmured.

"Don't make me murder you in your sleep, lad," McCarter quipped. "What's wrong, Barb?"

"The big new French interior intelligence agency has been comparing notes with itself, and they decided they don't want to play with American-sponsored Interpol investigators anymore," Price replied. "Especially in matters of French nuclear-energy security breaches."

"We've been on good terms with both French Intelligence in the past," Manning said. "What is the problem now?"

"I'll tell you what the problem is," McCarter growled. "The head of the new amalgamated agency has his head up his arse. Though it's not as if the bloody wankers sitting behind the desk realize that they're telling us to sit this one out and leaving it to the second or third best in the world."

"Pride is unbecoming of you, David," Price admonished.

"Bollocks," McCarter continued to snarl. "It's the same 'I know what's best' shit that happens every time we have to work with some department. We go somewhere and some half-wit thinks he's the cock of the walk when he's just a flounder in a bucket."

"Well, Hal doesn't want you to get caught. And if DCRI sends someone after you, try not to maim them," Price ordered.

McCarter sneered. "Just a dent on their chin and a slap on the ass to run home to mother."

Manning pulled out his Smart phone and began the process of ordering Chunnel train tickets. "Looks like you're going to have to grin and bear it with whatever your mate supplies you."

"I don't care if it's a wooden shoe that I have to break off in someone's bum," McCarter returned. "It's time to show the DCRI how professionals deal with infiltrators."

Manning grinned. It was good to see a flash of the cocky McCarter. It was also an indication of how much the enemy was going to regret pulling an operation that showed up on the Phoenix Force commander's radar.

CHAPTER TWO

Lyons stood in the hallway, battered forearm wrapped in an athletic bandage to secure it in case the blow it had taken had resulted in a hairline fracture. The bandage would serve as a temporary splint until the forearm could be x-rayed. The Able Team leader didn't intend to remove himself from the crime scene until the technicians had all of the data they needed to track down the escaped robot's murderous masters. He had seen the killer, but he didn't know its origins and who had sent it. The evidence linking Mare Hirtenberg's murder to the rash of security breeches at international nuclear power plants was purely circumstantial, but Lyons couldn't dismiss the possibility that someone had used a compact mechanical assassin to penetrate the Department of Energy's Washington, D.C., offices with the same ghostlike ability of the saboteurs at the other plants.

Lyons's leg was still raw from where the Taser darts had penetrated his skin and pumped twenty thousand volts through his body. The Justice Department crime scene techs had collected the contents of two Taser cartridges that had been loaded into the robot's head section. There might have been more in the mechanism, in case the mechanism had encountered multiple opponents. A security officer, assigned to protect the DoE offices, approached Lyons, his step cautious as he caught the grim darkening of the big ex-cop's face.

"No sighting of the robot?" Lyons asked, putting aside his rage to speak with a fellow lawman.

"No," the security officer said. "It'll take us a while to get our own camera-mount robot here, and even then, it might not fit into the air vents."

Lyons's brow furrowed. "I'd get a bomb-sniffing dog team here, just to be safe. If the device did have a self-destruct mechanism, it wouldn't do much damage to the infrastructure of this building, but it could harm a mainframe or more personnel."

"We've thought of that possibility already," the officer replied. "But thanks for confirming that we're not completely paranoid."

"My teammates think otherwise, but I appreciate the sentiment," Lyons returned.

The office door opened and a covered body on a gurney rolled into the hallway. The coroner walked beside the body of Hirtenberg, having claimed the corpse for release. The Justice Department medical examiner met Lyons's gaze for a moment before the brooding Stony Man warrior looked down at the remains of a woman whom he'd befriended over the past few days.

"Cause of death was fairly obvious," Alicia Khan said softly. Her dark, elfin face was serene and sympathetic, large and soulful brown eyes steady in the path of Lyons's disquiet and angry grief. "Exsanguination due to laceration of the throat by an unknown weapon."

"I saw it in action. It was a metal wire spun on an electric-motor-powered spool," Lyons said. "The crime techs picked up trimmings of it with blood transfer from her."

Lyons didn't want to give in to the queasiness in his gut at the description of a friend's agonizing murder, especially in front of someone as sympathetic and empathic as Khan. He swallowed his disgust at how clinically he spoke of her end. "You might find traces of the wire on her vertebrae, since the wire cuts flesh and thin aluminum easily, but might have been stopped by heavy bone."

Khan nodded. "I'll run an X-ray in that area. Metal from garrote wires or knife wounds often transfers to heavy bone. You going to be all right?"

Lyons took a deep breath. Khan, a gorgeous woman in her mid-forties, was no stranger to Lyons. She was one of a team whom Hal Brognola, director of Stony Man Farm, kept on hand to deal with the aftereffects of a domestic operation undertaken by Able Team, Phoenix Force or even the Executioner. The Justice crew kept traces of Stony Man's covert operations well out of the public eye, but kept data on hand in case there was a prosecutable case left in the wreckage of Stony Man's cleansing flames.

For a woman who interacted with the dead, her empathy was outstanding. She could endure even the worst of Lyons's legendary rages, never steering away from providing him with a bridge back to humanity. Lyons managed a smile for her. "Thanks, Alicia, I can deal with the grief."

Khan nodded. "Catharsis is one thing, baby. Just don't hang on to the pain for too long."

Lyons nodded. "Then get to testing, Alicia. I have murderers to track down."

Khan stroked his cheek, a brief touch of tenderness from tigress to lion. They were both hunters, different predators in the same ecosystem, tracking criminals. While the medical examiner took to her chase with microscopes and spectrometers, Lyons's tools of the hunt were measured in twelve gauge and .357.

"Good hunting," she told him and returned to escorting Hirtenberg's body to the coroner's wagon.

The Able Team leader glanced one last time at the receding gurney, then left the hallway to meet up with his partners, Hermann "Gadgets" Schwarz and Rosario "Politician" Blancanales, also fondly referred to as Pol. Able Team had gone from investigation and paper-pushing mode to full-on pursuit.

THE DOOR PANEL on the side of the van rolled open and Hermann Schwarz felt the mass of Lyons's muscular form tilt the vehicle. He opened his eyes after receiving a slap on the shoulder from his best friend, Rosario Blancanales.

"Look busy, the boss is here," Blancanales said.

"Carl knows that I'm a slacker," Schwarz replied.

"A slacker who calculates quantum physics equations the same way most people do Sudoko," Lyons mentioned. "Actually, no. You don't even need pen or paper. Do you need a description of the murder-bot one more time, Gadgets, or have you already cobbled one together out of soda cans and twist ties?"

Schwarz looked over his shoulder and looked back

at his commander, attempting to imitate Lyons's moments of annoyance. "Oh, fecal discharge, Rosario, my good man. The honorable Mr. Lyons just paid me a compliment and we haven't even blown anyone up yet."

"Gadgets, I'm being sweetness and love right now because I am under the delusion that you will put my hands around the throat of the scumbag who took out a fellow cop," Lyons explained. "Do you want me to return that anger back toward you and your snarky attitude?"

Schwarz pivoted in his seat and handed over a clipboard. "No. I did not build my own copy of the robot. Seems we were out of guitar picks necessary for the stegasaur-style ridge plates. But I do have technical drawings that hypothetically reconstruct the device based on your description of its movements and external dimensions."

Lyons rewarded Schwarz with a tight-lipped smile as he accepted the stack of papers with twenty pages of sketches of motors and circuits. He leafed through until he came to a page depicting himself, clad in a bearskin, wielding a massive thigh bone, ready to smash the robot that had escaped him. Scrawled in a cartoon word balloon were the words, "Carl smash shiny worm!"

"Can I keep this for my fridge?" Lyons asked Schwarz.

The Able Team electronics whiz raised an eyebrow. "Sure."

Lyons carefully ripped out the page, removed the sketch of the robot, then crumpled the rest of the page and hurled it out the sliding panel door, where it landed in the gutter. Lyons stuck it under the front clip as an impromptu cover for the robot design notes. "Do you know who built it?"

Schwarz looked out the door of the van, even though the wadded sketch was long gone. "Attempting to narrow down the original designer of a robot is next to impossible. There are entire schools of kids who build these things, not to mention countless amateurs who enter them into battle-bot competitions."

Lyons nodded. "I'm growing disappointed."

"Ah, but Mr. Lyons, you asked for a designer, while I applied my mental powers to a more productive course of action, I thought outside of the box," Schwarz said. "There is room in the robot for a 5.8-gigahertz transmitter that can maintain a remote link."

Lyons smirked. "You've been monitoring that signal?"

Schwarz rolled his eyes. "But of course. Unfortunately, I've only narrowed down the broadcast to a nearby relay module."

Lyons looked through the windshield as Schwarz turned wordlessly in his swivel seat. Halfway down the block sat a brown delivery van with a popular company's yellow logo painted on the back door. Lyons looked at the license plates. "They forgot to forge plates with the proper business coding on them. That vehicle's only got stickers for nonperishable food delivery, not air freight."

Blancanales shook his head. "You with the electronics, and him with the memorizing every possible type of license plate. Are you two attempting to make me feel like a fifth wheel here?"

Lyons winked. "Nothing could match your seven hundred years of experience, Methuselah."

"We hadn't run the plates yet," Blancanales said, steering the conversation away from the fact that he was the oldest man in the van and on the team. "We simply tracked down the signal and I realized that there was no one on this street that had received a delivery, and no one had left that truck."

Lyons looked along the sidewalks. "I might just make detectives out of you two jungle fighters yet."

Schwarz sighed. "Detectives. That's why God and Al Gore invented the Internets, Ironman. To make actual gumshoe work obsolete."

Blancanales regarded Lyons. "Not going to tear the doors off of their van?"

"I want to see if they make a pickup instead of a delivery," Lyons replied. "Gadgets, you have a camera focused on the undercarriage of that truck, right?"

Schwarz looked back at Lyons, sincerely offended this time by the implication that he wouldn't have done what his leader had suggested. "You trust me to plant a bomb in a microcomputer in the space of fifteen seconds before thieves can run off with it, but when I'm sitting right behind a suspicious enemy vehicle, you doubt that I've already been recording it for the time it took for the CSI team to run all their fingerprints and blood-spray patterns?"

Schwarz flicked on a monitor attached to the dashboard before Lyons could answer. A high-quality view of the underside of the van was visible. "The monitor would have turned on because I have a sensor in the camera set up to activate at the first motion."

Lyons patted Schwarz on the shoulder. "You just earned the weekends of the Consumer Electronics Show and the Electronic Entertainment Expo free. Barring end-of-the world crises."

"Yay," Schwarz droned, trying to seem unexcited,

but Lyons knew exactly the kind of electronic geekery that went on for those two weekends. The monitor flickered, indicating a change in the ground-level camera view. "Okay, something just moved a storm grating in the shadow of the curb."

Lyons squinted at the ten-inch monitor. "Come on, you son of a bitch, show yourself."

The metal grille tottered, then flopped over. A bulbous, silvery head emerged from under the sidewalk. As Schwarz muttered about a downgrade of hydraulic efficiency from Lyons's gunshot, movement on the sidewalk drew the Able Team leader's attention. A man was pushing a stroller down the street.

"It should have been able to push the grating over a little more easily," Schwarz commented.

"I'd hit it with my .357 Smith," Lyons said distractedly, watching the man and the toddler walk closer to the delivery van.

That brought a grin to Schwarz's face. "Able Team. Travel the world. Meet technological wonders. Shoot them to pieces."

"'Kin A," Lyons agreed softly.

The robotic inchworm crawled toward the center of the truck's undercarriage. A panel opened above it, and two hands reached down to grasp it.

"We've got the bas—" Lyons began.

"It's a segment too long," Schwarz cut him off.

Lyons's attention flitted from the monitor to the father and child on the street. He exploded out of his seat, jumping to the sidewalk and charging toward the delivery truck. He didn't need an explanation about the nature of Schwarz's grim, sudden warning. He took off from the Able Team van as if launched from the barrel of a gun as fast as his powerful leg muscles could propel him.

"Carl! Wait!" he heard Blancanales call out.

It was too late to stop Lyons as he drew upon his high school and college football conditioning to rocket him down the sidewalk with explosive speed. Each thrust of his powerful leg muscles carried him closer to the delivery van and the two bystanders who were now even with the stopped vehicle. The young father looked up from his child in the stroller, seeing the human freight train barrelling toward them both. Lyons unfurled his massive arms and scooped up father and infant. The Able Team commander twisted himself so that his broad back would absorb the shock wave that he expected to erupt. It came an instant later, the brown metal skin billowing out. Thankfully the hull of the truck was not pre-scored metal so that when it split due to the rupturing overpressure of the exploding robot, no shrapnel flew from the delivery van, though Lyons had his Kevlar on under his shirt and jacket. Lyons's forward momentum had carried all three of them past the torn vent in the side of the truck, sparing the trio exposure to a gout of flame that vomited through the wound in the vehicle.

Outside, in open air, the pressure wave had space to roll and disperse, sparing the Able Team leader and the two bystanders. The men inside of the truck would have had no such dispersal as the atmosphere inside of the vehicle could only compress so much before it crushed the bodies it was trapped with. Any living leads had been pulverized by the self-destruct mechanism in the robot.

"Y-you saved us," the man stammered.

Lyons set down the stroller, unhooking the crying

toddler within. He handed the girl off to dad after a quick examination for shrapnel injuries or possible burns. The father had suffered a scraped elbow, but the baby had been shielded from sidewalk rash by Lyons's body and her crumpled stroller. "Just calm your little girl down and go home."

"What…is this, a terrorist attack?" the man inquired.

"No. It's just a couple of crooks being silenced by their boss," Lyons explained. "You didn't see anything, but don't stick around, all right? Just make sure the kid's fine."

The girl's wails subsided as her father cradled her. "Thank you."

Lyons nodded and waved him off.

Schwarz and Blancanales had run up to the gutted van, but the heat of the fire inside kept them at bay. Lyons jogged back around toward his partners, phone already in hand.

"Barb, we have an explosion four blocks north of the Department of Energy offices. Get on the press and the Justice Department and start spinning that it's organized crime related, and totally independent of the murder of Mare. Keep this from being released as a terrorist attack," Lyons said to Stony Man.

"You found the robot?" Price asked.

"Yes, and it had a self-destruct mechanism inside," Lyons told her. "We won't get anything from the punks who delivered it."

"I'll put word forward to Calvin and Rafael," Price replied. "They're following another van with a mystery load in the vicinity of Inshas."

"Relay to them that the robot I encuntered had built-in Tasers and a wire whip that cuts through aluminum and flesh like butter," Lyons added.

"Given the Israeli situation at Negev, the robot they might encounter could have a firearm built in, as well," Price said. "You lucked out."

"Didn't seem so lucky for Hirtenberg," Lyons growled. "Send Alicia to pick up our crispy critters here. And give her my apologies for two call-outs in one day."

"You sound like you're not coming back to the Farm," Price mused.

"No. I know the van builders who might have crafted the fake delivery truck," Lyons said.

"We haven't even run the plates off of Gadgets's video footage," Price replied.

"I know the D.C. area chop shops and kinky garages like the back of my hand, Barb," Lyons countered. "We beat cops don't like waiting for slow shit like Web searches."

Price laughed. "All right. Khan's team is on the way to the blast site. D.C. Metropolitan Police has been advised to control the area and allow you egress from the crime scene."

Lyons looked up at the police helicopter that was already watching the area. "Good. Just to be safe, tell Alicia we may have a third corpse pickup for her."

"I'll convey your apologies," Price said. "Flowers and candy, too?"

"And reservations for dinner," Lyons added. He turned to Schwarz and Blancanales. "Mount up, soldiers. It's time to kill people and break things."

"Enough investigation?" Blancanales asked.

Lyons nodded. "Now it's time for prosecution."

Schwarz grinned. "Prosecution to the max, baby."
Able Team drove off, ready for war in the streets.

CALVIN JAMES, RIDING IN the backseat of the Peugeot
station wagon with "Atalanta" Kristopoulos, answered
his satellite phone's chirp on the first ring.

"Farrow here," James said, using his cover name.

"We have news from across the pond." Barbara Price
opened the conversation. "Ironman and his boys encountered some delivery men just like yours. Their
special present was a two-fold surprise."

"Whatever it is, it had a self destruct mechanism,"
James deduced. That brought sharp stares from the
others in the station wagon.

"All right. Only one surprise," Price corrected herself.

"It was a robot?" James inquired.

"Here's the surprise. It's been rigged with antipersonnel defenses, and was utilized for the assassination
of an investigator that Ironman was liaising with," Price
explained. "It gave Ironman a pounding with Tasers, a
wire saw and its tail boom."

"Tail?" James asked.

"It's a worm- or snake-shaped robot, which probably
allows for greater flexibility through vents and drainage
pipes," Price said.

"Okay. That makes sense. I was imagining one of
those modified radio-controlled cars or a rebuilt lawn
mower device like the battle bots that show up on British television," James said. "So the delivery men don't
control the robots themselves?"

"No, but they do sit on a remote signal relay," Price
told him. "Gadgets and Bear agree that the command
frequency is beamed through a tight focus point, which

allows the signal to penetrate concrete and steel over short distances."

"The usual structures of a nuclear power plant would interfere with the robot's reception," James agreed, following Price's logic.

"Precisely," she said. "A narrow-band, high-energy transmission allows for real time control in a power-plant campus or even your average office building."

"And these things are rigged for fighting?" James continued.

"Ironman was tased, and when the saw got snarled on a wastebasket he used for a shield, it nearly shattered his arm with its shield," Price recounted. "But that was the extent of its offensive weaponry."

"So it's agile and tough to escape our favorite caveman," James said.

"Carl put a .357 SIG round into it and was only able to take out the robot's Taser battery," Price described. "I'd hate to see what would happen if the Taser were replaced with a Glock."

"Chances are, that's what we'll have to deal with," James muttered. "Thanks for the heads-up on the destruct mechanism, as well."

"It's enough to kill everyone inside of a Grumman Kurbmaster," Price added. "But Carl was only fifteen feet from the van when it exploded, and came through unharmed. That's not to say the destruct mechanism can't produce its own shrapnel."

"Add in constant monitoring, presumably through built-in cameras," James said.

"Just built-in cameras?" Encizo asked from the Peugeot's shotgun seat. "Ask mother hen if she happens to have an eye in the sky over our position."

"Just satellites." James relayed her answer. "And they don't see anything in the air."

Farkas spoke up. "That's the point of remote observation drones. If they showed up on radar and aerial cameras."

"Figures," Kristopoulos grumbled. "Robots belly-crawling on the ground and flying in the air over our heads."

"It's only observing us so far," Encizo said. "But if they warn the Brotherhood members in the van or if it has weapons of its own, we're screwed."

"We are hanging back far enough that the drone operator may not think we're following their people," Farkas offered.

"If they are paranoid enough to put a set of eyes in the air, then they're too smart to leave our continued trailing of their deliverymen to chance," Encizo countered. "We were made long before I ever noticed their bird."

"Well, that's the end of a perfectly good surveillance operation," Kristopoulos said. "What would be their response?"

"Anything from scorched earth to the Brotherhood engaging in evasive maneuvers," James said. "But the deliverymen don't seem to have deviated from their normal course."

"Maybe they want us to know," Farkas said. "After all, how do you defend against armed, murderous robots?"

Encizo brought his field glasses to bear on the back of the Muslim Brotherhood van. "The back door just moved."

The Cuban drew his Glock 34 from its spot in a

cross-draw holster under his photographer's vest. He heard Kristopoulos and James do likewise in the backseat.

"We might not know how to prevent robots from infiltrating a nuclear power plant, but a pissed-off terrorist with an assault rifle is practically a Friday-night get-together for us," James said.

A hundred yards ahead, the muzzle-flash of an AK-47 burned. Even as the windshield cracked and deformed under the first impact, Farkas swerved hard to avoid the rain of shattered glass and steel-cored bullets tearing into their vehicle.

CHAPTER THREE

Rafael Encizo crouched tightly in the passenger's seat of the Peugeot as Farkas swerved. Bullets cut through the windshield and metal frame holding up the roof of the automobile before slicing the air over his head. Centifugal force and the anxiety of 7.62 mm rounds snapping past so close that his black hair flew with their passage made him grip the Glock 34 Tactical pistol tightly in his fist. Only his index finger resting on the dust cover kept the point-and-pull weapon from discharging from muscle tension. The idea of a handgun versus a Kalashnikov didn't appeal to the Cuban Phoenix Force veteran, even though the G-34's five-plus-inch barrel milked every ounce of range, power and accuracy out of the 9 mm round it fired. The polymer pistol still lacked the punch and reach of a .30-caliber rifle.

"Damn!" he heard Calvin James bellow from the backseat.

"Are you hit?" Encizo called back.

"Got cut by flying glass!" James snarled. "Farkas, pull over. We'll get our big guns from the trunk."

"No can do!" Farkas returned. "The Brotherhood is coming back around!"

The station wagon squealed its tires as Farkas spun the vehicle away from the enemy van. Its roof and all of its windows were blasted into a sieve of shattered glass and perforated metal. The hostile truck went into full reverse, backing toward them. The Peugeot ground to a halt, and Encizo realized that he was facing the stern of the Brotherhood's van head-on. If this was an old naval battle, Encizo would have been in position for an unopposed salvo on the vehicle, but in a modern assault-rifle battle where he'd only brought a side arm, he was a sitting duck, even behind the door of the station wagon. The gunman in the back poured on more fire. Encizo winced as a round, slowed by the car door, plunked into the Kevlar he wore. The body armor barely protected his stomach from the awesome punch of the Kalashnikov bullet. In response, Encizo thrust the Glock out of the passenger's window and blazed away. A half-dozen rounds jetted out of the extra-length barrel and speared through the night at the enemy gunner, each shot going off as fast as Encizo could pull the trigger.

From the back, James and Kristopoulos added their firepower to the fusillade of 9 mm clatter against the Muslim Brotherhood vehicle. The handgun rounds just didn't have the same oomph. Rather than punch through the door that the enemy gunman was using for cover, they merely dented the metal, and they weren't even able to smash the window through which they could see the silhouette of his head. The rounds only smacked starred impact craters in the glass. Sure, the fifty-yard distance lessened the penetrative punch of their bullets, but as the Brotherhood van drew closer, a second rifle-man poked his weapon out of the passenger's window.

"Hit the gas!" the Cuban shouted. The Peugeot station wagon shot forward, avoiding the twin streams of full automatic thunder. The rifles clattered as their owners swung the muzzles of their weapons in an effort to keep up with Phoenix Force and company.

Encizo levelled his Glock now that he had an angle on the open, passenger's-side window of the enemy vehicle. He ripped off four fast shots, and while he couldn't hit the head or the torso of the Egyptian gunman inside, he was able to break the killer's arm with three lucky hits. His last bullet clanged off of the AKM's receiver. Forearm bones splintered and muscles chopped into a bloody mess of shredded mead and the Egyptian terrorist let his weapon clatter into the dirt road.

The Brotherhood van swerved hard as the Peugeot swung for a brief moment, parallel to the enemy vehicle. Phoenix Force and their allies were the only ones able to open up, this time taking full advantage of the broadside they had been presented. At the space of ten feet, the Glocks had more than enough punch to tear through the van's thin metal skin. James, Encizo and Kristopoulos unleashed a torrent of rapid-fire handgun rounds into the hostile van, the Peugeot's interior filling with smoke and thunder. Though no handgun could be fired with the speed of a submachine gun or assault rifle, the three warriors were more than able to pour on a storm of copper-jacketed lead that slashed across the van's passenger side. The wounded rifleman's head snapped violently as it caught a 9 mm slug cored through his temple. The enemy vehicle jerked violently as blood and brain matter flew into the driver's eyes, shocking and blinding him.

"That got him," James growled as the Egyptian radicals ground noisily against a roadside barrier in a spray of sparks from metal-on-stone violence.

The rear of the van vomited a tongue of flame and the roar of an AK-47 that blew the rear window out of their station wagon.

Kristopoulos glared at James. "They didn't stay screwed."

"Less bitching, more shooting!" Encizo snapped at the bickering pair in the back.

"I concur!" Farkas agreed as he cranked the steering wheel, pulling the group out of the line of fire of the enemy assault rifle. "Kill him!"

Once again, Encizo, James and Kristopoulos opened up with their side arms, but Farkas, in his instinctive effort to avoid the withering bite of the enemy gunman's full-auto assault rifle, had pulled their station wagon out of direct view of their target. Their 9 mm bullets clanged against the side of the Brotherhood van, but there was no way to tell if they had struck the gunman in the van's cargo compartment.

"We don't have a shot, Farkas," the Cuban complained.

"If we get a shot, we'll be taking fire, too, and this car's already more collander than transportation," Farkas countered.

Encizo glanced back up the road. "Then drive back to where we jousted with the Brotherhood. One of them dropped their rifle."

Farkas looked doubtful for the space of a heartbeat, but threw the Peugeot into gear and spun to where

Encizo had pointed. Clouds of road dust and loose sand kicked up as the wagon fought for traction, providing the Egyptian-Israeli-Phoenix Force alliance with a smoke screen.

The Cuban commando opened the door and hung his hand down to almost road level to scoop up the Kalashnikov, but Farkas drove too quickly for Encizo to snag the AK on the first pass. The Brotherhood radical in the van took that moment to step out onto the street and open fire. The Peugeot's back tires exploded as rifle slugs smashed into them. Farkas found himself battling against a wild spinout that hurled Encizo into the road through the open car door.

"Rafe!" James's voice cut through Encizo's awareness. The stocky Cuban tucked his chin down to his chest and hit the dirt on his shoulders, rather than his neck or head, sparing him a spine-crushing impact. The powerful muscles of his well-toned swimmer's body cushioned his landing as he rolled in a somersault that bled off the momentum of his launch. Though he was not nearly as powerful as his Phoenix Force partner Gary Manning or the leader of Able Team, Carl Lyons, he was still possessed of a phenomenal musculature that shielded his body from crippling injury, and the added agility of his smaller size enabled him to recover from the rough landing. He saw that he was close to the fallen Kalashnikov carbine. Encizo's powerful legs kicked hard and threw him the ten feet to the equalizing weapon he'd sought. A deft scoop and Encizo swung the AK onto the Egyptian Brotherhood gunman. Kalashnikov steel-cored slugs tore into the violent radical, ripping him from crotch to throat, and the horrendous gash of autofire spilled out ropey intestines that looped down around his thighs. The gunman staggered for a moment, looking down at entrails pouring out of his torn-open torso. It took a few moments, but finally his strength gave out and he collapsed in a puddle of guts and gore.

James, Kristopoulos and Farkas scrambled to Encizo's side, finally armed with their rifles, recovered from the station wagon's hidden compartment.

"You all right, Rafe?" James asked.

"I'll be good, Farrow," Encizo answered, accepting the SIG 551 carbine from his partner. He didn't have to check to see that a magazine was in place and a round chambered. Phoenix Force operatives rarely went anywhere without a weapon ready for instant action. A sanitized rifle was as useful as a blunt-edged sword.

"Their driver isn't moving," Farkas reported. "We made a clean sweep of the scumbags, but that leaves us with nothing in terms of intelligence."

"There's always the crates inside the can," Kristopoulos said. "If you're willing to deal with a self-destruct mechanism that's killed at least two members of this robot conspiracy."

James sighed. "Stay here. I'll check the van out."

"Alone?" Kristopoulos asked.

"Alone," James emphasized. He glanced over to Encizo. "Rey took a nasty tumble, and I seriously do not want to piss off the Israeli or Egyptian governments by losing either of you two to a booby trap. That just leaves me."

Encizo patted his SIG carbine. "We'll provide cover fire for you if the robots wake up, or if our eyes in the sky takes more than a passive role in this bit."

James smirked. "Well, I was hoping you'd say that. I'm risking my life, not throwing it away."

"I've got your back," the Cuban said.

Farkas gave his rifle a pat in silent agreement with the Phoenix Force veteran.

James looked at Kristopoulos, who fumed but eventually nodded her assent that his plan held merit.

James kept his SIG 551 carbine at low ready, and made the approach to the wrecked enemy van. The driver looked as if he was out of the fight, but he could have been playing possum in the wake of his comrades' deaths. There was also Lyons's warning of the lethal antipersonnel capabilities of the infiltrator robots. At least one American was dead because of the weaponry bristling within the deadly little automaton's form. James glanced skyward and saw a dim flicker of movement in the night overhead.

The Unmanned Aerial Vehicle stalking in the dark, starless velvet of night cover was another risk that James added to the dangers on this quiet Egyptian road. The unmanned drone in the sky was visible, but only barely. James knew from experience that the converse was vastly different, thanks to built-in infrared and light-amplification optics that transmitted even in the darkest pitch of night. James had seen UAV camera footage and he knew that to the machine's operator, he was a glowing, bright target, easily followed and destroyed, especially if the drone was armed. The warriors of Stony Man had gone against too many UAVs with weapons ranging from machine guns and antitank missiles to payloads of nerve gas and even nuclear warheads. The drone, nearly invisible and totally silent, maintained its ghostly watch on James and his companions, not drawing closer to the grounded prey.

A clatter resounded from the cargo compartment of the van, and James snapped his rifle to his shoulder, his eyes and muzzle covering the same space. He checked the driver's seat first, but the Brotherhood wheelman was only just stirring, dazed and confused. He was in no position to do anything that would have precipitated the metallic sound James had heard. James crab-walked sideways to get a better angle on the open rear doors. He paused and stepped back to avoid tripping over the gory mass of twisted flesh and bone that used to be a hostile enemy rifleman. The man who had caused them so much trouble was nothing more than a messy puddle now. As James moved past the corpse, something slithered out of the back of the van.

James searched for the source of the burst of movement, but the robot had disappeared beneath the undercarriage of the van. He checked his hands-free radio to reach the others left behind, but had to endure the screech of static that blasted out of his earphone. The former SEAL was alone against a hostile mechanism with the power to kill, thanks to the enemy's ability to jam electronic signals.

A gunshot rang out and James felt the impact of a 9 mm slug against his upper chest. He collapsed to the dirt, but rolled to avoid further fire from the hostile robot. He was glad that he wore his Kevlar body armor under his shirt, despite the oppressive Egyptian heat. The armored material had stopped a bullet meant for his heart, fired with deadly accuracy by the stealthy infiltration automaton. James triggered his SIG from where he had landed on his back, 5.56 mm rounds kicking up dirt where the muzzle-flash had originated.

James was rewarded for his efforts by a bullet glanc-

ing off of his carbine. The impact rammed the receiver
into his cheek, dazing him for a moment, but Encizo,
Farkas and Kristopoulos opened up to give the stunned
Stony Man medic a chance to recover his senses. The
only problem was that a robot operating via remote
control was not intimidated by incoming rifle fire. It had
no need to flinch, even if it was operated by someone
on the other side of its camera feed. The undercarriage
lit up as the automaton turned its attention to the trio of
human operatives who dared to attack it.

James dumped the magazine on his SIG, working the
action by hand. There seemed to be no interference, but
considering that this was a life-or-death battle, the
Phoenix pro wasn't about to take any half measures
with his survival. He fed in a new load, chambered a
round effortlessly and cut loose on the gap beneath the
van. Sparks flew as 5.56 mm rounds impacted on the
segmented robot. The curved steel compartments of the
machine's body readily deflected the 5.56 mm rounds
that struck it.

James saw a flare light and he knew that a ricochet
had punctured the gas tank. Dripping gas was ignited,
and the robot was now lost in a roaring cauldron of fire.
If this had been a movie, the van would have rocketed
skyward on a column of blossoming fire, but that
usually occurred with the assistance of several pounds
of plastic explosives and hydraulic rams. The reality
was that there weren't enough fumes inside the van's
gas tank to cause an explosive situation as the liquid fuel
poured and kept the enflamed gasoline from detonating.
As the gas burned in open air, it had room to expand
without increased pressure.

James had hoped that the blazing heat would have

hindered the enemy robot, but another gunshot hammered into the dirt close to him. The rebounding slug clipped him across the collarbone, only striking the Kevlar vest's shoulder strap. It was a stunning blow regardless, and his rifle dropped into the dirt. He rolled away from the fallen weapon, another round only missing by inches, plucking the cloth of his pant leg.

Cut off from communications with his partner and under fire from an enemy robot obscured by a wreath of flame, James rolled, scurrying out of the path of the hostile mounted weapon. Somewhere in the crackling blaze beneath the van, the robot swiveled and turned to keep its aim directed at the prone Phoenix Force fighter.

It wasn't much better than the rifle at this range, but the former Navy SEAL pulled his Glock and cut loose with it. The wide-mouthed hollowpoints, however, would have a better chance to snag on the smooth, curved skin of the enemy mechanism and cut into its electronic guts. James grimaced as he realized that he was no better than shooting blind into the harsh glow of the burning gasoline, but he emptied a half-dozen shots, cranking the trigger as fast as it reset against his finger.

A burning figure scurried out from under the van. James swung his point of aim to pursue the fiery mechanism when a second round of gunfire burst out of the van. Two robots were applying pressure on the Phoenix commando now, and this one had been shielded from the flames by the interior of the van. He pushed himself to his feet and charged out of view of the back of the vehicle. Bullets kicked up sand at his heels as the second infiltration mechanism cranked off rounds at him. Encizo, in the distance, opened up with his SIG carbine, 5.56 mm rounds able to pass through the skin of the van as if it was made of paper. James skidded to a halt to avoid crossing his partner's line of fire. The full magazine tore a precision burst through the vehicle, and a limping, floppy mechanism crashed out of the rear doors into the dirt.

James swung his Glock toward it when a bullet hit him just above the solar plexus. Fortunately, the Kevlar prevented a catastrophic injury again, but the impact knocked the wind out of James's lungs. Farkas and Kristopoulos turned their rifles against the muzzle flash, which originated from a flaming copse of grass where the first robot had escaped. The two robots swung and cut loose with their weapons. Kristopoulos jerked as she took a round in the thigh, outside of the protection of her body armor. The bullet only struck muscle, not bone or artery, and she somehow managed to find the strength to continue to stand and fire. Farkas slipped his arm around her waist and triggered his AK from the hip. James whirled back to the machine that Encizo had damaged. It writhed in an effort to target the closer Phoenix Force commando. Together James and Encizo concentrated their fire on the machine as its operator struggled to choose between the two Phoenix targets.

A storm of 9 mm and 5.56 mm slugs tore into the silvery form and chewed it into confetti, knocking segments apart. James had reloaded his 17-round magazine twice in rapid succession and Encizo had fed a new magazine into his carbine.

"The other one's still moving!" Encizo relayed across from the pair of Farkas and Kristopoulos. "How much punishment can these things take?"

"Not that much when you can concentrate fire on

them," James said. "But it's not like shooting an animal or a human. These things probably have redundant motors and electronic systems that make them harder to incapacitate. Throw in their metal covering and the fact that they don't have the breath—"

"Enough lecture! Get your rifle!" Encizo snapped. He reloaded his spent SIG's magazine and ripped off a full automatic fusillade against the burning shrubbery. James scooped up his weapon and added his firepower to the final knockout. Four people with automatic weapons had expended almost 500 rounds in unison against a pair of these mechanisms, and had unhindered fields of fire against them.

James knew that any attempt to hunt these down in the confines of a nuclear facility would be a nightmarish struggle, even if they could manage to spot such robots in ventilation ducts and access pipes. The Chicago Phoenix Force warrior continued to pound out the contents of a second magazine into the writhing mass of machinery until it stopped twitching. He held his distance, not wanting to be caught in a self-destruct mechanism blast radius, but since the robot had been torn to shredded metal, he wondered if any detonator would have been still in operation after such a hammering.

"Farkas, are you and Atalanta all right?" James called.

"We'll be fine," the Egyptian said. "I'm applying first aid to her leg. She only took it in the meat, nothing structural or circulatory harmed."

James nodded. "Let me handle that. We need a bomb team here, just to be certain."

Encizo walked closer to the robot that he and James

had poured nearly a hundred bullets into. "How many times did we have to hit the other one, after you'd lit it on fire?"

James looked up from Kristopoulos, medical kit in one hand. He looked at the Greek Israeli woman. "How many magazines from you?"

"Only one from my rifle before that bastard smacked me in the leg," Kristopoulos growled. "Then I transitioned to my SIG-Sauer."

"Farkas?" James asked.

"Two magazines from my AK. Then what you two threw at it," the Egyptian said.

Encizo held up his hand to cut off James's estimation. None was needed. "We're looking at devices that possess a remarkable amount of durability. If it takes at least ninety rounds of 5.56 mm, not counting the stuff that managed to hit with Farkas firing his AK from the hip, these things require the same kind of firepower that's reserved for anti-aircraft or anti-matériel purposes."

James frowned. "Then again, Carl did disable some of its mechanism with a .357 SIG round."

"He disabled the Taser," Encizo countered. "One component in an arsenal. And that was a high-pressure, near-Magnum round at a range of less than five feet."

"So we utilize more appropriate weaponry," James said.

"Like what?" Farkas asked.

"Shotgun saboted slugs?" Kristopoulos suggested.

"You read my mind," James returned. "Then I've also seen bomb disposal robots which utilized a .44 Magnum Redhawk."

"That's old school," Kristopoulos said. "How old are you again?"

James looked at the Greek woman, then smiled. "I'd tell you, but it'd depress me."

"Give me some credit, Mr. Farrow," Kristopoulos replied.

Farkas was on the phone to his allies in Unit 777. Encizo scanned the air overhead, frowning.

"Is the UAV still up there?" James asked.

"It's moved on," Encizo replied. "Just the same, I wouldn't go close to the robots until the bomb squad has dealt with them."

"At least it wasn't armed," James returned.

"No, but now whoever is in control of these machines knows what we look like," Encizo said.

James frowned. "General appearance."

"So how many tall African-Americans and stocky Hispanics have you seen running around with weaponry in Egypt?" Encizo asked.

James sighed. "I'll get back on the horn to Barb to see if we can get some sanitization of our identities."

"Paranoid much?" Kristopoulos asked.

"Says the woman using a code name plucked from mythology," James said. "I thought Mossad and Unit 777 trusted each other and didn't have to hide behind fake identities."

Kristopoulos wrinkled her nose. "Point taken."

"A demolitions team will be by to deal with the carcasses," Farkas announced. "And an ambulance if our Israeli visitor is inclined to go to the doctor."

"It was far from my heart," Kristopoulos answered. "I'll deal with the pain."

"Stubborn as one of us," Farkas sighed.

"Help me up, Farrow," Kristopoulos said. "I don't want to look hurt in front of our hosts."

James nodded and assisted her to her feet.

Encizo continued to watch the night skies, as if he could penetrate the gloom and his sense of dread to find the mysterious foes who had caused so much mayhem on this quiet Egyptian street.

CHAPTER FOUR

The Paris bakery was run by a friend of one of David McCarter's friends. A network of people around the globe could give the Briton access to weaponry when he needed it. Sure, there was a long streak where Phoenix Force had military flights or passes through customs with huge suitcases of rifles and grenade launchers, but the truth was, such free rides weren't always reliable. More than once across the long and storied career of the team, they'd had to rely on utensils found on-site.

Daniel Mittner was one such supplier of wares in McCarter's network of European contacts. In Europe, it was becoming more difficult to find reliable, decent arms dealers with access to the kind of gear Phoenix Force required in the field due simply to harsher regulations. Not that the less scrupulous dealers had such qualms, but when it came to gun runners that McCarter could trust with quality equipment and privacy, Mittner was a rare deal for the team.

Mittner glanced up from his counter in the nearly

empty bakery, his bleary eyes recognizing McCarter instantly. "Oy. Three unsavory chaps like you blowing through my door? It's a bloody good wager someone would think you'd come looking for guns. Lord knows you'd draw a touch of interest from John Law."

McCarter looked around the bakery and saw a lone man, disheveled with a jaw covered in stubble, take a sip of coffee. The reaction on his face told the Briton that whatever he had just drank ranked with Aaron Kurtzman's worst pots of brew. The coffee drinker was a local Frenchman, and from his state, McCarter could tell that he was an armed, undercover police officer. McCarter glared at Mittner, making his look as dirty as he possibly could.

The Frenchman took a bite of a scone that crunched as if it were made of plaster.

"What? Just because we came in here with a dumb American Southerner…" McCarter began.

Manning tapped McCarter on the arm. "You're being redundant."

Hawkins nodded. "And wrong. I might have been born in the dirty South, but I was raised in Texas. There's the South, and then there's Texas. Never the twain shall meet, got it, hoss?"

McCarter rolled his eyes at the interruptions. "Sorry. Just because we have a redneck idiot—"

"Redundancy," Manning interrupted again.

McCarter gave Manning a scowl. He looked at Hawkins, who merely nodded in approval over the latest appelation the Briton had given him. Presumably after the faux pas with stereotyping the French, he was accepting pennance for his Texas cliché.

"Just because we have a Texan with us does not

mean we're gun-obsessed morons with no sense of awe and wonder," McCarter finished. "Can't a bloke walk into a bakery for biscuits and tea?"

Mittner nodded at the lone patron, who nodded in return as he stood. "If you will excuse me, I must retire to the men's room. This coffee runs through a man as if it were a flood tide."

"You know where to go, Bertrand," Mittner stated.

Bertrand nodded to the counter man and walked down a hallway.

"We don't have much time," Mittner said. "He's paid well to ignore certain things, and he doesn't agree with the current administration of intelligence services in this country."

"So he knows, but he can't say what we're doing here if he's in the loo for the bulk of our conversation," McCarter concluded.

"Makes things a little simpler," Hawkins said, standing in the hallway leading to the washroom. "You know him, David?"

"No real names, Texan," McCarter cut him off.

Mittner nodded in agreement. "He knows the type. A no-bullshit officer. You'll want locker FP5."

Mittner slid a key onto the counter that McCarter took, exchanging it for euro notes with numbers written into the margins. Mittner looked them over. "You'll inform me of the replacement code when you're satisfied?"

"I'll be satisfied with combat Tupperware?" McCarter challenged.

"I told you, finding a Hi-Power in France at this time is like trying to find a public official who takes a shower," Mittner returned.

Hawkins stifled a snort of laughter at Mittner's comment.

"Which package did you provide?" McCarter asked.

"Your first option," Mittner told the Phoenix Force commander.

"Well, can't be too bad, then," Manning said. "If it's your first choice—"

"It's not locked and cocked and made of steel, but it'll do," McCarter cut him off. "Thanks, Mittner."

"Whatever you do, don't get caught. It's all well and good being an outlaw to do the right thing, but the French government doesn't have much patience for outlaws," Mittner warned.

"I promise not to kick their asses too badly," McCarter replied.

Mittner handed the trio a small plate of almond croissants and three lattes. "On the house."

"Thanks," McCarter replied.

Hawkins took a bite of his pastry reluctantly, after remembering the condemnation Bertrand had given to Mittner's cooking. He was surprised at the flavor and freshness of the croissant. "Where does Bertrand get off insulting his cooking?"

"Bertrand is on a budget, and he can't justify spending money on Mittner's good cooking, so he's forced to eat the day-old baked goods," Manning said. "Besides, if Mittner were to start making good stuff for the French agent hanging out at his shop, watching for arms deals, his supervisors would think that there was some form of collusion between them."

McCarter took a sip of his latte. "Which there is, but the appearance of propriety makes up for a lot in terms of French collaboration."

"Collaboration sounds pretty negative," Hawkins noted.

"Not in this case," McCarter said. "Mittner informed us directly that Bertrand was on our side. If we do happen to get nicked by the gendarmerie, we can call on him for a voucher. Though, if that does happen, we're shit out of luck."

"In other words, since we're cheating, we better not get caught," Hawkins mused.

"Precisely," McCarter said. "We scored pretty well. I had Mittner pull a set of Steyr AUG A-3 rifles with Aimpoint scopes and a selection of alternate barrels. For side arms, we have SIG-Sauer SP-2022 pistols."

"Ah. Plastic pistols with hammers." Hawkins spoke up. "Why not a Heckler & Koch USP?"

"The French don't like German guns," McCarter said.

"But SIG-Sauer is…" Hawkins began.

"Once more, the image of propriety," McCarter returned. "Plus, the SP-2022 is the new side arm of choice of French law enforcement. We can score ammunition and magazines easily if we have to."

"Point taken," Hawins affirmed.

"Now, we've got leads to check out," McCarter continued.

"You've been getting updates from Barb?" Hawkins asked.

McCarter tapped his phone. "Of course. Plus, Gary used to do business with some chaps in France's nuclear power security back when he owned his own company. We'll tap them, as well."

Hawkins looked at Manning. "Man, I wish they'd picked someone with more real world contacts than a silk jumper and ground pounder like me."

"Don't worry, son," Manning replied. "Stick with us, and you'll get a real education."

Phoenix Force hit the streets to pick up their weapons.

AARON KURTZMAN PINCHED THE flesh between his eyebrows, tired of looking into the depths of the Department of Energy database for signs of electronic penetration by hackers. Lyons had been adamant that there was the possibility that the infiltrator robot had also been capable of introducing either a tap on the DoE's files or planted some form of logic bomb that would cause problems with the emergency protocols intended to prevent a hacker from endangering a nuclear power plant by remote control.

The threat of a hostile computer takeover was something that the Department of Energy was aware of since the old DARPA days of the Internet. Not only did the agency have on-call Nuclear Emergency Special Teams capable of countering terrorists like a national SWAT team, but they had electronic warfare and cybernetic infiltration experts on hand to keep the control apparatus of the nation's nuclear power secure. Even then, Stony Man had to work with the DoE on multiple occasions against threats too great even for the NEST squads to deal with, such as the ninja-skilled Tigers of Justice or KGB-backed forces out to force meltdowns of reactors.

Kurtzman shot a glance to Huntington Wethers, who was at his workstation, his unblinking eyes focused on his monitor. "Hunt, did you notice any errant lines of code in the system?"

"None so far. I'm barely halfway through my search, however, Aaron," Wethers replied. He gnawed on the stem of his pipe, not looking away from his monitor as he scanned the DoE operating system for any recent changes.

Kurtzman rubbed his forehead and rolled his wheelchair over to the coffeepot where Carmen Delahunt was mixing cold water with the freshly brewed chai tea she'd brought to the computer center. "Anything on the crispy critters that Lyons and the boys left behind in D.C.?"

"Not a thing. The explosion removed everything that could have identified them quickly. We're stuck with DNA coding, and CODIS is nowhere near as fast as it appears to be on TV crime procedurals," Delahunt answered. She took a sip of her tea and licked her lips.

"So, we've got at least three days before we can figure out if the dead perps are somehow in the DNA database," Kurtzman murmured. He sighed. "By then, we could have a China syndrome incident four times over."

"Which is why Carl and the boys are pounding the street and going through the likely goons who would have made a fake UPS truck," Delahunt told him. "Sometimes, all we can do is pore over computer programs looking for kinky programming and viruses left behind. All the satellites and computerized search engines in the world aren't going to replace shoe leather on a sidewalk and a shotgun in your fists doing the real work."

"Nope," Kurtzman said. "But don't tell Barb that. She thinks we can do anything." He paused to pour himself a mug of his high-octane sludge, then took a sip and sighed. "I'm going to see what Akira has on the French situation."

"The new Directorates talk a big game about operational security, but Akira's been tap-dancing through their systems pretty easily," Delahunt said.

Kurtzman nodded. "It's all that twitchiness in his reflexes. He's too fast for their system to adapt to. Quick and low profile is the way things work best, at least when you're in a hostile land."

"The same applies to David, Gary and T.J.," Delahunt noted. "They slipped into France, and now they're gearing up with a nonstandard supplier. Akira's doing his best to give them targets to look at, but mostly, it's up to those three."

"Once again, we're batting cleanup and doing the boring work," Kurtzman complained. "Any word from Cal and Rafe?"

"Nothing after they took out the probe team," Delahunt explained. "Right now, they're with Unit 777 looking over the infiltration robots, but considering how badly they damaged them, we're not going to have too much success figuring out the origins of their components or who built them."

"How badly damaged?" Kurtzman asked.

"Each took about 120 to 150 hits from rifle and handgun rounds," Delahunt replied.

"That much?" Kurtzman exclaimed.

"That's how long the robots kept shooting back," Delahunt explained.

Kurtzman frowned. He remembered the faxed scans of the designs whipped up by Schwarz based on Lyons's description of the robots. "Okay, that makes sense. It also makes them scarier. You'd need a heavy machine gun to take out one of those things."

"Wouldn't that be the point? You don't want a soap bubble sent in. It takes a knock in a vent, and you've wasted the effort. Force four people to pour bullets into one robot, maybe even more, and you've tied up half a SWAT team," Delahunt replied. "They probably have redundant communications, as well, making it harder to jam whatever signals are being directed toward them."

"Encizo also noticed a UAV over the truck, correct?" Kurtzman asked.

"Extra complication," Delahunt admitted. "Akira's got a search running for missing UAVs in the area, but this might be some leftovers from the last missing bits from a U.S. military shipment to Egypt that Striker encountered."

"I thought we tied up all of those loose ends," Kurtzman groaned.

"You put a lot of military tech on the black market, you have to deal with trickles of it for years," Delahunt grumbled.

"Well, at least we have records. I'll see if we can find back-door commands to get into the UAV CPUs," Kurtzman said. "There's a possibility that they haven't gone completely over to a new operating system to run the stolen birds."

"Though if they're good, they'll have gone through and closed those loopholes," Delahunt noted. "And they might well be the best. They found the DoE agent on their case."

Kurtzman grimaced. "I'll see what I can scrounge up. Maybe they've left a hole as bait for us. They'll know that someone would be on their case in cyberspace. It's a good bet they'll want a shot at their competition."

"So there's a chance we might have to go on viral lockdown again?" Delahunt asked.

"Better us than someone who can't handle a worm or logic bomb," Kurtzman explained. "We can cordon off any infection. The FBI or CIA get hit, and there's a chance we lose half the intel that Homeland Security somehow managed to gather."

"Half of nothing, you mean?" Delahunt asked. "I fail to see how bloating the intelligence-gathering process does anything for securing our national security."

"Don't say that too loud," Kurtzman replied. "There are still types who'd rather trade their freedom for security up the road."

Delahunt made a face. "You'd have thought after eight years of that kind of ineptitude, we'd be done with it by now."

"Promises made are just pillow talk. Politics is still the Greek term for many blood-sucking insects, not many truth speakers," Kurtzman growled.

"Back to work?" Delahunt asked.

Kurtzman sighed. "The bad guys aren't going to find themselves for us, are they?"

"Nope," Delahunt answered.

The two computer experts returned to their workstations, toiling on in the search for any link to the robot masters.

DARRIN HOMM LOOKED OVER the UAV footage from Egypt. Though the images were grainy due to the lack of finesse inherent to night vision, he still had height and weight estimations thanks to computerized parallax analysis relating the images to known objects on the ground around them. He entered the data into a search program that contained dossiers for known current and past agents of a half-dozen governments.

With that particular information, the computer mastermind turned to his partner, Mischa Shenck, putting the pictures down in front of the engineer. Shenck looked at the printed photos, then raised an eyebrow.

"An African in Africa?" the Russian-born cyberneticist asked.

"African-American," Homm replied. "But black Americans are usually tourists, and Egypt doesn't let tourists run around with state-of-the-art assault rifles."

Shenck looked at the picture. "So, he'd be an American CIA agent? Special Forces?"

"Special Forces is straight Army. Get the facts straight," Homm growled.

Shenck sighed, knowing the computer expert's obsessive-compulsive disdain for improper terminology. "Sorry. Special operations."

"Likely special operations. I put that face through recognition software, but it's come back as a null return," Homm said. "That marks him as a sanitized operative since he doesn't even register on recognition patterns."

"So, you want me to help you figure out who he is?" Shenck asked. "He's been sanitized by professionals if he's a nonentity in your recognition program. Whoever wiped him out of the database would have been thorough."

Homm nodded. "If anything, they are working closely with the Egyptian authorities. Their driver is a member of Unit 777."

"It's not much to go on," Shenck said.

"Bullshit it's not. Somehow, two Americans brought

their own personal weapons, because SIG-Sauer is not standard Egyptian gear, even for their high-speed, low-drag units," Homm said. "And they were on watch for our robots."

"Which means we're not talking about a large agency here," Shenck said. "The Americans at the Department of Energy had only encountered the other robot a few hours ago. Intelligence agencies take days to get word to units in other cities, let alone other countries."

"Hence the logic of a small agency or a tightly knit department," Homm suggested.

"Something around twenty people," Shenck mused. "Half in the field, half working cyber support. They undoubtedly have an efficient and secure communications network, as well, so tapping them will be nearly impossible."

"They might be hard to trace, but they have their own contacts and allies abroad," Homm stated. "So we should be able to tap whomever they're working with."

"Breaking the DoE and Egyptian military intelligence networks to figure out who they're interfacing with will be your job, but this group does sound sort of familiar," Shenck said. "Did you only get a picture of the black man?"

"There was an Israeli woman. I managed to pry her identity from Mossad's computers," Homm said. "And she was with another man."

"Did you run him through?" Shenck asked.

"He also had a zero response," Homm answered. "He was of average height and build, though."

Shenck looked at the second American's photo. He smiled. "Just what I expected."

"Who did you think you would find?" Homm asked.

"The Latino member of the team," Shenck answered.

"One black. One Latino. And three sort of average white men as partners?" Homm suggested.

"Exactly," Shenck replied. "We've come up against the urban legend known as Phoenix Force."

Homm punched the desk between them. "Damn! That means the big blond guy who didn't even stop when we hit him with the Taser must have been from their so-called sister team, Able."

"Presumably the same Mr. Stone who my former friends in the KGB despised so deeply," Shenck said. "Stone or iron or some such invulnerable material fits the description of a man who shrugged off twenty thousand volts through a Taser."

"So those two groups are allied?" Homm asked.

"Considering that they are aspects of the same myth, it is a likelihood," Shenck said.

"These groups aren't myths. We have photographs of them," Homm growled.

"We've seen the basis for the mythology," Shenck countered. "But the facts are not so clear in regard to what the nature of their organization is."

"Their agency is large enough to operate in Washington, D.C., and outside of Inshas, Egypt, but they are still small enough to quickly communicate across the Atlantic Ocean. They also have their pulse on things, because Hirtenberg was investigating our touches on the DoE's security system and they hooked up with the Mossad after the Negev near-incident," Homm speculated.

"So they know all about our infiltration, the nature of the attack robots and our deal with local terror groups," Shenck mused.

"They also know that we have Global Hawk UAV drones," Homm said. "Otherwise we wouldn't have excellent face shots if they weren't looking directly at the drone."

"How screwed are we?" Shenck asked.

"It all depends on operations in France," Homm replied. "And if they have their teams granulated enough to have a presence in Europe, as well."

"You believe the teams have split?" Shenck asked.

"There's only two visible in Egypt. We can't discount the remainder of Phoenix Force being elsewhere, especially in the wake of the violence committed in Paris," Homm sighed.

"What do we do?" Shenck asked.

"Adapt. Which means I call in some extra help on my side, and you utilize some of those upgrades which I thought would be too flashy," Homm replied.

"What about Inshas?" Shenck asked.

"It gets hit with upgraded robots, but only once we've made certain that everyone is locked into Washington, D.C., and France," Homm told him.

"So the Middle East will start suffering meltdowns, while our efforts in the U.S. and France are blunted?" Shenck asked.

"The U.S. operation is too widespread to be easily stopped, and France right now is on high alert. They're not accepting help from the U.S.," Homm said. "France might just be pulled off, and we have the flexibility in the States to do whatever we want."

"Just have to know what we're dealing with," Shenck said. "All right. I've got some quick module ideas that we can send out."

Homm smiled. After this, the panic against nuclear

power would paralyze alternative power technology around the world.

The nightmare would only make them the most influential men in future technologies. If they somehow managed to survive the effort.

CHAPTER FIVE

David McCarter watched T. J. Hawkins finish scrubbing down and lubricating every bit of mechanism of the high-tech, polymer-composite Steyr AUG A-3 rifle in his possession. When the Southern Phoenix Force pro was concentrating on his weapons maintenance, there were few things that could distract the young man from his task.

Gary Manning turned off his cell phone and removed the wireless headset from his ear. "The Security Directorate isn't aware of any outside investigation occuring within Paris at this moment. We're pretty much in the clear."

"Wouldn't asking about their awareness put them on alert?" Hawkins asked as he reassembled his rifle.

"There is that worry, but don't forget, not every organization is Stony Man," Manning returned. "By the time they send through memos and requests for recognition, it will have been two or three days before we encounter any official interference."

"That's from the authorities themselves," McCarter

mused. "The DoE is the same kind of bloated, fragmented beauracracy as the new French internal security agency, but our opponents discovered the agent looking into their backtrail fast enough to send a killer robot snake after her."

Manning nodded. "Which is why I routed the phone call through my cabin outside of Toronto. Whoever the opposition is, they might be genuinely misdirected for a few hours."

McCarter watched the mechanical precision with which Hawkins worked on the AUG A-3 carbine. "I wouldn't underestimate them. If Stony Man could catch a whiff of their interest in Europe's nuclear reactor programs, then there's a strong possibility that we're going to have some drama on our end here."

"So why are you looking at Hawkins's rifle like it were some long-lost lover?" Manning asked.

"'Cause I cleaned it so well that it shines like a diamond," Hawkins answered.

"No. I'm worried that according to Rafe and Cal, a 5.56 mm doesn't have enough immediate punch to slow down one of those robots. The round's fine for antipersonnel use at close range, but we're dealing with small, tough-skinned mechanisms which contain redundant systems," McCarter corrected.

Manning nodded. "Which is why you're not the only one here who has friends in France with access to powerful guns."

McCarter raised an eyebrow. "What are you thinking of?"

"We want a big, metal-crunching punch, so I arranged for a friend of mine to drop off something," Manning said.

There was a knock at the back door and McCarter glanced toward it. Manning rose and went to answer. Over the big Canadian's shoulder, the Briton could see a pretty woman with long, sable dark hair and glimmering blue eyes hand him a rectangular, gift-wrapped box.

Manning greeted her in French, and McCarter could hear enough to know that the brawny Canadian was telling her sweet nothings. Whatever compliments that Manning had for the woman could hardly be classified as lies, judging from the brief glimpses he caught of her. Manning gave the woman a kiss on her cheek, and closed the door.

"How do I arrange a delivery like that?" Hawkins asked.

"You know a beautiful, intelligent woman? Shame that you can't find those with your looks and manners," Manning responded.

"Southern charm mean anything to y'all?" Hawkins asked.

"You've never shown it," Manning said with a wink.

McCarter grinned at the jab as Hawkins waved off the Canadian's verbal barb. "We going to give the robots flowers and hope they contract hay fever?"

Manning sighed. "You know, that's a good idea. Too bad my plan was more pedestrian."

He opened the box and McCarter looked at the pistol-grip, folding-stock pump shotgun within and nodded. The Briton picked up a box of ammunition that was sitting next to the weapon in the gift-wrapped container. "Twelve-gauge slugs. Innocuous for deer hunting, but it's also strong enough to smash what passes for engines in European automobiles."

"Or smashing the self-destruct charge out of a killer snake robot," Hawkins noted.

"Really?" Manning asked. "I never would have thought of that."

Hawkins rolled his eyes. "Did you ever do this to James when he was still the youngest member of the team?"

"No. But then, Cal's laid-back, experienced and worldly," McCarter replied.

"Plus, we're jealous of Gadgets and Pol and all the piss they take out of Carl," Manning added.

"That, too," McCarter agreed. "Can't let the Yanks have all the fun."

Hawkins rolled his eyes and went back to fieldstripping his SIG. "Pistol-grip pump?"

"With a Knoxx Comp-stock and a folding shoulder stock," Manning said. "It can be fired like a handgun if need be. Lyons thinks the world of his Remington with the Comp."

"Lyons also has been known to break coconuts in two with his bare hands," Hawkins grumbled.

"Can't everyone?" Manning asked.

"I forgot. You've got more muscles than Paul Bunyan. You just dress to hide 'em," Hawkins said.

"All right. Enough chin wag." McCarter cut his friends off. "We've got leads to run down and people to beat up."

CARL LYONS LET THE BEAST out, and right now the rage he felt against the conspiracy that murdered a fellow investigator came down in concentrated agony on the shoulder and elbow of Darius Morrison. The chicken-wing armlock applied to him bent the two joints at angles they could barely support, tendons stretched to the snapping point.

"I know you have something to say to me, Darius," Lyons growled, his gas mask distorting his voice to make it even more animalistic. "The only question is whether you'll ever be able to use your arm again after your rotator cuff is permanently torn."

"You didn't even ask a question!" Morrison howled in pain. Tears and mucus ran from his eyes and nose as capsaicin burned the tender tissues of his face. He coughed and sputtered, suffering from the effects of riot control gas and feeling the ache from where a neoprene baton had battered several ribs.

Lyons looked toward Schwarz and Blancanales, also disguised and concealed behind their own gas masks protecting them from the remaining wisps of burning chemical smoke. "I didn't ask him anything?"

"Nope," Schwarz answered.

"Well, you did say hit the floor when we poured tear gas, flash-bangs and riot batons into this bunch," Blancanales pointed out. "But you haven't asked a question since you crippled Mickey Giardelli."

"Giardelli?" Morrison asked. "But he has an army—"

"Had an army," Lyons snarled, the gas mask turning the response into a gutteral reply from a ferocious beast. "They're being hosed off the concrete, along with Giardelli's arms and legs. Pol, you have the rubber tubing?"

Blancanales held up the pale yellow tourniquets. Morrison saw Schwarz stroke the blade of a blood-crusted saw.

"The fuck you going to do?" Morrison whined.

"Keep you from bleeding to death," Lyons told him. "That way, we can tell our boss that we didn't kill anyone this week."

"Not personally," Schwarz added. "How was I to know that someone switched the first batch of tear gas for high-explosive fragmentation?"

"Don't tell me that it's your fault we have a half-dozen bodies jammed into the back of our van to dump in the river," Lyons snapped at Schwarz.

Morrison twisted and struggled in the ex-cop's grasp. "Wait! Wait! What vehicle are you looking for?"

"A brown delivery van," Blancanales said.

"Don't tell him before we take his legs off at least!" Lyons bellowed. The hollow echo of the gas mask amplified the yell to a roar against the side of Morrison's head.

"No, the brown van? Man, they picked that up two days ago! Look in the office!" Morrison said. "You want the password? Ecclesiastic!"

Schwarz tilted his head. "What?"

"From that movie. Where they wanted the safe word…but had to go with snakebite 'cause the snitch was too stupid?" Morrison asked.

"Spell it," Schwarz said.

Morrison did so. He didn't even realize that Lyons had let up the pressure on his arm.

"Aw hell, you're going to shoot me in the head," Morrison muttered.

Lyons shrugged. "Why would I do that?"

"And, for our edification, Mickey Giardelli coughed you up, and we didn't even have to pretend to be a SWAT team," Blancanales said.

Morrison's eyes widened. "Aw shit…"

"You've got a choice, son," Lyons told him, slapping him on the shoulder to focus his attention. "Stay free, and maybe have the pricks who you delivered the truck to think you gave them up—which you did—or do some prison time for running a chop shop. One ends with you sitting safe in a box for six months. The other has guys willing to murder federal agents wanting to shut you up so you don't testify."

"I'll take the safe option, thank you very much," Morrison stated.

Lyons smiled. "Beautiful."

Morrison mopped his brow as Schwarz broke into his computer.

KURTZMAN PICKED UP THE secure, direct connection from the field. Schwarz had activated an encryption protocol that turned the line his computer was on into a shielded transmission conduit. Hackers attempting to penetrate the electronic security locks and creating interference with the direct connection would alert Stony Man Farm to the intrusion and render themselves open to a salvo of countersurveillance programs guaranteed to crash even the most powerful processors set to the task.

"Gadgets," Kurtzman greeted over the tight-band video chat. "Nice design extrapolation on the robot snake."

"Thanks," Schwarz replied. "You should have seen the picture of Carl as Captain Caveman that he destroyed."

"I bet it would have been a hoot," Kurtzman admitted.

Schwarz grinned. "Since I drew it on a tablet computer, I'll upload it to you for a screen saver."

Kurtzman chuckled. "Lyons would take my head off if he found that."

"You told him how to understand the magic box?" Schwarz asked.

There was a grunt on the other end, and Lyons appeared on camera as Schwarz winced and rubbed his shoulder.

"There'll be time for jokes later," Lyons grunted. "You have access to Morrison's hard drives?"

"Yeah," Kurtzman said. "We've located the account which paid for the delivery truck, but we're looking at an offshore bank with some paranoid security."

"Paranoid is a walk in the park for you guys, isn't it?" Lyons asked.

"Not these banks," Kurtzman replied. "They've been upgrading their black ice, and I'm not afraid to say that they're making us work for our paycheck, even if it is just a false front."

"So, the conspirators dumped cash into an account for their dead buddies to pull out," Lyons said. "How'll you be able to track the money trail?"

"By diligent, meticulous observation once Akira breaks a hole for us into the bank's security," Kurtzman stated.

"What about the robots?" Lyons asked. "I hear that Cal and Rafe transmitted digital photographs of what was left of their encounter with two of them."

"Same design. Two sets of parallel bow-coiled legs off of a central, flexible spine. The legs are fat little plates, and the body ends in a large head that fits an interesting firearm design," Kurtzman told them.

"How so?" Lyons asked.

Kurtzman looked at the picture. "You know how the

FN P-90 has that pivoting magazine that turns bullets at 90 degrees to keep the gun flat?"

Lyons nodded. "It's been used on other designs, as well."

"This one was hooked up to a Glock 26 barrel. The end result is that the head of the snake is about six inches long, and only four inches in diameter, but holds 17 shots," Kurtzman said. "It has no means to reload itself, but stuck in there, parallel to the Glock barrel are two small cameras, and two Taser modules, whose capacitor batteries are further down the spine, tucked between the legs."

Lyons blinked. "I saw the picture that Gadgets made. The batteries look like oversize watch batteries, right?"

"Yes. More than capable of producing enough voltage to paralyze a grown man," Kurtzman said. "You're lucky that you're as strong and prepared for Taser shocks as you are."

"I'm also lucky I was too stupid to keep my finger off the trigger. If my muscles hadn't seized up and applied enough pressure to drop the striker, I'd have been carved up by that weed-whacker in its tail," Lyons snarled.

"The cutting monofilament," Kurtzman noted.

Akira Tokaido waved at Kurtzman to get his attention. "Hunt's inside running the finances on the account," Tokaido said.

"Good news," Kurtzman answered. "You heard?" he said to Lyons.

"Yeah," Lyons replied. "Is anyone watching Hunt and Akira's six inside the bank?"

"Carmen's way ahead of you on that," Kurtzman told him. "After the DoE was penetrated, we're on extra-high alert about any impropriety."

"Good," Lyons said. "You done with Morrison's records?"

"Yes. You can shut down the computer," Kurtzman answered. "He tries anything in the future, we've got a tap on his records."

"I think he could be used as a local resource," Lyons said. "I'll stop by and rap my knuckles on his dome for a few answers every so often."

Kurtzman nodded. "I was thinking the same thing, except I'm talking about aiding anyone on the terrorist watch lists."

"Those things work?" Lyons asked.

"Not for Homeland Security, but those of us here with brains can determine the corn from the shit," Kurtzman replied.

Lyons smiled. "Spoken like a true cop."

Kurtzman winked. "Farm out."

ONE OF THE ADVANTAGES that Phoenix Force had over the Directorate of Security and their investigation was that they didn't have to worry about coordinating multiple raids after assembling a half-dozen teams in and around Paris. The Directorate needed to pull off each raid at the same time, in case the conspirators were in communication with each other, and more than one enemy site was actually part of the guilty party. The agency also needed to assemble warrants, scope out approaches and gather much more intelligence before they could make the first move. That all also depended on putting aside the bureaucratic differences that put the brakes on their moves.

McCarter looked at the latest data gathered from the French by the computer hackers at Stony Man Farm, and applied his years of counterterrorism investigation and operation to narrowing down Phoenix Force's target as Manning drove them through the streets of Paris.

"I think that we're looking at the neo-Nazi cell just off of the Seine," McCarter said.

"What makes you think that?" Manning asked.

"The warrants are moving especially slow on them," McCarter said. "Considering that we're dealing with expert computer hackers, as well as the robots, I'm betting that the conspirators are looking to keep their asses covered until their patsies can get out of the way."

"Or be gotten out of the way," Hawkins mentioned. "The bad guys in Inshas and Washington were both sacrificial lambs, and they didn't seem to care about the robots, either."

"So even if we hit the little Hitler lovers, they might already be corpses," Manning grumbled.

McCarter's brow furrowed. "I like our chances."

"What?" Manning asked.

"The conspiracy seems to be cleaning up its back-trail with almost paranoid efficiency," McCarter replied. "But they left the lead to the neo-Nazis hanging out there."

Manning nodded. "I see."

"I don't," Hawkins replied.

"The conspirators want to take the piss out of us. In two places, they've had Stony Man teams on their asses," McCarter said. "They noticed Able shadowing their deliverymen in Washington, D.C. They caught Rafe and Cal in Egypt. They're dangling bait for us here in Paris to see if they can catch a nibble."

Hawkins grimaced. "So they're aware of Stony Man."

"They're aware of a particularly efficient agency on their tails. They don't know the details, but the specifics of who we are doesn't matter to them," McCarter told him. "What matters is that someone has managed to cut through the red tape and bureaucratic bullshit to know that there is a conspiracy out there messing with nuclear power plants across three continents."

"And we're looking at a trap for us," Hawkins sighed.

"The neo-Nazis are in all likelihood dead," McCarter said. "But there will be an elimination team on hand, waiting for us to make our move. Once we do, they drop the hammer."

"An ambush won't work too well if we're aware of it," Manning said.

"The enemy might be anticipating that, as well," McCarter said. "Depending on who they hired to hit us, it could be a feint, or it could be a hard-kill force."

"A test for us," Manning said. "Or a distraction."

Hawkins took a deep breath. "Either way, we're going to have our work cut out for us, or is this mental chess game hinging on making us look less capable than we are?"

"Screw that," McCarter snapped. "If we're going to encounter some drama, we're going to bring our A game every time. Whoever they send after us, we treat them as professionals and we don't let up on them. Taking it easy on any asshole we meet is a fast ticket to an unmarked grave."

Hawkins nodded. "For a moment, I was wondering if you were a Cockney brawler or Sherlock Holmes."

"There's times for being smart, and there's times for being the deadliest bastard on the sidewalk," McCarter said. "The time for being smart is done now. Let's be bloody and deadly."

CALVIN JAMES POKED A pencil at the burned shell segment remaining from the snake-shaped robot that had been such a menace to him and his allies earlier. He glanced at his Phoenix Force partner and friend Rafael Encizo, who merely shrugged as he sat at the table. James was a scientist, but his fields of expertise were anatomy and pharmacology, not electronics or robotics. Encizo had more experience with robots, but only through his work with them during oceanic salvage expeditions. The fields of underwater archaeology and marine biology were rife with the use of subaquatic remote devices that could transmit images of the ocean floor or sea life, or had manipulator claws that enabled the recovery of living specimens or lost artifacts.

Still, there was a difference between the camera bots and recovery drones that Encizo worked with and manipulated on his salvage expeditions, and the compact, nearly organic device that lay before him.

Colonel Assid gave James a clap on the shoulder. "Nothing?"

"Just a pile of shot-up and charred metal that doesn't leave much in the way of forensics," James said. "The only things we know for sure is that they have enough redundant systems to survive a hundred rounds of rifle fire and still continue shooting and moving for the bulk of that barrage."

"Farrow had better luck going over the dead men," Encizo admitted. "Thanks for letting him stand in on their autopsy."

Assid nodded. "It's always good to have an extra set of eyes present. What about the digital images you transmitted back to your agency?"

"They're still running checks on the few markings

we discovered on the wreckage," James said sullenly. "But the components are common devices with pre-formed metallic shells. Trying to pinpoint their source of manufacture is like trying to find a particular grain of sand in the desert."

Assid nodded. "We're assembling a squad to pay a visit to the rest of the corpses' cell members. I thought you two might want to stretch your legs and give your eyes a rest."

Encizo smirked. "I'm all for that. Anything's better than being kept out of my element."

"Where did the cell originate?" James asked.

"They're operating off of a fishing trawler," Assid said. "Part of the reason why I'm hoping the two of you would help out. Normally, the unit would look for assistance from the Egyptian marines or navy, but right now, we're trying to keep everything in-house."

"Because of the drone we spotted?" Encizo asked.

"I remember the troubles we had with Egyptian military tanks and Predator UAVs falling into the hands of radical Palestinian and Syrian forces a while back," Assid mentioned. "I don't want to risk a leak of our raid getting back to whoever is running this show."

James nodded. "According to what the home team told us, the conspirators seem to be on the ball. Any investigation pointing in their direction gets flagged and bogged down with paperwork."

"So they do have monitors internationally, as well as moles?" Assid asked. "How big is this conspiracy?"

"Probably small," Encizo said. "Whoever the leaks are, they're probably just garden-variety bureaucrats with open palms and the willingness to look the other way or misplace paperwork."

"A couple of smart people with a good bank account can do as much as a worldwide organization," James said. "We work on brains and connections ourselves, so we can see where holes can be exploited in any security system."

"A bribe or two in the Egyptian government, and they have the drop on us if we go outside the family," Assid mused. "That explains why they're working with the Muslim Brotherhood."

"The local muscle they've hired don't know what's really going on, likely," Encizo offered. "But the conspirators have given them the promise of their goals of confusion and government disarray."

"That's worked well enough," Assid said. "Despite the fact that the Brotherhood didn't get the robots anywhere near Inshas, the press caught word of an attempted attack. People are nervous, and they're calling for an end to Egypt's development of nuclear energy."

James nodded. "The same news leaks have shown up across Europe and the United States. Israel was smart enough to clamp down a hard moratorium on printing the news about the Negev incident, so your neighbors aren't getting frightened and antsy yet."

Encizo frowned. "Israel isn't nervous over Israeli nuclear energy. But you just have to know that the Inshas attempt is all over their headlines. Just imagine that your neighbors had a gas leak, Cal."

"I'd be worried about fires or monoxide poisoning in my own house, just because of our proximity," James muttered.

Assid's brow furrowed in concern. "So even though we've been incident free, at least as far as a reactor being threatened with a critical incident, just the very act of stopping their infiltration accomplished whatever goal our enemy wanted? That's insidious."

"That's the type of Machiavellian manipulation that we encounter on a regular basis," Encizo sighed. "I miss the good old days when if it wasn't simply a local group of psychotics, then the ones responsible were the KGB holdouts."

"Or Nazi revivalists," James mentioned.

Encizo rubbed his forehead, tracing the faint scar he'd received on a mission years ago. "Thing is, with the world in such flux today, there are dozens of groups with the money and motive to pull this kind of panic mongering."

Assid nodded. "This could easily be a ploy of the Saudis to dissuade their customers from abandoning oil for nuclear power."

"Not necessarily the whole Saudi government," James said.

Assid sneered. "I wouldn't put it past those fanatics. They've given their nephews millions in order to fulfill their religious fantasies of Islamic dictatorships."

"You're Muslim, aren't you?" Encizo asked.

"And you're Christian. Does that mean you endorse homophobic freaks who claim that tidals waves are messages from God that Christians aren't murdering enough gays?" Assid asked.

Encizo smiled. "Okay. I was fuzzy on the specifics for a moment."

"I never call the Brotherhood by the official name they want to be called, because they are no more Muslim than members of the Ku Klux Klan are good, decent Christians," Assid stated. "The sad thing is, the so-called justice those maniacs endorse is the only reasonable response for killers and terrorists such as themselves."

James looked at Encizo. "I knew there was a reason why I loved hanging out in Egypt with Unit 777."

Encizo grinned. "Come on. We've got an amphibious assault to plan."

CHAPTER SIX

Clad in a long black duster, David McCarter was taking the one certain path that he always chose when faced with the possibility of a trap. He charged directly into its jaws. As he walked toward the abandoned youth center in the suburban Paris slum, his instincts were on high alert, even though he knew that he had the protection of Gary Manning and T. J. Hawkins a hundred yards behind him.

Manning was loaded for bear, having fitted his AUG-A3 with the 24.4-inch heavy barrel. As the longest Steyr barrel was meant to be used both for precision marksmanship and light machine gun support, Manning would have more than enough reach to take out targets anywhere within five hundred yards of his position. The M-1913 Picatinny RIS rail atop the A-3 allowed the Canadian marksman to mount a Leupold Mark 4 scope, which, when tied in with Manning's familiarity with the heavy 77-grain Sierra Match King out of the AUG's barrel, made him the deadliest thing for a thousand-meter radius.

Hawkins's AUG A-3 was set up with the more standard sixteen-inch barrel and an EO Tech holographic sight. Under the barrel was an MP-203 grenade launcher, a nine-inch tube and firing mechanism that turned the assault rifle into an explosive tool capable of evening the odds against heavy firepower. As Manning's spotter, Hawkins was less concerned with razor-fine accuracy than the ability to put a lot of bullets into anyone attempting to charge their position. The holo-sight was meant for quick target acquisition, and the integral foregrip made up the difference in stability and control in the smaller, lighter carbine.

Conversely, McCarter had gone with the stubby sub-carbine barrel for his AUG. The twelve-inch barrel was meant for close-quarters work, and he wore shooting glasses and electronic hearing protection that filtered out noises that would harm his eardrums. Stripped down to only the flip-up iron sights installed on the stubby Steyr, without even a T-handle in front of the trigger guard, the weapon was designed for speed and brutality. If fired inside a room, it would produce a blinding flash and a thunder crack that would cause bleeding. Armored against the muzzle-blast, McCarter would have a serious advantage in tight quarters. It would be as if he were commanding thunder and lightning. The short length of the weapon enabled him to keep the rifle hidden under his trench coat yet still pour out lead at 850 rounds per minute. McCarter also had a pair of SIG-Sauer SP-2022 pistols, one on each hip, to keep him in the fight.

By making himself a target, he'd need to throw out a ton of lead to keep himself alive, which would mean pulling another gun, rather than spend time reloading a weapon. McCarter loved being bait. It put him in the most certain position on the battlefield, on the receiving end of enemy guns. With that, he'd be free to react with as much violence as necessary.

Already McCarter knew something was wrong with the neo-Nazi safehouse. It was run-down, plastered with grafitti, and garbage was strewed everywhere, which was as it should have been. It was too quiet, however. The usual French hate rap or white superiority metal didn't rumble and echo from darkened windows, and while McCarter could smell traces of marijuana, it was stale, hardly the fresh clouds laid down by "on the clock" neo-Nazis pumping up their unfocused rages against society.

As the young skinheads had driven off non-European immigrant kids from this recreational center by violence and presence of numbers, it was unlikely that the neo-Nazis would leave the building unattended. There would be a constant presence, with loud music thrumming through the windows. Lights would burn and drug smoke would pour through broken glass, informing the unwanted Africans and Arabs that they were to keep away, or risk being attacked.

"They cleared this place out," McCarter told Manning and Hawkins over his throat microphone.

"Not totally clear," Manning returned. "Movement, side two, level two. Count at least three heads watching your approach."

"Throw in four scumbags, stacking at the corner of side four," Hawkins added. "Submachine guns and black outfits. No insignia, and their kit looks all wrong for official French SWAT."

McCarter nodded in response to their warning.

"These lads are here for a show. Let me accommodate them. Gary, hold off unless you know I'm in trouble."

"Shit, David…" Manning hissed over the radio as McCarter broke into a run toward the front door. The Briton's duster opened and his hand slid down the sleek polymer shell of the compact rifle hanging from its sling. He threw his foot in front of him like a battering ram and smashed the door off its hinges.

With the cracking of wood, he heard a sudden cacophony of cries, both through the electronic filters and over his headset.

"Scumbags in motion!" Hawkins announced.

McCarter was through the doorway even as the first of the enemy submachine guns kicked up bullets at his heels. He pivoted and skidded to the floor, dropping prone as gunfire slashed the air over his head. The AUG A-3 was jammed forward like a pistol, ready to greet all comers.

By firing through the walls, the enemy confirmed to McCarter that they were professional killers. They had tracked his motion from where they had last seen him, knowing that their guns would penetrate the walls to take out their targets. SWAT and other police agencies were discouraged from engaging in firefights through materials that they couldn't see, simply because the officers of the law were held accountable for every round fired. Putting a bullet through a thin sheet of wood was an invitation to a lawsuit if an innocent bystander was harmed by the stray shot. These men were soldiers who had engaged in house-to-house fighting, and from the looks of things, they weren't constrained by American military rules of engagement.

McCarter kept his aim on the door, despite the fact

that he knew that someone with that kind of experience wouldn't rush into his sights simply because he'd disappeared into the shadows.

"They're stacking," Manning announced to McCarter over the radio. "One's reached into his belt for a flash-bang grenade."

McCarter sneered and realized that while his eye and ear protection would shield him against the flash grenade, he was going to be dealing with a team of trained gunmen who would enter on the bang. That meant he needed more cover than the shadows. With a lurch, he hurled himself over the top of a counter, landing hard amid the clutter of liquor bottles and beer cans lying on the floor. Luckily for him, he wore too many layers of ripstop nylon and heavy fabric to receive more than a scratch or two from the broken glass.

The flash-bang detonated with tooth-rattling power, even through the protective barrier of the counter. Though his hearing was shielded by the electronic earmuffs, the overpressure was enough to send spikes of pain through his sinus cavities. He was nearly blinded by the shock force, but he jerked to his feet. Like true professionals, the enemy kill squad moved in on the bang of the grenade.

Such sudden entry would not allow most people time to recover from the explosive thunderclap they had dumped into the room. David McCarter, however, was not most people. As soon as he could make out the murky shadows of the armored gunmen, framed by the leaves of his AUG's front sight, he held down the weapon's trigger. At 850 rounds per minute, the Steyr belched out its deadly song.

The first of the assault team stopped as if the bullets

that tore through his armored load-bearing vest were the bricks of an invisible wall. The 77-grain open-tip slugs tore through his Kevlar vest and slipped between trauma plates, churning through his upper rib cage. The heavy slugs deformed in fluid mass, shredding the gunner's lungs. His partners, shielded by his corpse and their own protective armor, shoved his limp form forward as a mobile barrier despite their shock at the sudden lash of fire and thunder that rocked them.

McCarter lowered the A-3's front sight to leg level and ripped off a second burst through the thighs and knees of the dead body at their forefront. The 5.56 mm bullets drilled through muscle mass and caromed off of femoral bones, slashing through dead flesh and cutting down to the living limbs of the man behind him. The second armored attacker stopped, then flopped gracelessly onto the back of his dead partner, upper legs shredded brutally as his BDU pants were not sheathed in Kevlar and trauma plates. The second man had been wearing knee guards, tough polycarbon shells that could protect the joint from violation by gunfire, but McCarter noted them and had adjusted his aim slightly higher. The Briton's rifle circumvented that protection with precision shot placement. The wounded attacker had lost his grip on his weapon as he fell, and was temporarily taken out of the fight.

The last of the assailants in the squad was still framed in the doorway. He jerked violently as Gary Manning launched a hollowpoint through the gap between his Kevlar helmet and the collar of his armored vest. The gunner's head was all but torn off of his shoulders by the spine-shattering bullet. He crashed to the floor in a useless tangle of unresponsive arms and legs. The broken shards of vertebrae lacerated arteries feeding the hapless man's brain, and merciful death spared the would-be murderer a life of imprisonment in a crippled body.

The remaining attacker threw himself to the floor and away from the doorway in a desperate bid for survival. His submachine gun chattered angrily as he dived for cover, but the wild movement had ruined his aim and spared McCarter to fight and die another day. The Briton, however, stable and pivoting with precision skill, tracked the sprawling gunman and didn't return the favor of missing. His AUG's lethal message of copper and lead ripped brutally into his target's gut. A stream of 5.56 mm tumblers somersaulted through the ambusher's bowels and kidneys like acrobatic saws, slicing through muscle and organs. The downed, black-clad shooter vomited a torrent of blood before expiring with a harsh rattle of a dying breath.

McCarter dumped the spent magazine from his Steyr and pushed home a full one. He didn't have time to waste recharging the empty weapon, considering that Manning had reported other figures upstairs. The extended 42-round magazine was designed for the AUG in its light-machine-gun mode, but for now, the Phoenix Force commander just wanted to hold off a speed reload for as long as he could. Now the compact bullpup was in bullet-hose configuration. When the Steyr ran dry, he'd switch to the twin 16-shot SIG-Sauer in his belt. If that wasn't enough, then he'd use the empty pistols as clubs to acquire a loaded weapon.

He walked toward the man he'd shot through the legs. As he did, McCarter keyed his throat mike. "Thanks."

"I couldn't let you have all the fun," Manning replied. "Targets on the second floor haven't moved."

"Two vehicles approaching. No headlights, no strobes, no sirens," Hawkins announced. His implication was clear to the Phoenix Force leader. If the approaching SUVs were official, they'd make damn certain that McCarter knew who they were. Noise and light would have been their tools to rob him of his willingness to fight.

McCarter took a deep breath. "Probably why the blokes upstairs haven't moved. Backup's on the way."

"Leave anyone to talk?" Hawkins asked.

McCarter felt the throat of the man sprawled over his partner. No pulse. "Thought I might have, but a holed femoral artery determined otherwise."

"Hold off a blooper on the SUVs?" Hawkins asked.

"Light one up if you like. Leave the second one intact," McCarter ordered.

"Affirmative," Hawkins replied.

Outside, one of the approaching SUVs blossomed from black steel and glass into a flower of fire and pillowy charred wreckage as Hawkins landed six and a half ounces of high explosives into it. The blazing hulk ground angrily on the concrete, not stopping until it slammed into the youth center. The other vehicle swerved hard, skidding to a halt not five yards from the front door.

Hawkins popped off a pair of rifle rounds toward the halted SUV, keeping himself the source of the enemy's attention. Leaning out the windows, the enemy gunners returned the favor, in exceedingly larger volumes. The couple of shots that the Southerner had unleashed had provided the muzzle-flash necessary to anchor the attention of the commando squad. They were focused on where the initial flashes had come from, but Hawkins had sidestepped, moving behind more solid cover as their submachine guns sparked uselessly against the wall he crouched behind.

Manning held his fire, and Hawkins popped off a few more shots around the corner to keep the SUV team distracted.

Forgotten and invisible in the enemy squad's blind spot, McCarter was free to rush up to the stopped SUV. Along the way, he'd drawn a flash-bang grenade off one of the dead men, priming it as he ran. As the gunners inside the SUV unleashed sheets of autofire toward Hawkins, the Briton dropped the concussion bomb in through an open window.

McCarter hit the floor just before the distraction device produced 150 decibels of pure thunder. The sound burst like a tidal wave, crashing into the gunmen as it flooded the vehicle's interior. The pulse of pressure and noise rendered every person inside the SUV unconscious.

The Briton got to work quickly, throwing open the doors and hauling the knocked-out shooters to the floorboards. The four men were too staggered and blinded to resist as he slid cable ties around their wrists and ankles. Hawkins raced across the open ground and joined him at the vehicle, providing close cover for McCarter as he finished binding and gagging the nearly lifeless death squad.

"Gary? Any movement upstairs?" McCarter asked.

"Haven't had to take a shot. No one even flinched with the second flasher," Manning said. "Give me a moment."

McCarter heard the cycle of the Steyr's action through Manning's throat mike.

"The bodies up there are either corpses or mannequins. One took a round in the shoulder with no reaction."

"Bugger all," McCarter growled. "T.J., take this SUV back to the safehouse. Stay under the speed limit. Gary's driving me home."

"You're going up there alone?" Hawkins asked.

"I've got him covering me with his rifle," McCarter said. "Gary could be on the moon, but with the right rifle, I'll never be alone as long as he's behind the scope."

"Get going, T.J. David's too ornery to die of a few bullets anyhow," Manning added.

Hawkins slid behind the wheel, setting his AUG into the footwell against his leg. "If I have to vet two new assholes into this team, I'm pissing on your graves."

McCarter winked. "I'll miss you, too, redneck. Scat!"

The SUV pulled away and McCarter hung a spare MP-5 submachine gun around his neck on a sling. With the AUG and the spare machine pistol, McCarter gave himself some room in case he encountered serious opposition. The battle against the robots that would have infiltrated the Inshas reactor was foremost in his mind. Human intervention had failed. Maybe now the conspiracy would attempt to try its mechanized forces.

So far, there hadn't been any evidence of the presence of the robotic infiltrators in France, except for a few hushed rumors. The Farm was still trying to pry open the seals on the real facts, but the situation could have been akin to one that they'd faced too many times before. All the data in the world couldn't give McCarter a magical robot-destroying set of firepower right now. Out of touch with the Farm and with the upper floor of the recreation center dark but manned with lifeless semblances of men, the Briton could be walking into an empty floor or stumbling into a den of treacherous automatons capable of turning themselves into bombs if their weaponry proved insufficient to clear out the Phoenix pro.

"Passing out of incident perimeter," Hawkins announced from the SUV. "Soon to be out of radio contact."

"Sit on the prisoners until we get back," McCarter growled.

"Just make damned sure you get back," Hawkins returned.

McCarter remembered Encizo's description of how hard it had been for them to put one of the robots down despite two rifles emptying their loads into the metal shells. He regretted not taking Manning's shotgun along with him to deal with the enemy mechanisms, but a rifle, two handguns and a shotgun would have been too much for him to carry. As it was, with the borrowed MP-5 hanging around his neck, he felt slowed down by a surplus of gear.

As he mounted the steps, he heard the whirr of an electrical motor. His fingers tensed on the handles of his Steyr rifle, and he saw a squat object moving across the floor. Two blocky shapes poked out of the top of the flat patrol bot, and it rode on trapezoidal conveyors that were miniaturized versions of tank treads. As McCarter brought up his rifle, the boxy machine spun to face him. The two shapes atop the robot were the familiar square slides of Glock pistols, sights removed. But neither produced the bright, eye-searing strobe that burned McCarter's darkness-attuned retinas. Pure survival instinct kicked him backward down the stairs as the unmistakable rattle of Glock 18 machine pistols snarled from the second floor. The blue-white flash wasn't a gunshot, but bullets chased the Phoenix warrior and sliced through the air where he had been a moment ago.

"David!" Manning bellowed over McCarter's earbud. McCarter winced, nearly deafened as his comm receiver was inside the protective earmuffs.

"Bloody hell, Gary! I'm already blind!" McCarter snapped as he scrambled laterally along the landing halfway between the first and second floors. He didn't want to be in the open while all he could see was a glowing blob of brightness hanging in his vision. "Shit, it's not like I need more than one ear."

"Sorry," Manning replied.

McCarter's good ear picked up the motors of the boxy bot that had blinded him just before the machine opened up with a pair of automatic pistols. There was no doubt that the deadly automaton would be able to pursue him down the stairs, given its grabby, all-terrain treads and wide track base. There was a heavy thump above and McCarter opened fire at the sound. His night vision had been destroyed by the robot's luminal attack, but the cooler, milder fireball issued by the AUG didn't make things any easier. Sure, he could see the armed machine rolling down the steps, guns tracking in the flicker of the Austrian rifle's muzzle-flash, and he could even see the holes punched into it by 5.56 mm rounds as they appeared in the dull steel box of its body. But he was also slowed enough by blindness that he could feel the thud of 9 mm bullets as they plunked into his chest, their impacts jolting him even through Kevlar.

The robot, sensing McCarter's counterattack, threw itself into reverse and disappeared behind the top step. The Briton took a few deep breaths. The robot's guns hadn't broken any ribs through his protective armor, but he could feel the bruises that would turn his chest a purplish black by dawn. He wondered how his rifle had done against the hostile device. Odd sounds, like coins clinking, issued from the top of the steps, and McCarter knew that there was at least one other type of murderous machine accompanying the boxy ambusher.

He bit off his dread and opened up with the AUG again. The muzzle-flash illuminated a serpentine infiltrator, its skin a dull gunmetal color, its body sinewy and writhing as it poured over the top step. The stubby gun barrel in its cyclopean head flashed, the first round sizzling the air over McCarter's shoulder, the bullet's passage a dull crack through the hearing protectors. Had the veteran commando not sidestepped at the first appearance of the new opponent, the slug would have cored his skull. McCarter leaned into the butt of the Steyr, his rifle a flaming lance that speared the oncoming mechanical serpent with metal-rending hot bullets.

The snakelike device twisted under close-range, violent impacts, splitting it in two. The battered segments twisted wildly as McCarter let the emptied Steyr drop on its sling and he transitioned to the MP-5. He turned on the underbarrel flashlight as stealth was no longer a consideration in the wake of the brief, violent firefight. He needed the spray of light to see any subsequent targets now that his night vision had been ruined by strobes and gunfire.

The front half of the snake machine tumbled toward the landing where McCarter crouched. The Phoenix Force commander immediately recalled the self-destruct mechanism that Schwarz had described, and that it had the equivalent killing power of an M-26 fragmentation grenade. The memory of the internal bomb set off alarms in McCarter's brain as the tumbling segment grew closer. He spun around on the landing and threw himself wildly down the steps to the first floor. As he crashed to the tile floor, knee and elbow protection shielding his joints from crippling injuries, the stairwell landing sprouted a new sun of fire and concussive force. By hitting the floor, McCarter had avoided flying shrapnel, and his electronic earmuffs kept his head from feeling as if he'd been struck by a bellowing rhinoceros. The pressure wave slapped against his back, knocking the wind out of him, but other than that, it was no worse than a run through Selection back at Hereford.

The ceiling flexed under a second detonation, chunks of masonry slapping the tiles around him hard enough to break them. McCarter tucked his legs in as a fifty-pound slab broke loose and nearly sliced off his feet.

"David! Get out of there!" Manning warned.

McCarter didn't need to be told twice. More detonations smashed holes through the ceiling above him, and rubble crashed to the floor where he'd been only moments before. Had he not charged out of the rec center at maximum speed, the explosion-weakened building would have crushed the Briton beneath collapsing chunks of roof and ceiling. The abandoned building, racked by self-destructing robots, imploded behind McCarter as he skidded to a halt.

On his knees, gasping for breath, he watched as the former den of French skinheads folded in on itself, blown to hell. Wiping his brow, McCarter hoped the conspiracy's plans for Europe had suffered a similar fate. From the amount of blasts that had gone off, it was likely that a supply of infiltrators large enough to hit every nuclear plant in France had been stored up there, then destroyed to prevent capture.

The destruction of an entire building would bring the authorities down en masse, making things harder for Phoenix Force's European contingent to conduct its investigation clandestinely. However, that much heat would mean that McCarter wouldn't need to be the sharp end of the spear against the conspiracy's efforts in France.

As Manning drove up with their rental car, McCarter wished the authorities good luck. He would have to confirm his suspicions with their captured prisoners.

CHAPTER SEVEN

The fishing trawler was 120 feet long and had seen better days. While the rust and peeling paint made the old hulk appear to be a well-worked, currently employed fisher, the terrorist operators of the ancient rustbucket didn't take into account that the winch mechanisms were so crusted and in disrepair that they were completely useless.

The stench of rotted fish made Rafael Encizo glad that he had a strong stomach. Though he had plenty of fishing boat experience from his younger days, Encizo knew that the nausea-inducing cloud wafting off the decks could only be from a worthless load in its hold. Even the gulls that should have been drawn to the smell of an operating fishing boat were too savvy to approach a craft that promised only ill stomachs, and this for birds which regularly sought out landfills and all manner of fish carrion.

Around the Zodiac boat shadowing the Muslim Brotherhood vessel, dorsal fins broke the surface and gave proof to the deadliness of this trip. The sharks didn't mind even the most rotted of carcasses that washed out of the hold, but if either Phoenix Force or their Unit 777 allies received an injury, a fall to the waves would be instantly fatal as the blood-and-carrion-frenzied scavengers sought a fresh meal.

Encizo and James were regular dive partners, so they would form one team for this part of the mission. Despite the fact that Kristopoulos had worked well with Farkas back at Inshas, the Egyptian had a designated swim partner, and in shark-infested waters, you wanted that particular person—who knew your swimming tempo, strengths and weaknesses—on your side. Kristopoulos had no such partner in Egypt, which was why she had been left on the helicopter that had dumped the inflatable raft into the Mediterranean.

She now rode on the MAG-58 heavy machine gun mounted in the door of the Blackhawk helicopter that was flying overwatch on the mission. It was hard to feel worthless when you had control of a belt-fed 7.62 mm NATO bullet hose that could belch out heavy slugs at 3000 feet per second at a rate of 800 rounds per minute. Due to Kristopoulos's Israeli military training, she was familiar with the MAG-58 design, and could make the big machine gun do everything she wanted it to, especially dealing with hostile forces that would be within feet of Unit 777 on the deck of the trawler.

Relying on the amplification on her night-vision goggles, Kristopoulos was able to inform the assault team that there was no activity on deck. The stern of the trawler provided the best location for the Zodiac inflatable to dock, as it was clear of equipment where an ambusher or an enemy robot could be lying in wait.

Farkas worked the throttle and the Zodiac caught up

with the trawler, its high surface speed enabling it to run rings around the fishing boat if necessary. Their target vessel only plodded along at a meager eight knots, meaning that even with seven men on board, keeping pace with it was no problem.

Farooq, one of the biggest Egyptian men that Encizo had ever seen, and Brassha, a lean man easily as tall as James, threw the grapnel hooks of the caving ladder onto the railing in unison. The rubber-tipped metal hooks made little sound as they snared the rail of the boat. Luckily, as the trawler was moving along at its maximum speed, its engine sounds and the groan of its flexing hull covered whatever impact was made.

Encizo was the first up the ladder, climbing with apelike skill and speed, his MP-5 cinched tightly across his shoulders. As he somersaulted onto the deck, he drew his Heckler & Koch USP-45. His MP-5 was loaded with heavyweight 147-grain hollowpoints, chosen for their penetrative power and excellent performance against automobiles. The slithering snake robots might have been much smaller and generally a bit more fragile than a one-and-a-half-ton car, but most automobiles didn't have a mounted weapon and a built-in self-destruct mechanism that packed the power of a fragmentation grenade.

"I'm not getting any movement whatsoever," Kristopoulos announced over their hands-free radio as all the Egyptians except for Brassha followed Encizo's example. James was the last on deck. "I'm not even picking up a heat source through the pilothouse's construction, but that might be due to all the metal in there."

"Autopilot?" Encizo asked. He holstered his .45 now that there were others on deck with him.

"I assumed as much," James answered. "But this is moving awfully quick for an unmanned boat."

The African-American Phoenix Force veteran scanned the deck, his Saiga 12 shotgun following his gaze as he swept for movement or enemy targets. The Izhmash-built 12-gauge came from Russia and was based on the classic AK-47 receiver. The Saiga had swiftly become a popular combat weapon for close-quarters encounters. With a five- or an eight-round quick-reloading magazine that could chamber 3-inch 12-gauge Magnum shotshells, it could spit a dozen pellets with a single pull of the trigger or fire a .72-inch bolt of heavy lead that could smash the engine of an enemy vehicle. It was one of the ultimate power tools, despite being only semiautomatic. The Saiga 12K that James carried was especially handy, combining a seventeen-inch barrel and folding stock, allowing for swift movement inside of buildings or ships.

The collapsible Saiga had been chosen for its machine-smashing capacity, as well as the potential utility it possessed against human opponents. An ounce and a half of copper and lead, either in shot or slug form, would be more than enough to take out an enemy robot easily or instantly stop a human gunman.

So far, they had only encountered opposition armed with conventional weapons, men with rifles or robots with modified handguns. Of course, those machines were small infiltration devices that weren't meant to encounter enemy commando teams head-on. If they were seen while slipping through a nuclear power plant, they could quickly lose themselves in ventilation ducts or access pipes. If there were other forms of robotic opposition, the Phoenix commandos wanted to be ready for them. They were familiar with remote-controlled drone tanks that had more than sufficient firepower to easily destroy the eight-man force.

"The question we have to answer is whether this is a trap or a diversion," Encizo mused. "They could be drawing us away from something else."

Farkas flipped down his night-vision goggles to look for movement. "If it were a distraction, wouldn't there be crew present? There's been no indication of life. And from this angle, I can see that the pilothouse is empty."

Asslid spoke up. "The Blackhawk's radar is peeled, and there's nothing in the air. And we're keeping a sharp eye out for unmanned aerial vehicles."

"Nothing visual, either," Kristopoulos added.

"There's no guarantee that they'd require a UAV to relay commands to the robots," James noted. "And there's always the chance that there's someone on this ship, out of sight belowdecks somewhere."

Farkas nodded. "What's the plan?"

"Clear the deck, by the numbers, as if this were a normal takedown," Encizo said. "No changes. Business as usual. Farooq, anchor us here and give us cover fire if necessary."

The Egyptian giant didn't look pleased to be stuck in the babysitting role, but the man was a professional and would perform his assigned duty. He nodded and lowered himself into a squat that rested him below the top of the railing, safe in the shadows. Night vision would not catch him as the extradense shadows provided nothing to amplify. Motionless, he'd only be noticeable if he was swept by an illumination beam, and their night-vision goggles would pick up any such strobing lights, even if they were in the infrared range.

Encizo led James, Farkas, Sayid, Hussar and Belloq in single file along the deck, confident of Farooq as he kept watch as their designated marksman. On point, Encizo had his eyes and ears peeled for the first indication of ambush. His MP-5 followed his gaze, ready to empty its payload into any target he spotted. His darkness-attuned eyes were augmented by his night-vision goggles, but hearing was not as easy. The fishing trawler's engines rumbled, creating an ever-present undertone, and caused loose equipment on the deck to vibrate. Each wave that lifted the trawler made the hull groan as it flexed. The hull was not as rigid as would be assumed by a layman because a stiff-spined keel would mean that the craft would splinter atop a turbulent ocean. The hull required just enough spring so that it wouldn't shatter as a mountain of seawater pushed upward beneath it. What kept the boat afloat also made it far too difficult to make out stealthy footsteps. Encizo had to make do with his sharp eyes.

With the bobbing deck and bouncing rigging, there were dozens of slithering, snakelike forms on the deck. It took every ounce of discipline that Encizo possessed to prevent a pull of the trigger. Shifting cables or swaying rope looked too hauntingly similar to their serpentine robot enemies. The Cuban's back teeth ground furiously with tension. It was one thing to look for human opponents in a stalk such as this, but against stealthy robotic snakes that could hide anywhere, his nerves were as taut as tripwires.

An inhuman, small and deadly enemy had triggered Encizo's paranoia, which was a bad thing when he had a firearm in his hands. His own concern over his edgy nerves only increased their rawness. Natural fear was a lifesaving mechanism, a biological response that fed the body extra oxygen while closing off smaller vessels to reduce the potential for blood loss. That extra oxygen also sharpened senses and increased his strength and resistance to injury. Calvin James had quantified the bonuses of the fight-or-flight reflex, one of which was an increased heart rate, giving Encizo an intellectual anchor for his racing thoughts. Still, the robotic slithering enemies that could crawl through shadows and mimic coils of rope were an imposing form of opponent that didn't conform to his usual enemy. The infiltrator robots defied the usual logic of combat that his life had depended on.

"Fuck the panic," Encizo whispered to himself. "We killed two of these things already."

"Telling yourself that, too?" James asked. "Just use your inside voice…"

Encizo smirked. "Thanks."

Something jingled softly, almost musically, and the two Phoenix Force commandos froze, focusing on the sound. Their weapons both locked on to the same stretch of deck. The Egyptians wanted to aim there, too, but training forced the quartet to establish a covering perimeter for the pair.

That both James and Encizo reacted identically was all the confirmation needed that it was more than overactive nerves or imagination. The Unit 777 counterterrorists covered their Phoenix Force allies as they closed with the tinkling of metallic spring mechanisms. James held up a closed fist to stop their movement. Encizo looked at him questioningly.

"Why would an infiltrator make noise?" James asked.

Encizo turned on the IR illuminator mounted under his MP-5's barrel. The sudden flare of light in night vision inspired lateral movement on the part of a serpentine mechanism. "Back to back! It's an ambush!"

The Unit 777 commandos backed up tightly against James and Encizo, as much for their own protection as for that of their Phoenix Force allies. James's and Encizo's body armor and torsos would slow down any bullets that went through them, providing extra cover from behind as well as keep an opponent from sneaking up on them by surprise. It was a bit bloodthirsty to use your own teammates as living shields, but as all six members of the team were heavily armed, it wasn't like the same tactic of ruthless dictators or armies putting helpless civilians in the line of fire. The six sets of eyes would also prevent an infiltrator from slithering between them and detonating its self-destruct mechanism to take out the whole team.

That threat became readily apparent when Hussar opened fire with the Israeli Desert Eagle he'd chosen for his side arm. The Egyptian's mammoth pistol bellowed a heavy, hard-cast 158-grain load that tore through metal skin. The raw power of Hussar's two-shot string of fire, guided by an underbarrel, infrared illuminator, was more than sufficient to shear through the robot's shell and burrow into its destruct mechanism. Hussar and his partner, Sayid, were shoved backward roughly, but Encizo, James, Farkas and Belloq provided enough buttressing that they stayed on their feet. Luckily the Egyptians' armor held against the wave of shrapnel thrown out by the serpentine infiltrator.

Sayid triggered his Saiga 12K as another of the snakelike automatons popped into view. The Saiga's roar flung the robot back so that when it detonated, its concussive splash was deflected by a low bulkhead. The Phoenix and Unit 777 operators had no time to enjoy their momentary victory as scattered robots slithered into view and opened fire with their head guns.

Muzzle-flashes betrayed the serpentine infiltrators' positions, allowing the mixture of shotguns and machine pistols to rain lead into them. James and Encizo saw multiple targets emerge around the decoy that had almost drawn them into a trap. Like metallic cobras, the infiltration units lunged at the Phoenix pair. Encizo cut one off with his MP-5, deep-penetrating 147-grain bullets tearing into one of the enemy mechanisms.

Head unit wrecked, the decapitated robot slammed into the Cuban's chest. Encizo snared the attacking device and hurled it with all his prodigious strength. The robot flew through the air, but detonated at ten feet, right at the apex of its flight. Only the Cuban's goggles kept his eyes from being punctured by shrapnel. As it was, his cheeks were peppered with slicing fragments. James's Saiga dealt with a second lunging steel serpent, pinning it back to the deck where its detonation rocked the Phoenix pair, but hurled the infiltrator's robotic kin in all directions.

James swept the muzzle of his semiauto shotgun, triggering 12-gauge thunder as if he were a bronze-skinned Zeus. His thunderbolts slew the enemy snakes, buckshot and slugs both proving to be effective against the thin skins of the automatons. Buckshot crippled mechanisms, while slugs simply obliterated segments with one hit. The seven-round magazine had run empty, but James was able to quickly slam home a second five-round magazine and continue pouring out concentrated, deck-sweeping fire. The Russian thunderer ripped off five more rounds before James let the shotgun drop on its sling, transitioning to the 14-shot Israeli Bul 5, a high-capacity variation on his favored Colt 1911A1.

James drained the 14-round reservoir into two infiltrators that continued fighting ground despite being chopped in two by the shotgun's shredding fire. As 9 mm rounds plucked his torso armor and glanced off his protective helmet, James managed to tag a single destruct mechanism inside one of the enemy infiltrators. The detonation destroyed its ally, but also knocked James off of his feet, where he landed on his back between Farkas and Belloq.

By now, their safety was being bolstered by Tanya Kristopoulos and Colonel Assid in the Blackhawk helicopter, as well as Farooq back in the stern. Kristopoulos was putting the MAG-58 and her training with the heavy metal blaster to good use, utilizing precision bursts to tear into any of the slithering forms that her night-vision goggles picked up. The 7.62 mm rounds tore down onto the hostile devices with relentless killing power. Where the boarding party couldn't see a crawling robotic serpent concealed on the deck, her aerial point of view helped her to plug their blind spots. Detonations of the machines flared in her goggles, but the blasts only served to illuminate further targets.

Muzzle-flashes at the stern indicated that Farooq was in the fight, though a swift glance showed that the robots had chosen to ignore him and concentrate on the six men who had formed a protective ring. That meant that Farooq must have been invisible to whatever mind was coordinating the deadly infiltration automatons.

The enemy swarm was intent on Phoenix Force and their Egyptian allies. Kristopoulos bit off the urge to ask the embattled warriors to look for a camera on the deck. Instead, she glanced to Assid.

The Unit 777 commander was already on the hunt. "The camera has to be in the pilothouse. I'm taking it out!"

Assid shifted from his rifle to an AGM-6 40 mm grenade launcher. He shouldered the huge revolver-style piece of portable artillery, looked through its scope, then triggered two fat rounds into the bridge of the trawler. The high-explosive grenades thundered mightily, smashing two gaping craters into the pilothouse.

"Robots still active!" Kristopoulos announced.

Assid triggered the AGM three more times, blowing the bridge into a cloud of splinters. Finally reduced to a sunken crater, the incessant robot horde simultaneously detonated, their self-destruct mechanisms triggered by a lack of fresh data beamed into their receivers. Fortunately, as many had already been destroyed or swept off of the deck into the sea, only a half-dozen robots remained to detonate around Phoenix Force and their allies.

James staggered to his feet, hooking an arm under Belloq to help him rise. The man had taken shrapnel or bullets to his legs, and he could barely support his own weight, let alone scramble to safety. The Egyptian's face paled with effort, but Farkas shored him up on the other side. Sayid was injured, as well, his upper right arm lacerated deeply by shrapnel. Encizo and Hussar scooped him up. All of the men who'd been in the middle of the deck were sporting cuts from flying metal fragments, but Sayid had four deep gashes that cut down through muscle.

Encizo handed Sayid a compress, which he clamped over the carved flesh to prevent bleeding until the Cuban was able to tape it in place. The pressure dressing would compress any severed blood vessels, without the crippling, mangling power of a tourniquet.

There wasn't going to be any time for plucking out shrapnel, since the fishing trawler lurched radically. The boat was starting to sink, probably due to either the self-destructing robots that might have been below-decks, or perhaps Assid's hail of grenades had punched deeper than intended. Either way, the Muslim Brotherhood's illicit craft was going to rest at the bottom of the Mediterranean, and they needed to get off before it sucked down the Zodiac in its wake.

"We've got smoke issuing from multiple parts of the hull," Assid informed them. "The conspirators are scuttling the craft."

James and Encizo looked at each other. James grumbled. "So much for getting any information out of this trip."

Sayid and Belloq were lowered gingerly down on ropes to the Zodiac boat, where Brassha untied them and settled them into the inflatable power raft. It was a slow process to keep from aggravating their injuries, but by the time they were done, the railing had dropped from fifteen feet above the waves to only seven. Brassha sliced away the caving ladder as the remaining five warriors, Farooq included, leaped over the rail and swam toward the Zodiac.

"Go! Go!" Farkas shouted as he grabbed a loop of material on one of the inflatable pontoons.

Brassha hit the throttle and twin Mercury engines

roared to life. The suction of the sinking trawler kept the Zodiac from launching like a rocket. Horsepower that would normally hurl the inflatable along at nearly seventy miles per hour with a full load of men barely gave them enough escape velocity as water surged over the deck of the swamped ship.

"Move, you piece of shit!" Brassha growled as the Zodiac's engines snarled violently.

Encizo was surprised, as most times he'd been on a Zodiac raft, which was almost a weekly event for him, the big motors were silent, even stealthy. The strain of the engines against the whirlpool formed by the mass of a thousand-ton trawler sinking below the waves had increased the roar of the engines exponentially until finally the Zodiac shot away.

The Egyptians, James and Encizo clung to the heavy nylon handles on the pontoons, their arms securely hooked through the loops to keep from being left behind and yanked beneath the waves.

The Cuban glared back at the whirlpool left in the disappearance of the deadly, robot-infested boat.

Another lead was gone, and the conspirators had proved that they were aware of Stony Man's presence. The trap laid for McCarter and his contingent, and now this ambush, showed a frightening prescience on the part of the nuclear plant saboteurs.

A grim grin crossed Encizo's face, however.

That meant that somewhere in the United States, the enemy was laying a death trap for Able Team. If anyone could turn an ambush into a resounding victory, it was the singularly intense Carl Lyons and his brothers in arms.

The conspiracy was about to pull the tail of the tiger and receive a face full of claws.

CHAPTER EIGHT

While Aaron Kurtzman and the Stony Man cybernetics team scrutinized the meager clues provided by Morrison's hard drive and navigated the treacherous security systems of offshore bank accounts that paid off the D.C. chop shop owner, Able Team decided to do some research the old-fashioned way. Since the enemy seemed to have an excellent team of hackers on its side, electronic intelligence was going to have to take a backseat to standard research.

Luckily, Stony Man Farm's blacksuit program had a large number of alumnii among the ranks of nuclear power plant security teams. It was no coincidence that SWAT teams and elite soldiers were drawn to duty at power plants by hiring incentives. With relative ease Lyons, Blancanales and Schwarz were able to scour the nation for information that wouldn't make it into electronic intelligence databases. As Lyons and his partners helped to provide the advanced training for most of the blacksuits who had gone through the Farm, their calls were happily received and information flowed freely to the Stony Man trio. Still, three phone calls at a time, coast to coast, took enough hours for Able Team to receive word of the two ambushes conducted against their comrades working overseas.

"You three look like you could use a break," Price told them, looking down at a list of power plants whose security team resources had been bolstered with private contractors. She handed Lyons, Blancanales and Schwarz the after-action reports filed by McCarter and Encizo.

Lyons looked at McCarter's report first, nodding with approval that his Phoenix Force counterpart was utilizing "wall-to-wall counseling" in retrieving information from the mercenaries captured in France. As it was, their fingerprints and faces were run through the database by Huntington Wethers, who had identified them through their Interpol files. While James's medical experience would have been necessary for Phoenix Force's usual brand of chemical interrogation, utilizing the anti-inhibitor known as scopolamine, wall-to-wall counseling was a brute-force means of achieving the same results.

The men's background files had been expunged and they were listed as dead. Only through Wethers's meticulous investigative skills had the eldest member of the cyberteam discovered the last entries on each of the dead men's passports—Morocco. It was standard operating procedure for men who joined the French Foreign Legion to be listed as dead, to allow the men who entered France's service to begin anew with a clean slate. While many considered the Legionnares nothing more than mercenaries and cutthroats, Lyons had encountered enough of them to realize that there was a strong line of discipline that went through those who lasted long enough to receive the phoenixlike rebirth afforded by the military service.

The prisoners were dropped off a few blocks from where the Paris police had been investigating the prior battle against the mercenaries and the robots, drawing the cops to the hired guns by firing a few shots into a concrete embankment.

"So these are men who may have been in the French Foreign Legion?" Lyons asked, looking over McCarter's data.

Price nodded, then caught Lyons and Blancanales sharing a knowing glance. "What have you discovered?"

"We've been making calls to nuclear power plant security teams around the country, and we've had a name pop up quite often," Blancanales explained. "One of the plants that isn't on Lyons's list of tested facilities is Calvert Cliffs Nuclear Power Plant."

Price's brow furrowed. "Why would that draw your attention?"

"Come on, Barb. Think geographically," Blancanales pointed out. "Calvert Cliffs not only feeds Washington, D.C., with the bulk of its electricity, but it's also close enough to the capital that a full-blown nuclear incident could produce a Chernobyl-like evacuation of the national government."

"Remember, the Negev and Inshas plants were small infiltrations. Negev only runs about twenty-two megawatts, and Inshas is about the same. Calvert Cliffs runs two 2700-megawatt reactors," Lyons said. "When the Israel and Egypt plants went too hot, they wouldn't cause a catastrophe. But two reactors capable of putting out a total of 5400 megawatts of thermal energy is almost half again as large as the power Chernobyl ran at its peak. If Chernobyl required an eighteen-mile radius evacuated around it, and was responsible for 200 to 270 thousand cases of cancer and nearly 300 immediate deaths…"

Price looked to Schwarz. "I thought you were the math wizard."

"Carl's no dummy. Chernobyl was an accident, and only one reactor went critical," Schwarz said. "We're looking at the potential for widespread sabotage on two high-powered reactors at the peak of their operation."

"But no one has run any tests on their security according to Hirtenberg's investigation," Price replied.

"You want to cause a nuclear disaster, and you're not going to make an effort to hit Washington, D.C.'s source of electricity, and possibly get the bonus of a cloud of radioactive contaminant that could kill off half the federal government?" Lyons asked. "Besides, we spotted something else."

"Don't keep me in suspense," Price complained.

"Well, Calvert Cliffs has had some subcontracting work to a firm called Second Sphere, which was allowed to operate peripherally to the main security force for the facility," Blancanales explained.

"Second Sphere?" Price asked. "That's not a security company. It's a private military contract firm."

Lyons nodded. "While the blacksuit program has alumni seeded around the country in various police and military units, Second Sphere is the reverse. The owner of the corporation, Jacob M. Stern, has been picking up those who are washing out of the kinds of groups we're looking into."

"Washouts is a polite way of putting it," Price said. "Kurtzman had run a check on Second Sphere a few months back. While none of the men they hired were actually charged or convicted of wrongdoing, it was only because of timely resignations or the disappearance of evidence and testimony."

"Violent disappearance of testimony," Lyons mused grimly.

Price shook her head. "If that were the case, the Department of Energy would have dropped their contracts a lot faster. No, Stern's managed to clean his men up until they look respectable."

"So?" Blancanales asked. "Aaron's been able to make David and Carl look presentable to honest law enforcement or real military."

Lyons scratched his temple with his middle finger, the not-so-subtle flip-off directed at his elder partner. Blancanales smirked, but Lyons had already returned to the discussion. "So David picks up a group of men who most likely had been sanitized by the French Foreign Legion, and we have similarly clean rent-a-cops working for Second Sphere. While the ex-Legionnaires are definitely connected to the robots, we only have circumstantial evidence tying Second Sphere to any wrongdoing."

"Well, it's not as if you three need a warrant, do you?" Price asked. "We're not working on a case that will go to court—we're trying to prevent the donation of a nuclear power plant that could pump lethal radiation into our nation's capital."

"In the meantime, I think you'd better drop some ears into the French authorities, in case they receive any photographs of David," Lyons warned.

"You saw that about the strobe flash, too. While the building was blown to hell, there's a strong possibility that David's picture was transmitted via wireless modem," Price agreed.

"Even if the police haven't received his image, there's the possibility that our enemy has been distributing BOLO fliers on him among their contacts," Lyons told her. "The conspiracy can't afford to have the French police receive information directly from them, but there's nothing that could compromise them if a bunch of young, hungry punks end up with a piece of paper with his face on it in their pocket. The conspiracy gets cheap and easy cannon fodder to throw at Phoenix Force, and the aftermath of a failed hit still puts an easy-to-follow stink on David and the gang."

"BOLO... Be On The Lookout," Price translated from her mental cop-to-English dictionary. "You know, it's bad enough that I have to keep tabs on acronyms and contractions from military, espionage and political slang."

"Sorry, Barb. Once a police, always a police," Lyons returned. "I wonder if Cal and Rafe are also on the enemy's known-faces list."

"You could be, too, considering your robotic encounter," Price said. "Calvin and Rafael are most definitely going to have their faces handed out to whatever gunmen the conspiracy can wrangle in Egypt. Unmanned aerial vehicles are notoriously good at providing real-time, crystal-clear imagery. Even night-vision photographs would come out sharp enough to hand out for targeting purposes."

Schwarz frowned. "I'm sure that Cal or Rafe brought this up..."

"They're looking for places where a UAV could be stored, supported and launched. The trouble is, we're looking at technology that can fit in any garage," Price said. "Between dealing with the money trail to Morrison's account for the fake delivery van and tracking down components from charred remains of the robots, we're pretty thin on aerial investigation of likely launch points for the eyes in the sky."

"We'll need to look for UFO reports around Calvert Cliffs," Lyons stated.

"UFO reports?" Price asked. "As in flying saucers?"

"Barb, you've heard reports out of Groom Lake and Area 51 enough to know that the average citizen is going to see a quiet, silent craft hovering in the sky and think little green men, not high-tech military-intelligence-gathering technology," Lyons told her. "I'd like to have someone tap UFO reports all along the East Coast, because Calvert Cliffs is not the only nuclear power plant that we have to watch over."

Price nodded. "Good point. And here I thought we only hired you because you're too stubborn to die."

Lyons winked. "I'm full of surprises, lady."

Schwarz shook his head. "Robots and flying saucers in the same mission. I love my job."

"Keep your nerdgasm in check, Gadgets," Blancanales replied. "So far, every UFO we've encountered has tried to kill us."

"Not to mention hostile robots, zombies and skinwalkers," Lyons added.

Schwarz nodded. "Tried to kill us. And two out of three of those were bald-ass forgeries. But this time, I've got some ideas of my own. Langley Air Force Base has a unit of remote intelligence devices and operators back from a run in the Sandbox," Schwarz explained. "Barbara, if you can mobilize them, we could definitely use the assist."

"I'll see what we can do," Price replied. "Until then, what are you three going to do?"

"We're heading out to Calvert Cliffs," Lyons told her. "We'll be low profile."

"To check on some rent-a-cops who are performing cafeteria and dormitory security for the nuclear plant staff," Price added.

"Totally innocuous," Lyons agreed.

Price was about to say something when her phone rang. She picked it up and listened, then relayed the news to Able Team.

"We've got some news coming in from Indian Point, New York," Price said. "Any testing of the waters at that power plant?"

Schwarz frowned. "That's quiet, too, and it feeds New York City, which is between eight and thirteen million people in the path of a meltdown's fallout."

"What's the deal with Indian Point?" Lyons asked.

"We've been running digital photographs through matching programs on electronics components recovered from the robots which have somehow survived their encounters with your two teams," Price said.

"I thought they had self-destruct mechanisms that stopped that kind of information getting out," Lyons said. "That's if they haven't been hosed into scrap metal by concentrated streams of automatic fire."

"On the trawler that Encizo and James hit, they managed to cut some of the serpentine robots in two," Price explained. "Shotguns and high-powered handguns managed to leave recoverable components."

Lyons nodded, then looked at his after-action report.

"Checking to see if Calvin left you some notes on the effectiveness of the Saiga 12K?" Price asked.

Lyons nodded. He circled it. "No jams under actual amphibious combat situations."

"You've already used the Saiga in the field," Price said.

"Not on a ship raid. This is good news for me," Lyons replied. "All right. So they have components that they photographed and they're being run through online technology catalogs?"

"Precisely," Price said. "Also, Striker called to give us a heads-up about an incoming call with some new information about trouble in Calvert Cliffs."

Lyons looked at the notes that he and the others had assembled. "Indian Point has been quiet in terms of testing the waters, but we suddenly have a big technology connection to the area? Plus we've got some kind of bait that could lead us to divide our forces between Indian Point and Calvert Cliffs."

"It's not outside the realm of possibility that the enemy are looking to draw us in," Blancanales said.

"Why couldn't it be a trap for the Department of Energy teams?" Price asked.

"Because they have a million different security breaches that are their priority," Blancanales explained. "Because they're the ones in charge of keeping our nuclear reactors safe, they have to treat every bit of interference as a real and urgent problem."

"With them spread so thin, this kind of 'evidence' isn't going to be anything more than a worm on the hook for us," Lyons said.

"What was the technology tie-in for Indian Point?" Schwarz asked.

"The company announced that it had been robbed of a couple of hundred processors," Price said. "Those processors closely resembled the technology recovered from the fishing trawler."

"And this company provided pictures of their processors just in time for us to be able to identify them after capturing leftovers in Egypt," Schwarz mused. "That's no coincidence."

"What's the Calvert Cliffs problem?" Lyons asked. "Depending on which bait is which, we might just have to thin out our forces like Phoenix Force had to."

"Yeah, but there are five of them," Price replied.

"This isn't like triage. One target is our nation's capital—the other target is the largest metropolitan area in the United States," Lyons countered. "On the one hand, our government would be crippled. On the other, you've got twenty million citizens and visitors, as well as the largest financial institutions in the path of a radiation leak. Which is easier to allow to be permanently irradiated and filled with corpses?"

Price nodded. "Well, you might have help in Calvert Cliffs. Striker told us that we have an inside man informing us of the situation."

"Who?" Lyons asked.

"His thief friend from Baltimore," Price answered.

Lyons nodded. "I've heard of him. He's helped police in the past, and has never harmed a citizen. He's as good people as you can find for someone who robs and shoots drug dealers."

"So Pol and I hit up Indian Point." Schwarz spoke up. "You confer with Face, or whatever he's calling himself this week—"

"Ramon Biggs," Price said. "We checked his real

name. Used to be stoop kid before the bad guys decided he knew too much. So, he knew that life inside and out, and figured that if they wanted him dead, he might as well start taxing them. Any heroin he picks up, it ends up flushed or otherwise destroyed. All the money ends up in his pockets, though Striker decided to set him up with some bank accounts."

"All right, I'll try to connect with Ramon," Lyons said.

"We'll see what we can do," Blancanales said. "Barb, can we grab a couple of blacksuits to aid us?"

Price tilted her head, trying to figure out who they meant. "I know at least one who'd love to work with you two again."

"Righteous," Schwarz said.

Lyons chuckled. "Your baby Ironman?"

"Kid's got potential," Schwarz replied. "Maybe he can pull it off again."

"If he survives," Lyons said. "We go to the well too often, our friends end up in coffins."

"He'll just be a placeholder until you get to New York," Blancanales replied. "I don't want to risk his life, either."

"Good luck, you two," Lyons said.

Able Team was ready to put boots on the ground.

LYONS MOVED TO THE War Room just as Kurtzman declared the incoming phone call clear. Price handed Lyons a hands-free headset.

"All right, Ramon, you're on with Ironman," Price said.

"Thanks. I called this in to the Big Man, but he ain't on the East Coast. He got other business going on,"

Ramon Biggs said. "Folks be laying out a lot of green for trigger fingers here in Baltimore. We're also seeing faces from D.C., Raleigh and New York."

Lyons frowned. The Baltimore robber had come to Bolan's attention years ago as he waged his own personal brand of warfare against the drug dealers in his home city. Biggs was a lawbreaker and a multiple murderer, but then, so had Bolan been an outlaw when he began his war on organized crime. Biggs had proved himself as a fine ally and a resource for intelligence on the East Coast crime scene. "We're in the middle of something here, too, Ramon."

"Sure, you are, but the recruiters have us set to make a road trip to the middle of nowhere in Maryland. Calvert Cliffs to be exact."

Lyons grumbled at the revelation. "That's something that's popped up on our radar. It's the only reason we're listening to you now."

"That and my work with Big Man. But I figured that our destination would grab your attention. Talent all up and down the coast are here on this, and none of these shooters have a slice of conscience to share between them," Biggs continued.

"Just you," Lyons added.

"If all you ask is poison slingers, I'm the coldest mother born on Earth," Biggs responded. "But they think they hired some Islam sucker. I changed up my look. Suit, bow tie, spectacles and proper English. The slingers have been hiring me as a triggerman named Elijah. They point me to their competition, their snitches, and whatever slinger's got his hand skimming from the cookie jar."

"So you're cutting into informants who have a chance of taking down these bastards?" Lyons asked.

"Nah, man. I call your peeps there in the boonies, and Witness Protection scoop 'em up. They provide me with a headless corpse that I dress up and throw docs into," Biggs explained. "The informants live, the fuckers think I did them a righteous, and I continue killing poison dealers as long as I like. Plus, they pay me to do what I love."

"So when is the convoy leaving for Calvert Cliffs?" Lyons asked.

"A few minutes from now."

"Be careful, thief," Lyons warned. "The bad guys might be setting this up as just a trap for me and mine. And they could be listening in."

"If they suspicious, then you're going to hear a lot of shooting up in Baltimore," Biggs promised.

Lyons frowned as the renegade hung up. He looked at Price. "This is serious. If Second Sphere is involved on the U.S. side of things, why is the conspiracy hiring guns from the ranks of East Coast crime families?"

"This could be more bait, like what was hung out in Indian Point," Price noted.

"And we've now got two situations that need investigation. The factory in the shadow of one of the largest plants in New York State is too big a red flag to ignore, but then, so is an army on the march to Maryland's big power plant," Lyons replied.

"I'd say that they were trying to split our resources, but that would entail that they know a lot about the Stony Man operation," Price said. "And we've worked too hard to keep this a top-secret operation."

"They laid out two traps for Phoenix Force already, and the first infiltrator robot likely caught a good look at me," Lyons explained. "While the agencies we've worked with don't know our specifics, there are more than enough rumors flying around about a trio of bullet-proof Justice agents who kick ass and don't take prisoners."

"Just like the vague descriptions of Striker and Phoenix Force have built up legends about them," Price added. "So whoever we're fighting has stories about our operations from Second Sphere and whatever gutter scum are working for them in Europe and Egypt. Since every story about you and the others say that there's only three of you, two concurrent crisis points will split you up."

"Which is what I've already done," Lyons said. "But Pol and Gadgets have themselves an ace in the hole with their favorite blacksuit, and I have backup in the form of a hardcore Baltimore outlaw."

"I feel sorry for them," Price said.

"They don't deserve your sympathy," Lyons growled. "And they're not dead yet...."

CHAPTER NINE

Darrin Homm and Mischa Shenck waited for Jacob Morgan Stern to finish his phone call. The two technological wizards were going to report to him, but the big ex-military policeman had other business to attend to first. Stern was a huge beast of a man with a sharp, hatchetlike face and deepset, brooding eyes. On a less refined man, he'd seem almost like a Neanderthal, but he was immaculately dressed, and spoke clearly and cleanly on the telephone. He was in his mid-fifties, but his hair was still dark and his frame large and imposing.

Stern was the man who had gathered the two men together. Homm was a computer hacker, while Shenck was his technology expert. The two of them had worked hard at assembling Second Sphere's tech support for Stern's plan. Where Stern received his startup funds no one knew, only that he began forming the Second Sphere security agency in the late 1980s.

Shenck had worked under Stern back then, and had been hired since the young Russian's cousins had been left homeless and later riddled with cancer in the wake of the Chernobyl meltdown. Given their work at destabilizing Western nuclear reactors, Shenck and Homm had agreed that Stern's motivations originated with the Chernobyl disaster. They doubted that it was Stern himself who had suffered loss in the wake of the meltdown, since he was large, powerfully built and had been healthy in the decades since Shenck had first met him.

"Thank you, Barnabas," Stern said into the phone. "I'll talk to you later."

Shenck glanced to Homm. "Bolfrey?"

"It's none of your concern right now, Mischa. I commend you on your designs for the Paris and Mediterranean diversions," Stern said, hanging up the phone.

"There was nothing special about the remote camera system on the trawler," Shenck replied. "And the members of the covert strike team got away."

"There were injuries among their number according to the secondary observation platform," Stern noted. "And the infiltrators performed admirably against even a force prepared for them. I only wish we'd have been able to set it up for belowdecks operations. Their transport helicopter's guns were too much of a deciding factor in that battle."

"If you give me a week, I could set something else up," Shenck offered.

Stern shook his head. "Right now, we have to concentrate on our main goals. We've set up traps for the American-based contingent of our opponents."

"Traps?" Homm asked. "It's only a three-man team...if it's the group we suspect."

"It most likely is only three men, so that's why we've laid out two bits of bait," Stern told the pair. "I'm sorry,

Mischa, but we had to let them learn about the New York firm you used to build your prototypes."

Shenck sighed, his brow furrowing. "That's understandable. You're trying to split the enemy up?"

Stern nodded. "Not that it will make anything easier. Right now, we're looking at the team known as the Phoenixes split into smaller contingents, and they've managed to survive both human and robotic opposition."

"At least with the trawler, we've got their attention turned away from Europe for now. The recreation center's destruction signified the loss of our stored robots in France," Shenck said. "However, the ocean traffic of infiltrators points their attention down toward North Africa."

Stern raised an eyebrow. "And how do you make them think that Libyan reactors are a more juicy prospect for our destructive efforts than France's main power plants?"

"We simply applied logic. The trawler left a port in southern France with several other ships," Homm said. "I made up the craft, and it'll only fool them for a little while, but I made it seem as if we were transporting swarms of robots to northern Africa."

"So at the very least, their French contingent will be drawn away from Paris and Nogent Nuclear Power Plant to investigate the embarkation point," Stern concluded.

"Precisely," Homm replied.

"It's a thin premise, but by the time we turn Nogent into an inferno, it'll be too late for them to act. Besides, the threat to Libya's experimental nuclear reactors could spark an international conflict, even if nothing comes of it," Shenck said. "Qaddafi is trying to play nice with the Western powers, but if their experimental reactor goes up in a flash of nuclear flame, they will be pissed off and they will accuse Israel."

"I don't care for this plan," Stern said. "Libya's air force and navy are nonexistent after conflicts and embargoes, and there's not even much of a presence at the Libyan plant."

"It's not our real target anyway," Shenck said. "We're running Libya as a diversion while we make our move on Syria."

"There's one small problem with Syria fitting into our plans," Stern said. "The power plant that the North Koreans were helping them to build was blown up by the Israelis in 2007."

"Our main focus isn't their aborted nuclear power program," Homm said. "You wanted the Middle East to know the same kind of fear that Europe and the United States have. Unfortunately, the Arab states don't possess the atomic genie in a bottle."

"What they do have is one of the most intensive chemical weapons programs in the world," Shenck explained. "We can sneak our robots into a reactor, we can use them to sabotage nerve gas construction plans."

"And the joy of it is, Syria has dozens of facilities placed near populations under the premise of human shields," Homm added.

Stern frowned, then nodded. "So one of their chemical weapons plants goes up, it produces a tragedy of the scope of what happened at the Union Carbide plant in India."

"Though there were only three thousand initial deaths, in the long run, it grew to be twenty thousand,"

Homm said. "And that was with simple pesticide. Just imagine if it was designed to kill humans."

"Won't that take away from the message that Bolfrey and I have constructed?" Stern asked.

"We're working it into the final script for our announcement," Shenck stated. "The ruination of the planet not only takes the form of defiling the atom, but also in the production of chemicals that poison the world and slay all of its creatures. This way, if Syria somehow manages to pass off the attack as one on a pesticide production facility, their denial won't have a negative impact on the thousands lying dead in the streets."

"We're also going to utilize Israeli unmanned technology to give us oversight in the region," Homm said. "Israel and Egypt both have extensive fleets of unmanned aerial vehicles, but since Syria and Israel have the greater beef with each other, if they spot an Israeli drone, Damascus might do us a favor and demonstrate the level of chemical weaponry we have."

"Which is why we were interested if whether or not it was Bolfrey," Shenck said. "He's got operatives in the region who are coordinating our override programs."

"I'd prefer to keep lines of communication limited, but much more secure," Stern replied.

"All right," Homm agreed. "We'll give you the message traffic we want him to look over."

"Thanks," Stern said. He glanced to Shenck. "You also said you wanted to show me approved designs?"

"Since we're dealing with an enemy of extraordinary skill, I want to try something that can put us on equal ground," Shenck said.

"The Second Sphere operatives who are in on the

plan are highly trained," Stern said. "What would be able to even those odds?"

"First, we have more than a few pictures of our opposition," Shenck answered. He handed Stern four photographs. "The blond man is the American who discovered DoE Agent Hirtenberg. The man in the watchcap was in Paris, and of course, you're familiar now with the pair from Egypt."

"Robot duplicates?" Stern asked with a smirk.

Shenck sighed. "I wish we had that kind of technology. You'll have to wait about seventy-five years for that, barring some quantum leaps in robotics and artificial intelligence."

"So what do you have?" Stern requestioned.

"A variation on one of the U.S. military's new remote designs," Shenck said. "Essentially, its a standard ATV with a variant of built-in optics and a weapons turret. The chassis of the converted ATV provides enough room to support an internal transmitter and a processor with one of Darrin's artificial intelligence combat programs. The extra weight also means we can arm the unit with something heavier than a glorified Glock."

"Like what?" Stern asked.

"Something tough and simple. We've got some Romanian AKs," Shenck answered.

"I've heard about that style of drone," Stern replied. "So you have a supply of ATVs to convert?"

"We've managed to bring in about forty to our construction site. It won't take long with my staff," Shenck answered. "All you need to do is approve the redirection of my resources and we can have twenty ready up at Indian Point by the time investigators arrive. Wait a day, and you'll have that force to turn Calvert Cliffs upside down."

Stern frowned. "I'd like the opportunity to test them in Maryland, but right now, our main goal is New York. Washington, D.C., has sufficient resources on hand. Double the Indian Point forces if you can, though."

Shenck nodded.

"Dismissed, gentlemen. Excellent work," Stern told them.

Homm and Shenck left their leader to his plotting.

DAVID MCCARTER SHIFTED HIS weight uncomfortably in the backseat of Phoenix Force's rented sedan. Gary Manning and T. J. Hawkins had teamed up to convince him that, as their team leader, he didn't need to sit behind the wheel. Driving was grunt work meant for the lowest member of the team.

The truth was in face far different. McCarter's driving was a matter of legend among the operating teams of Stony Man Farm. While no one doubted his excellence as a driving instructor, teaching blacksuits evasive maneuvers behind the wheel of an automobile, the members of Phoenix Force and Able Team had enough experience with him on missions when he put the pedal to the metal. Even the unflappable Ironman, Carl Lyons, had been known to hold on to his seat with a white-knuckle grip when vehicular combat occurred and McCarter was in the driver's seat. Though the Briton had never lost a passenger due to his wild style of road wars, his comrades always looked green around the gills. Hawkins's admission of subservience was merely a ruse to allow both him and Manning to hold on to their stomachs.

The Southerner accepted the rookie role of chauffeur, and the burly Manning filled up the shotgun seat.

This put McCarter a safe distance from the controls of the BMW as it rolled along the road. The Phoenix Force leader put aside his impatience as his cell phone rang.

"David?" It was Mittner, and the Cockney's voice was tense on the other end of the line.

"What's wrong?" McCarter asked.

"Bertrand showed up this morning with a flier he'd received at headquarters," Mittner replied. "I'm transmitting a photo of it to your phone."

"You don't have to," McCarter answered. "I know that the enemy had a good look at my face. I saw the flash on the digital camera go off. I was just wondering how long it would take for my gob to get into the hands of the proper authorities."

"They got it midday yesterday," Mittner said. McCarter noted that this was around the time that he was extracting information from the captured mercenaries. The conspirators had a well-connected network if it had taken them twelve hours to get his likeness into enemy hands. "I certainly hope you're going to avoid places like Marseilles."

"That's one of the places where my people have picked up the stink of the ne'er-do-wells who have been snooping around France," McCarter replied. "Is that where the flier showed up?"

"A couple roughnecks were picked up there, and they had your picture," Mittner replied. "And it wasn't for one-handed pleasure."

McCarter chuckled. "Bloody French don't appreciate true beauty."

"Where are you?" Mittner asked.

"On the road."

"Shit!" Mittner growled. "Bertrand's mates have

people with their eyes peeled from Perpignan to Toulon for you and whoever you're with."

"Then we'll just have to avoid them," McCarter replied.

"The French don't want you bloody interfering!" Mittner snapped. "You blew up a building and dumped a bunch of battered thugs in their lap. And now, they've got word about contraband heading out by the boatload to Egypt! These lads don't dick around with half measures."

"Neither do we," McCarter replied coldly. "They bloody well either step out of our way, or they better hope that the sods who sent them against us will care for their widows and orphans."

"David…" Mittner began, stunned by the steel in his countryman's voice. "If they were listening right now, they would know full well that you just threatened to kill good men only trying to do their jobs."

"Tell it to someone who gives a shit, mate," McCarter returned. "Daniel, you do intend to tell Bertrand to pull out all the stops on the coast, right?"

There was a moment of uncomfortable silence. Finally, Mittner cleared his throat. "David, you don't seem like you are a cold-blooded murderer…"

"Well, I am. Stone cold. You tell Bertrand that his best bet is to turn the docks upside down," McCarter growled. "Tear up every ship, blow through every warehouse, look under every rock. Because his bosses are not going to stop me from doing *my* job!"

Mittner took a deep breath. McCarter hoped that the real message had gotten through. He and the rest of Phoenix Force didn't have the resources and manpower to search three hundred miles of waterfront on their own. He also didn't fancy being drawn into a trap so elegantly set up by their enemy so soon after the last fiasco with the recreational center.

Mittner cleared his throat. "From Spain to Monaco, there will be no spot where you can hide, David. You have forced the hand of the French government, and they will not tolerate the operation of a team of vigilantes on sovereign French soil. The south of France will be inhospitable to anyone associated with you."

"Good. You let them know. I welcome the challenge," McCarter snarled, hanging up.

Manning looked back over his shoulder. "You know, for a blunt instrument, you sometimes show remarkable adeptness at subtlety."

McCarter grinned. "There's going to be something waiting for us in the south. And our foes want us looking away from Paris if they're waving that kind of bait for us."

"So the French are going to be ready for the Horsemen of the Apocalypse, rendering whatever ambush the conspiracy is laying a moot point," Hawkins added. "Leaving us free to continue our sweet little trip to Nogent."

"Gadgets checked, and it's the most likely target for them. And I concur, Nogent's a big, juicy bomb waiting to happen," Manning replied. "There isn't much down by Marseilles that would benefit their meltdown tactics, while Paris and its surrounding environs are a population nightmare for a massive radiation leak."

"It's just too bad we can't let Bertrand know that we'll need a response team in case things get too hairy," Hawkins sighed. "But if we let the law know that we suspect Nogent is their target, then the conspiracy will know we haven't been fooled by their bullshit."

"He's getting a hang of this espionage stuff," Manning said.

"See? Soldiers aren't all thick," McCarter replied.

"Boy, I hope my sense of humor doesn't degenerate to your level when I get old and decrepit," Hawkins returned.

"You'd need one in the first place," McCarter replied. He gave the Southerner a friendly punch on the shoulder. "Good return fire, lad."

"It's starting to rub off on me, God help me," Hawkins sighed.

The team continued their trek to Nogent, satisfied that the conspiracy's presence in the south would be dealt with by overwhelming force.

ASSID CHECKED ON THE battered and bloodied members of his unit, and came across James practicing his bedside manner on the men.

"You don't have to do that for my people," Assid told him. "We have a very competent medical staff to attend to their needs."

"Well, these guys also guarded my back and kept one of those snake robots from crawling up my ass," James explained. "If it means acting like a nurse for 'em, then they've earned it…within reason."

Assid winced. "I did not need the mental image of you dressed as an American candy striper."

James laughed and then shuddered at the notion. "Oh man, even I'm going to have to get a hot poker to pry that out of my mind's eye."

Assid smiled and rested his hand on James's shoulder. "Rey sent me to inform you that you've gotten new intelligence from your home base."

"Intelligence? Or are we being misled?" James asked.

"Well, according to what he said, you're moving out to make a check on Libya. Your agency requested that we supply transportation for you to get across the border," Assid noted.

"And Rey?" James asked.

"You're doubtful of anything fruitful in Libya?" Assid countered.

"Damned straight," James told him. "As of now, on the American side of things, we have some major reactors that may be sized up as big targets. And in Europe, well, I won't give away any details of what my partners are doing there."

"When I heard about Libya, Rey and I agreed that such a direction of investigation was doubtful," Assid added. "The biggest reactor on record in Libya is a mere seventy-seven megawatts. Inshas and Negev were no larger than that, but in either instance, neither meltdown would do more than cause an inconvenience before emergency shutdown procedures took effect."

"You're thinking in terms of the amount of thermal energy emitted by the Chernobyl reactors," James said. "Each of those reactors produced four times as much energy."

Assid nodded. "On this side of the Mediterranean, there isn't much that will create a disaster situation. And even Libya, with its history of terrorism support, would not be stupid enough to act on a power plant accident. There was some possibility that Israel or Egypt would be sparked to increased tension, but luckily, we've been working together on this crisis."

"Libya doesn't have any allies that would make a

meltdown worthwhile, either. Back in 2007, Syria's attempt at a nuclear reactor was blown to hell by your neighbors, and Iran's got foreign eyes on its efforts at nuclear development," James said. "There isn't anything in North Africa or the Middle East that is like the power plants that supply electricity to major cities like Paris, New York or Washington, D.C."

James gave his Unit 777 allies a quick salute. The Egyptian comrades smiled and granted their American friend his leave. Continuing their discussion, he and Assid strode back to the command center, where Rafael Encizo waited.

"Still, if there is going to be something happening in Libya, we'd be remiss if we just let it happen," Assid said. "A small event in Libya might lead to an international incident."

"Like one of Libya's other allies going off the chain and smacking Israel. A reactor goes south there, and some place like Syria might get nervous as they could be next?" James asked.

"That's one theory," Assid mentioned. "Or someone could make it look as if Syria overreacted."

"That works, too. Anything to muddle the situation and draw us away from the main targets makes things easier for them," James admitted.

"So how'll we handle that?" Assid asked.

"Do you have anyone who owes you inside Libya?" James asked.

"I've got a few friends," Assid answered.

"Then we'll have our sources look for likely retaliation points against Israel," James said. "Syria, Lebanon and a bunch of other lesser possibilities could all be utilized. I like your idea for Syria as the main suspect, however, so we'll get some of our best on that."

"In the meantime, I'm going to do what I can to make sure that Libya's nuclear reactors remain safe," Assid told him.

"You two are about on track with what home base is saying," Encizo said as they entered the command center. He had just shut down the laptop with the communications link to Stony Man Farm. Tanya Kristopoulos was standing beside him. "But I guess I should make the official invitation to this party."

"The bad guys handed me a gold-plated RSVP the moment they pulled something at Inshas," Assid answered. "You'll head to Israel?"

"From there, my people will assist Rey and Farrow as much as they can," Kristopoulos answered. "The Mossad would like to thank you, but you know we can't say those thanks too loudly."

Assid smiled. "I can hear them just fine."

The Egyptian commander held out his hand to the woman. "Atalanta…"

"Sir," Kristopoulos replied.

"Good luck, and may God watch over you," Assid said.

"You, too," Kristopoulos answered.

The two looked at James and Encizo, who were smiling.

"Don't mind them—they get sentimental about Middle East peace," Kristopoulos grumbled.

"Just wishing I had a camera," James said.

Encizo made a show of wiping an imaginary tear from the corner of his eye. "Really. Good luck in Libya. I hope the next time we meet, it's just for cross training, not real work."

"Take care of yourselves, as well," Assid said with a bow of his head.

James's mood darkened. "I'd prefer just to take care of the conspiracy."

CHAPTER TEN

Rosario Blancanales showed up at the barracks to find Terrence "Baby Ironman" Aspen assembling his gear. The young man did a quick fieldstrip of his favored SIG-Sauer P-229 while a Texan heavy metal band growled from the headphones hanging around his neck. He'd earned the name "Baby Ironman" partly due to his resemblance to Carl Lyons—same height, build and blond hair and blue eyes. The "baby" aspect was due to his smooth, unlined face, carrying baby fat that kept him looking half his age, marred only by a multiply broken nose. The rest of it came from one particular factor— in a game of football held by the blacksuits, Aspen kept charging for the goal line while three other, much larger men hung off him. Red-faced and determined, with a broken nose from an inadvertent head-butt, he continued on toward his goal, dragging the opposing team's tackles until finally Blancanales and Schwarz had to tell the young man to stop.

"Hey, stubborn." Blancanales spoke up. "Ready to roll?"

Aspen nodded as he put the slide back onto his pistol. A member of the Texas Department of Public Safety, his preferred side arm was the .357 SIG-Sauer P-229, like Lyons's own .357 Magnum, but in a smaller package. "Never thought that I'd be called up as an alternate, sir."

"You've been vetted, son," Blancanales told him. "And we need the extra manpower."

Aspen slipped his pistol in its waistband holster, then flipped the hem of his T-shirt, emblazoned on the front with a red-and-gold-armored superhero, to conceal the weapon.

Blancanales raised an eyebrow. "That's not who we're talking about when we call you Baby Ironman."

"I know. But I've liked the dude since I was a kid. 'Sides, it's spelled different," Aspen returned with a wink.

Blancanales chuckled. The cartoon figure on the shirt wasn't the only armor the Texas cop wore. As Aspen had donned his holster, the Able Team veteran saw a concealable Kevlar-and-mesh vest, meant as undercover bullet protection, under the T-shirt. When the hem had been raised, Blancanales also noted that his belt was festooned with plainclothes police equipment, a cell phone, a handcuff case, a sheathed folding knife, spare ammunition and a collapsed ASP baton. The utility belt made his trim waist seem thicker, but the loose drape of the oversize shirt concealed it well. The load of equipment was another thing that reminded Blancanales of his partner. Aspen threw on a lightweight leather jacket over the ensemble.

"Looks fine," Blancanales said. He handed an Able Team communicator to the blacksuit. "Got room on your belt for this?"

Aspen nodded. He shifted his cell phone over and clipped the communicator in place. He knelt and wrapped an ankle holster around one leg, then slipped a .357 SIG-Sauer P-239 into the backup weapon shealth. "You guys don't mind me staying with my SIGs. They don't take the same magazines as your Smith and Wessons…"

"Whatever suits your fancy," Blancanales replied.

"Cool," Aspen returned. "So, how are we getting to New York? Am I driving?"

Blancanales smirked. "No. We're traveling by air. However, when we do arrive, you will be our wheel-man."

"I expected no less," Aspen said. "The guy behind the wheel always gets shot on these things."

"You've got your armor," Blancanales said. "And even if our guys get shot, they mostly survive."

"Mostly," Aspen replied. "So I'll be playing the averages."

"You've got the skills and you've got two top wing-men. Besides, you're Baby Ironman," Blancanales replied. "You don't stop."

"That's what could get me killed," Aspen brooded.

"Nah, we ride a tight rein on Ironman, and we'll ride a tight rein on you," Blancanales promised.

HERMANN SCHWARZ LOADED THE last of the crates into the airplane, then closed the cargo hatch. Colonel Rick Emerson marked off the inventory record and took a deep breath.

"I'll bring as much back safely as I can," Schwarz promised.

"Why not have our boys closer to the action?"

Emerson asked. "We can transport to New York state and be in the region."

"Because we're looking at the potential for fallout that could take out the entire eastern half of the state," Schwarz replied. "I don't want to risk any more lives than I have to."

"It's our job, sir," Emerson stated.

"I work for a living, Emerson," Schwarz returned.

"You're still putting yourself at risk," Emerson said.

"Look at it this way. I'll be making a proof run for your man-machine interface system," Schwarz replied. "This way you can operate at longer ranges."

"Longer ranges, getting shot at and taking the risk of radiation poisoning that my people have signed up for," Emerson countered. "Our people went to Iraq and Afghanistan, looking down some of the most dangerous holes for some very nasty shit."

"Right. And you just got back from that tour," Schwarz countered. He held up a computerized wrist cuff attached by a cable to an armored Kevlar vest. The unit was designed to allow an advance team member to control the remote drones, process data, and serve as a signal booster. It also allowed the robotic devices to be handled by more conventional means. "You deserve a little break."

Emerson winced. "We're not burned out."

"Which is why I'm using your team," Schwarz added. "Your kids don't have the kind of clearance to work in the field in the U.S. anyway. Remember Posse Comitatus?"

"That didn't stop U.S. troops from putting down gang bangers taking advantage of the Katrina disaster," Emerson said. "And if Indian Point goes into meltdown mode, that's going to make the hurricane's effects on New Orleans seem like a kiss on the cheek. We've taken the oath to protect our country…why won't you let us do that?"

"You will be doing it," Schwarz said. "And I'll be helping you."

Emerson sighed. "I wish I were coming with you."

"I know. Just be my link to the guys who are going to save the world, okay?" Schwarz asked. "You'll be where you need to be, not where you want to be. And as Mick and Keith once sang, you can't always get what you want…"

"But if you try sometimes, you get what you need," Emerson returned. "I'm younger than you, man, but not that young."

Schwarz winced at the barb over his age, then chuckled. "I knew there was something about you that I liked."

Emerson grinned. "Godspeed, secret agent man."

Schwarz tucked the interface vest under his arm as Blancanales and Aspen reached the plane. "Thanks, we'll need it."

RAMON BIGGS SAT on the bus with the two dozen other hired guns from Baltimore, staring absently out of the window as a book rested in his lap. He'd read *The Spook Who Sat by the Door* by Sam Greenlee half a dozen times in his life. It was one of his favorite books, since as a young boy, he had graduated from comic books to pulp novels that existed in abundance. He'd assumed that the Greenlee novel was another action book, but interspersed with the espionage training and the Chicago revolution against oppression and injustice, he found a strong satire of the politics of the late sixties and early seventies that was still relevant in racially tumultuous cities like Baltimore.

It was the book that sustained him morally when he first became a stoop boy, dealing drugs off a porch in a run-down Baltimore public housing project. The concept of gangs being protectors, not predators, resounded in the back of his mind, helping him to draw lines of demarcation between what he would allow himself to do and what he couldn't.

Biggs became a predator who fed upon other predators. That was the only way that he saw that he could come to terms with his conscience and rise to the goal of protector of the black community. Somewhere along the way, he'd come across a big white man who himself was a terrorist to terrorists, a shadow hunting shadows. Biggs had become one of a gigantic, faceless horde of people whom the Executioner counted on to continue their fight in the shadows. That meeting seemed like a lifetime ago, and dressed in his pristine suit, with his reading spectacles resting on the tip of his nose, deep brown eyes looking at the Calvert County countryside, Biggs was a completely different entity from the scarfaced, trench-coated robber that Baltimore's criminal underground recognized him as.

The novel sitting in his lap was the kind of complex, intricate thing such a self-educated man would be reading. It was part of the disguise, which itself replaced a different false visage. Ramon Biggs, a young gay man who had made one wrong choice that transformed into a very right decision, was nothing like the street thug or the crisply dressed American Muslim image that he presented to the world.

"That shit looks pretty intense," the young man sitting next to him said.

Biggs looked at him. Wearing a black sweatshirt with a hood, the kid couldn't have looked more out of place if he was wearing a school uniform and carrying a lunch pail. He was small, no more than sixteen, and despite the bagginess of the hoody, Biggs could see the handgun butt poking through the fabric. "My book?"

"Hell yeah," the kid said. "Sorry for readin' over your shoulder, but man, the National Guard getting owned by some revolutionary brothers? In Chicago?"

Biggs closed the book. "That is what I had assumed when I was your age. I saw a cover, similar to the poster they had for the movie made from this novel. I was looking for something hard and tough like *Shaft* or *The Iceman*. Instead, I found the beginning of an education."

"Education?" the kid asked, surprised. "Yeah. I can see that. You dress like a Herb, but word is that you're ice-cold."

Biggs wanted to break into a wide grin, but the identity of Sherif would not be given to such a narcissistic display. "I dress like a man. Not like a child."

"Sherif, right?" the young man inquired. "Name's Two-Tone."

Biggs tilted his head. "How so?"

Two-Tone pulled down his hood and tugged on his collar, showing off a patch of milky skin running from under his left eye down his neck.

"Eloquently explained," Biggs stated with a nod.

"Sherif. That got some double meaning. Sherif sounds like some Arabic name, except I seen it spelled Sharif in newspapers," Two-Tone began. "But you spell it with an *e* 'cause you're like the new sheriff in town."

Biggs narrowed his eyes. "Astute observation, young man. What's your real name?"

"Michael," Two-Tone replied. "But that don't fit me."

"Why, pray tell?" Biggs asked.

"Well, I ain't an angel," Two-Tone answered. "I'm about as far from it as you can get."

Biggs sighed. "But a sheriff represents law."

"And you do, home," Two-Tone said. "It might not be the real law, but it's the law of the street. You gotta do what the top says."

Biggs nodded. "Everyone has free will."

Two-Tone frowned. "No, they don't. That the case, I'd still be in school, not hiring myself out as muscle to care for my baby brother."

"What about your parents?" Biggs asked.

"Mom's is a crack whore. Would you let shit like that raise a kid?"

Biggs shook his head.

"So I do what I have to do," Two-Tone continued. "Be it slinging smack or putting lead in some nigger…"

"Don't say that word, please," Biggs said.

"Why not?" Two-Tone asked. "If anyone deserves that kind of disrespect, it's the kind of folk I am."

"You are kidding, correct?" Biggs asked.

"I make money off fools who've destroyed their bodies," Two-Tone said. "Or I make it shooting kids who're just like me, just working on the wrong corner."

Biggs rested his hand on Two-Tone's shoulder. The young man didn't shrug away from the comforting gesture. Biggs could feel the torment churning as the countryside rolled past out the bus windows.

"And now we're going to a dust-up in Calvert Cliffs," Two-Tone continued. "What kind of business is that? We've got peeps from D.C. and other cities throwing in, too."

"You do what you have to," Biggs repeated. "What kind of money did they promise you?"

"Five grand," Two-Tone said. "But I'm just a baby gee."

"That's the same I am receiving," Biggs answered.

"Listen, if I catch some lead, I need someone I can trust," Two-Tone told him.

"I will watch out for you," Biggs promised.

Two-Tone shook his head. "Not that. No. My brother. He's a good kid, and I've been keeping him away from the slingers. We've got a nice little apartment, and I've got the rent paid for a year, but if I'm capped—"

"You're going to live to see him again." Biggs cut him off.

Two-Tone handed him a slip of paper. "That's where he is now. The second address is for my aunt."

"Your brother will not come to harm," Biggs said.

Two-Tone lifted a closed fist and held it there. "Then we tight, Sherif."

Biggs completed the fist bump. "As you say, we're tight."

BARBARA PRICE LOOKED at the viewscreen and sighed. Through a secure cutout the Farm had received a text message from Ramon Biggs's cell phone.

"'Fifteen to seventeen years old,'" she read out loud. "'African-American. White coloration from left eye down side of face. Five foot eight. Wears simple clothing. Black hoody, no bling. Not a full criminal yet. Name Michael, also known as Two-Tone.'"

Price looked at Kurtzman. "Biggs must have found

someone on the raid team that his conscience doesn't feel should be a target."

Kurtzman nodded. "Striker trusts Biggs a lot, so we should pay attention."

"Anything that slows Ironman down while he's outnumbered could get him killed," Price said.

"You think that Lyons is going to not beat the hell out of himself if he learns that he pulled the trigger on an innocent kid?" Kurtzman asked.

"How innocent can he be if he's working with a crew of hired guns?" Price asked.

"Pretty innocent if all he's done is fire on criminals," Kurtzman said. "Just like a kid who's been to war, they're fighting for their lives, and as long as they don't fire on unarmed civilians, our military doesn't consider them breaking military law."

Price's brow furrowed at the thought.

"Biggs stays alive by robbing drug dealers. This boy, Michael or Two-Tone, stays alive by shooting the same kind of criminals who are trying to harm him," Price said. "You're right. It's just like a war. Michael was dragged into it probably for purely economic survival."

"Rationalizing this for yourself?" Kurtzman asked.

Price nodded. "Hal's going to want to know why I made the choice to put Lyons at further risk."

"Carl wouldn't have to rationalize it. He's gone wholeheartedly into alliances with all sorts of unsavory people," Kurtzman argued.

"Carl's had to explain himself to Hal enough times here in the States," Price continued.

"And most of it comes down to 'I did what I felt was right, screw politics,'" Kurtzman related.

Price folded her arms. "All right. Forward it to Lyons. Let him know the situation."

"Want me to clear the message traffic so Hal doesn't let us know about the breach in protocol?" Kurtzman asked.

Price shook her head. "If Carl can tell Hal to sit on it, so can I. It's the right thing to do, after all."

"That's my girl," Kurtzman said, forwarding the message to Lyons's cell phone.

Price said a soft prayer, wishing the Able Team commander good luck. Blancanales and Schwarz had the advantage of backup by a remote-control squadron of robots and one of the blacksuits that they felt possessed promise. All Lyons had going for him was a robber and a young street gunner for whom the robber felt a pang of sympathy.

However, knowing the history of the man they called the Ironman, if anyone could surmount such odds, it was him. Even with two unknown quantities as his allies, he'd turn the whole situation to his advantage.

CHAPTER ELEVEN

The President had called in Hal Brognola for a briefing on the latest crisis involving Stony Man. The leader of the free world always held his breath whenever he had heard that the small farm tucked into Virginia's Blue Ridge Mountains was on global alert. All that was known so far was that a mysterious conspiracy had been engaging in sabotage and covert intrusions into nuclear power facilities around the globe, utilizing remote-control robots that proved to be very deadly. Already at least three people had been killed in the United States.

As Brognola, a big, gray-haired man who looked as if his suits came off the rack already rumpled, was briefing, the head Fed's laptop burbled with an incoming comminique. The President looked at the machine as if it was the bearer of bad news.

"Excuse me one moment, sir," Brognola told him.

"You're kidding me with the hand raising, Hal. You're here to keep me updated, so speak your mind," the President replied. He sat back on the white leather couch, trying to hide the fact that his heart was pounding beneath his ribs. He'd been brought up to date on some of the recent missions that had been conducted by the covert operatives at Stony Man Farm. The thought of a new menace, unlike anything they had faced before, made him uneasy. The two Stony Man teams had waged war against opponents as varied as the low-tech, beastial Lion Warriors of Africa to the deadly artificially intelligent tanks and robotic missile systems that nearly turned Central America into a fortress of fascism. Still, this new threat would be difficult to counter.

Brognola had provided the President with photographs of damaged infiltrator robots, as well as their brutal effectiveness against human beings, either as an assassination weapon, as in the case of Mare Hirtenberg, or simply as a self-destructing bomb, as was the case of two hapless employees of the conspiracy, their bodies shredded and sprayed over the insides of a brown delivery van. The stealthy little devices had proved capable of penetrating the toughest of security measures, as they had shown when they had caused a serious malfunction at Israel's Negev reactor.

Brognola had also provided background on how each of the little drones could be utilized to turn a major American or European reactor into an out-of-control furnace that could pump thousands of kilowatts of thermal energy and radiation into the atmosphere. According to two of the team members, identified as Mr. Wizard and Gary Roy, who apparently were scientists as well as highly trained commandos, casualty projections would be in the five-figure range before cities could be evacuated. As it was, millions of American citizens would be left homeless, the targeted metropolises of New York City and Washington, D.C., rendered uninhabitable for at least one hundred years, given current technology.

The President thought of the carnage that had been wrought by Hurricane Katrina. The city of New Orleans, only a fraction of the size of either Washington or New York, had been little more than a ghost town for the space of half a year before people had rebuilt enough to move back to the homes and businesses they had been forced to abandon by flooding and wanton damage. In that time, and in the months of the repopulation effort, violent crime and disease were a factor, and nearby communities that had taken in the displaced refugees were also thrown into disarray.

The metropolitan population of Washington, D.C., was five times that of New Orleans, and at times, the city was considered even more violent and turbulent then the Louisiana city at its worst. The President considered the strain that would be put on its neighboring communities, not to mention the political and economic horrors inflicted on the country as the government was uprooted by a massive nuclear radiation disaster. The only place that could have caused a greater blow against the United States, indeed the rest of the world, would have been the other projected target, New York City.

Not only would twenty million Americans be forced out of their homes, but also one of the world's greatest stock markets, Wall Street, would be paralyzed in the wake of a disastrous release of energy from a melteddown reactor. Couple the Wall Street interruption with the fact that New York was one of the busiest ports in the country, where tons of goods were imported and exported, as well as the home base of the United Nations, and the President didn't want to think of the global implications of such a catastrophe.

The economic effects would be nothing compared to the horror of twenty million people sent screaming from their homes. Evacuation of New York City would be almost impossible, that those unable to escape the city in time would likely succumb to radiation poisoning. The survivors would have received such genetic damage that their lives would be shortened by cancer, or pass on deformities to their children if they survived.

The President thought of his wife and children, who would be safe from radiation poisoning, thanks to the White House's environmental safeguards. However, easily six hundred thousand people would suffer and die from a Calvert Cliffs reactor spewing radiation into the atmosphere. His wife and children would remain healthy, while the wives and children of people who didn't have such station in life were vulnerable to cancer and deformity if they weren't lucky enough to expire in the space of a few hours.

The President winced at that thought. "Lucky enough to die in a few hours…"

"Sir?" Brognola asked.

"Just thinking about what would happen if your people failed," the President explained. "I guess I was using my outside voice."

"It's all right, sir," Brognola replied. "We have the finest people in the world at work on it."

"Whether that will be enough is still up in the air," the President replied. "I wish that I could allocate more resources to dealing with this."

"The only thing you could do would be to begin an evacuation, but if that were to occur in New York and

Washington, you'd be doing nearly as much economic and political damage as if a leak were allowed to happen," Brognola stated.

"But no one would die because of radiation," the President countered.

"You read the reports of the casualties projected in such an evacuation," Brognola told him. "And those projections are incomplete, given the potential losses due to looting and rioting."

The President looked at the neatly scrawled numbers for the two cities. Washington, D.C., had a list of twenty-five thousand killed. New York City's violence was exponentially larger, with notations about the willingness of the NYPD to do what had to be done to contain violence.

"I sit it out, and wait for the disaster to pass," the President said.

Brognola nodded. "It's hard to do nothing. Right now, the Department of Energy is running down leads in relation to sabotage attempts and probative intrusions that may only be diversions, but also could be real. The DoE's Nuclear Energy Strike Teams are on call and ready to respond to a crisis at a moment's notice."

"What kind of timetable are we looking at?" the President inquired.

"An hour," Brognola returned. "However, we have Able Team covering both American targets."

"You're certain that it will be an East Coast crisis," the President replied.

"The team pored over all options," Brognola stated. "There are voids of activity in Indian Point and Calvert Cliffs. Everywhere else in the country has been prodded to raise Department of Energy awareness of a crisis."

The President nodded. "What about Europe? Phoenix Force has more members, but you've only informed me of robot sightings in Paris and in the Mediterranean."

"Initially, it appeared that the European contingent was sending the robots toward the Mediterranean to utilize them in North Africa and the Middle East," Brognola said.

The President frowned. "Those are only experimental reactors, not massive power complexes like the ones in Europe and the United States. Sure, a meltdown might wreck Libya's efforts at plutonium production, but it wouldn't create a crisis situation like they're attempting in the other regions. In fact, there's nothing, even in Israel, that approximates the plants that inspired this crisis."

"Chernobyl," Brognola clarified.

"But there's still something going on in the Middle East, and that has me nervous," the President said. "Egypt has the potential for chemical weaponry, but their production facilities are kept on standby, only as a deterrent to any escalation of a conflict with any of their neighbors. Libya is in the same boat, both with its experimental reactor and its chemical fabrication."

"Our Phoenix team in the Mediterranan, Rey and Farrow, are of the opinion that it's Syria, using the same process of elimination," Brognola said.

"I can try talking to Damascus so that we can put people on the ground without fear of an international incident," the President offered.

"The Mossad already is trying back-channel communications through Bahrain and Jordan," Brognola replied. "If the State Department can arrange something more solid, then fine. But we have a contingency in place."

"You're sending an undermanned Phoenix Force into a nation where they will most likely be executed if they're captured." The President sighed.

"They've got one ace in the hole," Brognola said. "We've shipped over a stealth helicopter with some remarkable capabilities."

"Code-named Dragonslayer," the President concluded, drawing from his briefing on the Stony Man Farm's assets. "That thing has managed to slip your man Striker into North Korea, and proved itself in deflecting an assault on O'Hare airport."

"It can go quiet, or it can go loud. And judging from the robotic opposition our people will be facing, we'll need every bit of loud it can bring," Brognola stated. "The Egyptians were only able to survive the assault on the trawler because they had a Blackhawk with mounted weaponry giving them support."

"That's on the deck of a ship, not amid tanks of chemicals meant to store nerve gas," the President said. "And you haven't told me about the new data you received from your people at Stony Man Farm."

Brognola looked at the printout, then took a deep breath. "While Able Team hasn't encountered any human opposition who weren't simply hired deliverymen, they have been able to do the research on the two nuclear facilities that haven't been probed by the enemy. There's a security firm known as Second Sphere, who I believe you are familiar with."

"They were one of the companies that protected me while I was on a fact-finding trip to Iraq," the President responded. "Very professional men. It turns out they're a mix of American law enforcement and French Foreign Legion veterans."

Brognola nodded. "They were on their best behavior for you."

"It forced me to change my position on them in regards to private military contractors," the President said. "You're not implying that they might be involved in this conspiracy…"

"Leonard Bolfrey and Jacob Morgan Stern are the heads of the European and American divisions of Second Sphere. So far, we've identified a group of mercenaries who clashed with Phoenix Force in Paris as members of Second Sphere Europe, though they were 'released from duty' months before the encounter," Brognola explained. "At the same time, Able Team has noted that Indian Point and Calvert Cliffs have their security forces bolstered by Second Sphere North American cadres."

"Then why would they need infiltration robots and hired gunmen to go after the American reactors if they already have inside men?" the President asked.

"Second Sphere NorthAm has only been relegated to secondary security concerns," Brognola said. "The Department of Energy hasn't authorized them to have anything directly to do with the nuclear reactors."

"It's circumstantial evidence which wouldn't hold up in a court of law," the President mused grimly. "But then, we don't have time to try a government prosecution against these people."

"Not with a force of hired guns on their way to Calvert Cliffs, no," Brognola agreed.

"So, Syria could be ground zero for the worst chemical weapons attack in global history, while our own country and France are at the mercy of runaway nuclear reactors?" the President asked. "What's the timetable for this countdown?"

"Twenty-four hours, and it should be over," Brognola said.

The President snorted. "One day."

"Just remember, Mr. President, unlike the TV agency, we are the gang that actually shoots straight," Brognola pointed out.

"That's news that makes me feel better. Anything the Farm needs to expedite matters, you have my carte blanche approval," the President told the head Fed.

"Right now, we're working so far ahead of the curve, even stopping to ask for permission would take hours," Brognola said. "All we need is your forgiveness."

The President frowned. "You've got it ahead of time. But according to how your people work, the only forgiveness needed will be for failure. And if they've failed, they won't be alive to need forgiveness."

Brognola nodded solemnly.

"How about I just send my prayers?" the President offered.

"Every bit helps," Brognola responded.

The rumpled head Fed folded his laptop and stood. He left the leader of the free world sitting alone in the Oval Office.

CARL LYONS PULLED UP to the gate at Calvert Cliffs Nuclear Power Plant and flashed his Justice Department credentials in the name of Carl Stone. He noted that the gate guard had an emblem on his uniform signifying that he was a part of Second Sphere NorthAm. While the rent-a-cop didn't have a firearm on his workbelt, there was a selection of communication equipment, as well as less lethal implements for restraining unruly visitors to the nuclear plant.

Lyons doubted that the man was in on the conspiracy simply due to the fact that he had settled so well into the role of sitting on a stool all day, monitoring card readers and looking at photo IDs. The man barely paid him any notice as he went back to sipping coffee and watching music videos on his laptop computer.

Lyons drove through to the campus. There was an area within the facility that had much tighter security. Department of Energy police in ballistic vests with holstered handguns patrolled a fence topped with concertina wire. A large SUV worked a circuit inside the fence, and from his experience, the ex-LAPD cop knew that there would be patrol rifles inside the vehicle, probably Colt 630 police rifles, in semiautomatic but still possessing the kind of firepower necessary to deal with a heavily armed intruder. As the DoE men's patrol rifles had full-length barrels, and they also had no limitation on the use of frangible ammunition, the guardians of the reactors would have no difficulty staging a holding action in the face of a direct assault.

Somewhere inside the security barracks would be two armored vehicles designed to shrug off hits from even a Soviet RPG-7 rocket-propelled grenade. The armored personnel carriers would have a top speed of fifty miles per hour and could hold a half-dozen men clad in body armor and packing fully automatic weapons. There were also towers among the reactors where Lyons had caught glimpses of men armed with bolt-action rifles. The sharpshooters would equalize any threat to the power plant simply due to the fact that they had the cushion of range and altitude blunting the effects of most assault weapons.

Lyons sighed. The plant was well-guarded, and they were putting on a good show for the guy visiting from the Justice Department to follow up on the rest of the Department of Energy's concerns. However, if an alert cop like Lyons was able to make out the basic defenses of the Calvert Cliffs facility, then the men who filed in and out working the "garbage shift" for Second Sphere NorthAm would also know what their people would be facing.

Somewhere among the retired cops and discharged military, Jacob Stern had at least one ringer who had fed him the information necessary to set up a successful raid, even with only a scattering of untrained gunmen as his main force. Lyons also couldn't discount that Second Sphere had stashed robot infiltrators to assist the hired hoodlums. There was every possibility that the men Ramon Biggs was hiding among were enlisted only as cannon fodder and a distraction for the real thrust of the conspiracy's strike.

It was a suspicion that Lyons had relayed to the Farm to throw back to Biggs. He owed the undercover outlaw a warning that the enemy would want a bloodbath between street thugs and Department of Energy SWAT teams. Lyons also wanted Biggs to watch out for Michael, the young man who had come under the robber's protective wing.

There had been a brief moment of skepticism that Biggs had stumbled upon a relative innocent among the stone-cold murderers for hire jammed onto several busses. That disappeared when Lyons heard the description of the young man from Biggs, with corroborating evidence from the Baltimore police department regarding the youth's activities. In Los Angeles, Lyons hadn't encountered the kind of stoop dealers prevalent in the more built-up East Coast cities. His experience was more toward crack houses and roving operations that worked out of the trunk of a car. However, Lyons had spent enough time riding with cops from Atlanta to Boston to become familiar with the situation.

At fifteen, a stoop kid was not real management material. He was a soldier, or a part-time supervisor who would take the heat while anyone with real authority stayed on the sidelines. That Michael was considered enough of a gunner to be brought into this battle meant that the kid had fired a few shots in anger, most likely during a beef between corners. Lyons also knew that, unlike New York City, Chicago or Los Angeles, Baltimore kids prided themselves on not being sloppy drive-by ambushers.

"Use the sights, that's the B-more way," he'd heard one say.

By aiming and hitting what they shot at, they kept the heat down for citizen deaths. Baltimore Homicide didn't care if they caught a murder case where the body belonged to someone with a rap sheet.

Lyons pulled up to the secondary security office where Second Sphere men stood around, smoking cigarettes. A couple of men had loosened their shirts and had opened a couple of beers, signifying that they were off shift, and getting ready to go home for the night. The ones still biding their time, either before going on duty or at the end of their break, puffed away as they envied their friends downing cold ones.

Everyone stopped sipping and puffing when Lyons

pulled up in the black sedan and stepped out. Lyons was dressed in FBI Special Agent chic, right down to the jet-black, impenetrable sunglasses and grim countenance that made most ordinary cops squirm.

The two beer drinkers downed the last of their brews and stuffed themselves into their cars. Engines fired up and the security men were on their way home as Lyons walked past them. If it was in character for him to smile, Lyons would have, noting the black rubber worn onto the parking spots that had just been evacuated.

"Sir?" one of the guards asked, shoved by the others to find out what was going on. "Can I help you?"

Lyons turned his head almost mechanically, the black lenses of his shades giving the impression that a soulless machine was staring into the bottom of his soul. The poor rent-a-cop paled and swallowed audibly, then Lyons showed off his badge.

"I'm running a check on conditions here with the contracted security," Lyons said. "There have been allegations of unprofessional conduct."

The man winced and coffee sloshed from the brim of his disposable cup. Cigarettes were thrown to the tarmac and stomped out.

"We haven't heard anything about that," the coffee drinker said. "We've been courteous and aware. The admin hasn't said anything that would indicate—"

"Which admin would that be?" Lyons said, pouring a little extra sneer into the word *admin*.

"That would be Mr. Edwards, our administrative director," the security guard said. He was almost successful in keeping a tremor of fear out of his voice.

Lyons glared at the rent-a-cop. "Take me to see him."

The young man led the way, and the Able Team commander followed, knowing that he could be stepping right into a trap.

The nice thing about a trap, though, was that you didn't have to worry about which direction the threat was coming from, when it was coming at you from all sides.

CHAPTER TWELVE

The twin cooling towers rose almost five hundred feet over the tree line as McCarter, Manning and Hawkins looked at them from a copse of trees across the River Seine. Getting closer would mean risking security in the woods across the great river, and even then, there was only one road in from the south that crossed the evacuation canal, where the runoff from the two 1300-megawatt reactors was allowed to cool before being cycled through the system.

"Seven hundred people in there," Manning noted. "Not counting tourists, and contractors hired on for odd jobs."

"Like staging a terrorist attack or operating remote-control robots," McCarter said. "We haven't gotten word back from Lyons and the others about how these bastards are setting up their operations in the States."

Hawkins ran his fingers through the water that sloshed on the shore, his mouth turned down in a frown. "There is a lot of water on hand."

"So?" McCarter asked.

"So Gadgets provided plenty of video of snake-style robots that are similar to the designs we've been encountering," Hawkins said. "And one of them seemed perfectly at home in a marine environment. They also didn't seem to be hampered by humidity and the saltiness of being on the deck of a rusted fishing boat."

Manning looked at his map. "The evacuation canal is connected to the cooling towers by small, mostly impenetrable pipes. They are far smaller than a man, and there are grates in the pipes to keep rodents and other animals from crawling through."

"But these things have been equipped with all manner of tools, including something with the capability to cut the head off of a human being," McCarter concluded, nodding. "Plus the designer of this robot doesn't seem to worry about outfitting each robot with different utensils."

"Schwarz pointed out that the design is modular," Hawkins added. "Different heads with mission-specific tools can be installed."

"Of course, you're going about this in terms of an outsider trying to obtain access," Manning said. "We've been having problems looking into the French energy administration records to see their dealings with Second Sphere Euro."

"They haven't had a chance to break into the company's computer records?" McCarter asked.

"They have a whole lot of nothing going on in there," Hawkins answered. "They're way too smart to have anything incriminating in public banks."

"'Bout time the bloody bastards went back to putting things on nonaccessible filing cabinets," McCarter said. "It gives us something to actually do mentally, rather than wait for the key twiddlers back home to pull some magic message out of thin air."

"Not everyone's advanced enough to use carrier pigeons anymore, old man," Manning said with a chuckle.

Hawkins's brow furrowed. He glared at the two older Phoenix veterans.

"Carrier pigeons, son," McCarter taunted. "Back when they wrapped messages around the ankles of homing—"

Hawkins's concern turned to agitation. "Shut up. Do you hear that?"

McCarter was about to offer another snide comment when he heard the whirr of a motor in the air. "You've got to be shitting me."

"Carrier pigeons, twenty-first century style," Hawkins replied. "And these don't attract hungry peregrine falcons."

Hawkins took off running toward the sound of the small electric motor. Pulling a pocket monoscope from his pocket, he swept the sky until he saw the small, silvery object buzzing through the air. McCarter and Manning caught up to him, and the three men watched as the remote-control airplane, no larger than a foot long with a one-and-a-half-foot wingspan, hung lazily in the blue sky. It had been almost invisible, hidden among the fat, pillowy cloud of smoke that rolled out of the open neck of one of the tall cooling towers. Now it had dropped down, coming lower to the ground.

"It could just be someone taking time out for a hobby," Manning pointed out.

"If all you have is a hammer, every problem looks like a nail," Hawkins said.

"And if you have a bloody big supply of remote-control technology, then your secure method of communication while in the field takes the form of a toy airplane," McCarter returned. The Briton patted his belt where the SP-2202 nestled in an inside-the-waistband holster. He doubted that anyone receiving a message plane would be too heavily armed, but there was always the possibility that the opposition would be on heightened alert due to the fact that Phoenix Force had already made a strike against their Paris operation.

Manning had been carrying his cut-down shotgun in a "man purse" and he slid his hand into its mouth. The brawny Canadian would save his 9 mm handgun for backup duty.

"Do we take direct action?" Hawkins asked, peering over a small hedge to see another trio of men standing in a field. One of them had the boxy remote for the airplane, while the other two were standing next to an off-road vehicle. The guard closest to the SUV was half obscured by waist-high grass, but he appeared to be leaning on something, and he didn't look like the sort of man to require a walking stick.

A quick scan with the pocket telescope and Hawkins saw that the "stick" was actually the two barrels of a side-by-side shotgun, not much different from the over-and-under that Gary Manning had, except that this one hadn't been hacksawed into an urban robot-smasher or door-breacher like the Canadian's. It wasn't unusual for a small group of Frenchmen to be in the field with a bird-hunting shotgun, but all three of the strangers in the clearing clearly had unnatural bulges under their jackets.

Concealed-handgun permits were not common in France. Hawkins knew that his pistol under his untucked shirt was a violation that would bring down the full force of law on him if he was captured. French authorities felt that their subjects were better off shielded by police officers, regardless of how long it took for them to come to the rescue. The fact that those three men were carrying concealed weapons in proximity to a nuclear power station meant that they were up to no good.

Hawkins thought of the conundrum that he and his allies were also packing concealed weapons, but he realized that the same truth held for them. Phoenix Force wasn't going to try to dissuade the conspiracy from its violence over tea and crumpets. They were going to stop the would-be mass murderers with fire and lead.

It was just a detail that the "no good" that Phoenix Force was up to happened to be in the defense of the very country whose laws they were breaking.

"Take 'em or observe?" Manning asked.

McCarter frowned. "The enemy knows my face, so I'll have to stay here and keep an eye on the plant. You two follow them and see what's going on."

Hawkins tapped his cell phone. "We'll keep in contact with you, then."

Manning and Hawkins tromped through the shrubs while McCarter was left in position. The two were on their way to a trio of parked, rented Vespa scooters that had been obtained for low-profile travel through the countryside. While their sedan wouldn't have been too out of place, the scooters had storage compartments that enabled the trio to store the kit borrowed from the Second Sphere mercenaries they had encountered in Paris. The trunks didn't have the room for even the

compact Steyr rifles, but the collapsed MP-5 submachine guns were sufficient firepower for most of what
they would encounter, aside from Manning's choice to
keep the cut-down 12-gauge shotgun on hand.

Hawkins's cell phone vibrated, and he answered.
McCarter was getting in touch with them over the
walkie-talkie function of the particular cellular units
Phoenix Force had chosen for the French trip.

"They're back in the car. The guy with the radio control sent the plane back to the Nogent station," McCarter
told them. "They'll be passing by you in about two
minutes."

"Roger," Hawkins replied. He fired up the scooter
and made certain that the bottom of his jacket was held
closed by a snap. While it would have been more comfortable to allow the tails of his coat to flap in the wind
as he rode the touring bike, such movement of his jacket
and the shirt beneath would reveal that he had a sizeable
handgun jammed into his waistband.

Manning secured his double-barrel shotgun between
his legs on the scooter. The zipper was partially open to
allow his hand to dip in, and the bag it was carried in was
fastened securely by carabiner links. With a plunge of the
hand and a pull of the trigger, the big Canadian would be
able to launch nearly twenty .36-caliber projectiles in a
single cloud, more than sufficient to excavate the interior
of a vehicle at close range. If more refined, less indiscriminate shotgun use was required, each barrel held nine
pellets of double-aught buck that would hammer into an
eight-inch circle at seven yards. Such raw power had
been proved on countless occasions, and Manning was
comfortable with it, even out of a stubby, foot-long
cannon.

Once the shotgun was empty, Manning intended to fall back on two handguns. One was an old Astra .44 Magnum revolver with a three-inch barrel, while the second was the SIG pro 2202 handgun. The stubby little Magnum was another hand cannon that the burly Manning liked, though he favored the American-built Ruger Alaskan and Smith & Wesson versions of the stubby revolver. However, for their current mission the Phoenix Force warriors needed to keep their weapons well hidden.

As the SUV passed down the road, Hawkins took the first leg of their tail, pulling out fifteen seconds behind the truck. Manning would follow another fifteen seconds later, and the two Phoenix Force operatives would take turns staying in line of sight with their quarry. By trading off and using the scooters' small size to slip them behind other vehicles in traffic, they would be able to allay suspicion by shadowing the conspirators.

That all hinged, however, on whether the Second Sphere members had fallen for McCarter's misdirection that they had taken the bait for the south of France. If it did work out that way, then there was the chance that the enemy skulkers would not be aware that Stony Man's eyes were watching their every movement.

BACK AT THE SEINE, McCarter pulled his satellite phone out of its pouch. The larger but more powerful device didn't need local transmission towers, since its signal would bounce off transmission satellites that would relay his message back to the Blue Ridge Mountains. It also had encryption that was several times as powerful as the pocketable units so that it was less likely to be tapped. He had to let the Farm know about the radio-control aircraft in touch with people inside of the Nogent plant.

"What's going on?" Price asked.

"We've got a little bit of news," McCarter said. "We've observed activity at the Nogent nuclear power station. There were people with guns in a field receiving a remote-control aircraft. I have Gary and T.J. following them."

"Guns," Price noted. "You know about the situation we have here in the States."

"Yes," McCarter replied. "Right now, we're only in observation mode. I was just wondering if you have eyes on the reactors."

"We had some satellites set looking down at the plant, but we weren't aware of the airplane. How large?" Price asked.

"A small hobby job, about a foot long by two wide," McCarter related. "Is it too small for the cameras to see?"

"That kind of information is classified," Price taunted.

McCarter sighed. "Give me a break, Barb."

"All right, we're replaying footage to see if we can spot the origin of the RC plane," Price said, suppressing a chuckle. After a brief pause she continued. "We've got the pictures. There was someone in the north parking lot. He loaded the plane into a burgundy Toyota hatchback. I'm sending the license plate to you."

McCarter looked at the alphanumeric combination. There were two variable numbers on the plate, which impressed the Briton over how sharp and perceptive the satellite cameras were that the Farm had hijacked. That, plus a visual representation of the color of the parked vehicle gave McCarter enough to locate exactly which car he had to check.

"Good enough for you?" Price asked.

"I'm on it now," McCarter replied. "Keep an eye on the lads while I go snooping."

"We'll do that," Price said. "But what are you going to do if something bad goes down?"

"For me, or for them?" McCarter asked. "Because if drama comes my way, I'll break off as many boots up asses as I can."

"And if Hawkins and Manning run into trouble?" Price asked.

"I'll steal a car from the parking lot," McCarter explained. "It'll be faster than this sputter mobile I've got. Either way, I'm leaving it behind."

"You're not entering the parking lot straight up?" Price inquired.

"The bad guys have my ugly gob plastered all over this country. They'd stop me with a dozen bullets if I show it at the gate," McCarter said.

"Be careful," Price cautioned.

"I'll do better than attempt to be careful," McCarter promised. "I won't get caught."

He could feel Price's smile over the phone. "Be a ghost, then."

"Ta, Barb," McCarter said softly, hanging up.

CIRCUMVENTING THE GATE GUARD wasn't going to be easy, especially if he was armed. Granted, the metal detectors on the main plant itself would sense the polymer-framed handgun if he went through a door. He thought back to when the Glock series of polymer-framed pistols was first introduced. Critics went into a panic because they felt the plastic frames wouldn't set off metal detectors and be invisible to X-rays of baggage, but they conveniently ignored the several ounces of steel that made up barrels, springs, slides and trigger mechanisms, not to mention the amount of metal in the ammunition for the handguns. McCarter had encountered porcelain and wooden handguns in his time, and the most invisible ones fired a form of caseless ammunition, but in all those instances, the weapons were crude, single-shot, manually cycled weapons and many could not be rechambered from an internal reservoir.

The SIG pro pistol was not invisible to detection measures, though it was flat and compact enough not to be noticeable when tucked against his hip under his waistband. Still, an alert gate guard would notice the slight bulge and be concerned. The best thing that the Briton could do was to enter the plant without attracting attention. He'd been studying the layout of the Nogent campus and its surroundings. In broad daylight, there wasn't much cover, and he had no intention of swimming through the runoff canal. It wasn't that the water itself was irradiated. Sure it was warm due to the fact that it had been used to cool down reactors that generated tremendous amounts of heat, but it was relatively safe. Indeed, the canal was teeming with life, as evidenced by its greenish tint from the algae that turned the waters murky. Here and there, he saw fish pop up to nibble at bugs attracted to this oasis of balmy warmth, and ducks paddled along on the surface.

However, being stealthy after swimming through a man-made marsh, dripping with water and smelling of mold and duck shit was impossible. The car that McCarter wanted to get to was in the northwest parking lot, and that was only accessible by a road from the southwest, which had its own lot. Since the direct approach was McCarter's favorite, he had maneuvered himself around to the northwest corner of the campus. The fields here were empty, with no sign of life for miles. The road he stood next to was more appropriately graded dirt rather than paved asphalt. There was overgrowth under the fence, but it was electrified to keep animals and unwanted snoopers from venturing too close.

That wouldn't stop the Phoenix Force commander. He had a set of insulated wire cutters that would protect him from the lethal shock, though he didn't think that it would be necessary. A couple of bushes he noticed had spread into the chain link, branches and leaves resting on metal that should have been inhospitable to the plants. The current that went through an electrified fence generally kept even the rudimentary plants from brushing against it. McCarter had always doubted the sensory abilities of grasses and bushes, but Hermann Schwarz showed him footage of how flowers turned to follow sunlight and how trees grew to avoid environmental hazards like crumbling slopes or electric fences.

The warning sign was probably a cheaper method of security than the wiring necessary to pump the section of fence with voltage. McCarter scurred to the bushes, looking for cameras or security guards who might notice his movement. Nestled in the shrubbery, he had crouched out of sight and touched the tip of the wirecutters to one of the links of fence.

No spark leaped between the two metals, and McCarter touched it. Scanning left and right, he saw that this was the only section that had such growth snug up to the bare chain link. On a whim, McCarter felt around under the branches until he felt the loopings of cable ties. He squirmed closer to it and saw an improvised hatch had been cut into the chain link. The gap wouldn't be man-size, but it was certainly enough to allow various remote-control robots to slip under it. McCarter set to work on increasing the size of the flap to slip through himself.

Second Sphere Europe had been listed as a security contractor for Nogent, and according to Kurtzman's discoveries, they were in charge of the perimeter fence maintenance.

That made sense. While the security contractor would not have the authority or clearance to have anything to do with the main reactor, the peripheral jobs afforded access to enough holes to allow infiltrator robots to penetrate the plant. Inside the fence, the Briton made certain that the links were secured with some of his own cable ties. He didn't have enough to deny his robotic opposition entry, but he'd slow them down for a moment.

It took him a few minutes to find the burgundy Toyota hatchback that Price had noted. Utilizing the pommel of his knife, a conical glass breaker, McCarter knocked out the driver's-side window, unlocked the door and slipped into the vehicle. He found a machine pistol stuffed under the driver's seat, Second Sphere contractor identification and the radio-controlled airplane with controller in the back. He looked around to make certain that no one had detected his break-in on the car, then shuffled into the backseat and investigated the plane.

There was a digital camera on board the remote plane. Under the storage compartment behind the rear seats, in the place of the spare tire, was a compact but powerful-looking transceiver unit. McCarter knew that this had to be the robotic control relay point. Using the glass breaker on his knife again, the Phoenix Force commander smashed it into so much electronic garbage with a few well-placed blows. He set the floorboard back over the relay transmitter and rearranged things to how he'd found them.

He sat in the driver's seat and contemplated his next move.

Destroying a radio was such a small task, and he doubted that Second Sphere would possess only one means of controlling their murderous machines. He looked over the contractor identification papers, studying them closely.

His cell phone hummed, set on vibrate so as not to give away his presence during the infiltration. He opened it up.

"Our quarry's gone apeshit," Hawkins advised. "What did you do?"

"What makes you think I did anything?" McCarter asked.

Hawkins groaned. "Because only you can turn a group of disciplined, undercover operatives into a pack of shrieking chimpanzees so quickly."

"I took the piss out of their robot communications," McCarter confessed. "I didn't realize that they were monitoring things that closely."

"They were, and now they just took off in their SUV," Hawkins said.

"Cut them off. Try to take one of them alive, but if not, you know their headquarters at least," McCarter said. "I've got some more sneaking around to do."

Hawkins sighed. "Have fun. Don't do anything I wouldn't do."

McCarter chuckled. "Shit, T.J., you're depriving me of ninety percent of my game plan if I stick to your methods. How could I have fun if you put that stipulation on things?"

"Then do what you gotta do, hoss," Hawkins replied.

McCarter hung up, pulling out a spare badge and a baseball-style cap. His dark jacket looked enough like a uniform coat that the hat and a clipped-on badge would make him fit in. All he had to do was take a premade photo sticker of himself and slap it onto the front of the badge. He'd taken to carrying the flat, inobtrusive little sticker around, like the rest of Phoenix Force. It made on-the-fly forged badges like this ridiculously quick and easy to make, and he would withstand scrutiny for at least ten seconds.

Slipping out of the Toyota, bringing a clipboard with him, McCarter decided it was time to blend in with the bad guys, and try to locate their primary communications and remote-control relay.

When McCarter saw two Second Sphere security men run out into the parking lot, concerned looks on their faces, he knew that he wouldn't have to look very hard. Not if he could beat the answers out of two of the conspirators.

CHAPTER THIRTEEN

"What's the plan?" Manning asked over the radio as he shadowed the conspirators' SUV as it raced back toward the Nogent plant. The men inside seemed to be in a hurry, but speed laws kept them in check, allowing his scooter to keep pace with the vehicle.

"David says take 'em out. It'd be good to get a prisoner, but not necessary," Hawkins replied.

Manning took a deep breath. "Stay back at the headquarters and check it for any stragglers. I'll deal with the SUV."

"Sure?" Hawkins asked.

"Positive," Manning replied. "I've got a plan to take out the vehicle with minimum disruption and danger to surrounding traffic. Can you handle their safehouse by yourself?"

Though Hawkins was the youngest member of Phoenix Force, and with far less experience at solo operations, he was a highly trained soldier, having received education from McCarter and Manning, in addition to Mack Bolan. The conspirators' safehouse was a restaurant and bar with a second floor devoted to residential use. On examination, they knew that the basement was utilized for food storage and offices, meaning that Hawkins would have to secure all three floors by himself.

Right now, though, the restaurant was listed as closed for renovations. Workmen's vans had parked around the back of the building, allowing the conspirators' allies to cart in boxes of all different sizes. It didn't take much imagination to see that the Second Sphere's allies would have a good stockpile of automatic weapons and crated robots.

"I can take it," Hawkins said. "You just be careful on that scooter."

"I know what I'm doing," Manning answered. "Just remember, because David let us go weapons free, that doesn't mean..."

Hawkins cut him off. "I know." Frustration ground under his laconic drawl. "Believe it or not, I've paid attention the past few years, and even if I were completely oblivious, I'm not going to drop the hammer on a noncombatant. However, you're on the road, and one wrong swerve can cause casualties where you don't want them."

"Fired up," Manning told him. "Good. Take that anger and put it in your fuel tank."

"Thanks," Hawkins replied.

Manning unzipped the bag between his feet, the taped round handle of the over-and-under shotgun poking out unobtrusively. He thumbed the safety off on the stubby little boomstick, and once it was primed and ready to go, he hit the throttle on the Vespa.

Its motor buzzed into higher gear and he shot toward

the right side. Manning's plan was to knock out the SUV by dumping both barrels of the 12-gauge into the driver's-side window. Acceleration launched the big Canadian on the scooter. The conspirators had stopped at a light, which was the opportunity that Manning wanted. Taking out the driver while the vehicle idled at a red light would keep the truck from veering into traffic.

The snarl of the Vespa drew the attention of the Second Sphere driver. Manning could see his alert features in the side mirror, but the brief moment of concern was too short for the driver to do anything but widen his eyes in horror as the two cavernous mouths of the Canadian's shotgun were shoved through his window.

Both hammers fell on the sawed-off double, and a storm of buckshot bellowed. The recoil jammed up Manning's powerful arm, a shock wave that would have knocked any other man off balance. The roar of the shotgun was accompanied by a sudden cloud of pink mist as the Second Sphere wheelman's head and shoulders were transformed into chopped meat. The man riding in the front seat with him howled in pain and dismay as he was covered in a patina of blood and pulped flesh, clutching his torn cheek and shoulder as a few pellets had torn through the body of the driver.

The SUV lurched a few feet as the dead man's foot slipped off the brake, but cars and pedestrians scattered to escape the sudden act of violence in their midst. Manning hated creating terror in the streets of a French town, but considering that the three men in the vehicle were part of a plan that would unleash lethal radiation that would kill thousands, and render millions homeless, it truly was the lesser of two evils.

The mercenary in the backseat recoiled in horror from the thunderous shotgun blast, but he ripped open his jacket after his second of shock passed. Manning lunged through the driver's-side window, having traded the empty 12-gauge for the stubby little .44 Magnum Astra.

"Don't do it!" Manning shouted in French, dragging the pulped corpse behind the wheel up as a shield.

The gunman in the backseat triggered his pistol, bullets tearing through the back of the seat and stopping cold within the corpse's torso. Manning snarled and extended the Astra, its two-and-three-quarter-inch barrel right at the end of the shooter's nose. Before the passenger could move his head and continue firing, the Canadian triggered the powerful revolver twice. The rear window of the SUV was coated with a fountain of shattered skull and stewed brains

The blood-covered remaining passenger stopped screaming, looking at the powerful mass that was inside the driver's-side window. He opened his mouth as if to say something, but Manning pivoted the Magnum snub around, raking it across the man's wounded cheek. Flesh tore violently under the impact, and his head bounced off the passenger's-side window.

Out cold, he was no more of a threat, and would prove to be useful if Hawkins hadn't secured any data or prisoners. With a powerful surge, he yanked the corpse of the driver out of its seat and threw it in the road. He took a moment to grab the MP-5 and its spare magazines from the scooter's storage compartment, and slashed the empty shotgun and its bag from its moorings. He dumped them in the well at the unconscious prisoner's feet, then fired up the truck, spinning it down side streets even as sirens bleated in the distance.

The Nogent policemen were going to have their work cut out for them, investigating a mutilated corpse and an idling rental scooter, but the distraction would give Manning time to reunite with Hawkins back at the enemy's safehouse.

Manning could only hope that they could do the job without causing such a ruckus that the authorities would come crashing into the abandoned restaurant.

As he accelerated down a side street, keeping out of sight of the police, he resigned himself to cross that bridge when he came to it.

HAWKINS KNEW that going into the restaurant with an MP-5 would bring down enough official heat that any effort he took in securing the enemy safehouse would be wasted. The police would sit on whatever data they discovered in the building while analysts tried to fathom the secrets within. It would take stealth and audacity to do what he had to do.

The first thing he did was to take one of his spare SIGs and attach a suppressor to the prethreaded barrel, then hung that in a shoulder holster. He hoped to avoid a gunfight, but if he couldn't, he wanted to keep things as low profile as possible. His primary tool was going to be a piece of kit he'd recovered from the Paris-based Second Sphere mercenaries.

The Halligan tool, sometimes called a hooligan tool, was an improvement on the crowbar, featuring a sharp, spiked end with which to create a gap to jam the forked crowbar end into. The tool was in use with fire departments around the world, and could rip a door off its hinges with ridiculous ease. Hawkins also saw this as a quiet and brutal weapon, a modern-day equivalent of a spiked morningstar. It could be utilized with any one of a dozen other disciplines of melee combat, from less-than-lethal butt-strokes to jaws to skull-crushing strokes with the rugged spike sticking out of the hammerlike end. It was heavy, but not so much that he couldn't maneuver it in close-quarters combat.

Having recovered the Halligan tool from their sedan, he tucked it between his knees on the scooter and drove around to the back of the restaurant. As he pulled up, a pair of men who were busy smoking stubbed out their butts and glared at him.

"The place is closed," one of them snarled in French.

"I was just looking for some day work," Hawkins replied in his passable French. He got off of the scooter, leaning on the Halligan tool as if it were a cane. "I'm touring—"

"We don't give a fuck about your life story, idiot," the other man grunted. "This is a union job, and you're not wanted here."

Hawkins took a deep calming breath. He looked the two "workers" over and saw the butts of handguns bulging in their belts. One of the men swept his jacket aside to show off the handle of his weapon. "We don't like scabs around here."

"Shame," Hawkins said in English, turning back toward his scooter. "Really bad that you hate scabs."

"Why is that, American?" the other asked, following his language change.

Hawkins whirled swiftly and violently, the hammer-block at the end of the tool smashing one, then the other with unyielding momentum. The Halligan tool opened ugly gashes across their faces and deposited them on the ground in senseless heaps. "The two of you, if you wake up, will be nursing scabs all over your faces."

Hawkins knelt by the pair and quickly drew the pistols from their belts. He tossed them into a waste can and buried them beneath trash. It took another moment for him to bind the wrists of one of the unconscious guards when the back door of the restaurant opened.

"What's going on?" a newcomer asked in the middle of lighting his cigarette. The new man froze in shock as he saw one of his partners hogtied on the floor of the alley. He shot a glance at Hawkins, who had been in the process of restraining the other guard.

Hawkins swung the heavy metal tool with a hard snap as the newcomer's hand darted toward the weapon he had concealed. The metal-punching spike connected with the Second Sphere conspirator's cheek and caved it in with all the power of a charging rhinoceros. Facial bone structure collapsed under the force of the blow, the spike continuing into the gunman's brain. His lifeless body tumbled back through the door he'd just exited, eliciting a yelp of surprise from the kitchen.

Hawkins dived through the battered door, staying at waist level as he entered the building.

"We've got trouble!" a guard shouted. "Get upstairs!"

Hawkins sneered in disgust that his plan had gone to hell, but he managed to get some revenge on the alarmist by using the cutting table as a weapon. The edge of the countertop hammered into the Second Sphere gunman's belly and pinned him against a stove. Hawkins felt the crunch of a pelvic bone through the metal of the table, a grinding that he wouldn't have heard with the howl of agony elicited by the wounded man.

The open basement stairwell threw up the thunder of stomping feet, alerting Hawkins to the fact that he was going to be outnumbered and overwhelmed if he didn't take swift action. Hawkins spotted an open can of paint and hooked its wire handle with the spike on his Halligan tool. With a powerful pivot, he hurled the can toward the stairwell. The gallon of paint weighed in at eight pounds, and when it struck, it cracked the ribs of the first of the mercenaries up the stairs. The sudden deceleration of the open can spewed the container's contents out in a blinding cloud that had the Second Sphere guards clawing at their faces.

Unlike in a comedy movie, the men wouldn't be blinded for long, but the sudden maneuver had bought the Phoenix Force commando all the time he needed to close with the blinded thug at the top of the stairs. With a solid swing, he shattered the man's clavicle. The man dropped to his knees, screaming in pain, giving Hawkins an easy shot, bringing up the block hammer under the jaw of a second guard. The mandible shattered under the crushing impact, and the unconscious mercenary tumbled back into his two remaining partners, arms tangling them up.

Hawkins leaped off the top step and came down with all his weight, boots smashing into the trio of bodies at the bottom of the stairs. One of the guards managed to get his pistol out, but the Halligan tool swept the man's hand, forearm bones splintering under the deadly stroke. The last of the Second Sphere hired soldiers squirmed to get out from under Hawkins and his unconscious partner, but the Phoenix Force commando kicked him in the throat.

"Don't hit me!" a voice cried from a computer station. Hawkins spun and faced the man. A quick examination showed that he was unarmed, but that didn't mean the man was harmless.

"On the floor, face down, hands interlaced behind your head," Hawkins ordered.

"Yes, yes," the computer operator said, complying with Hawkins's orders. The Phoenix Force commando looked around the basement and saw that it was empty. Most of the desks had been shoved against the wall, except for the one that served as the platform for the setup that the operator was using. Having spent enough time in the Stony Man Farm computer annex, he knew that the hardware on hand was sufficient to operate a slew of robots if necessary.

"Who are you?" Hawkins asked.

"I'm Roberto Alemeda," the computer operator said. "Please, don't hit me with that thing."

"Stay put and behave, and I won't," Hawkins said. "Don't behave, and I get to clean your brains off of this thing."

"All right," Alemeda said.

"This is for controlling the infiltrator robots?" Hawkins asked.

Alemeda looked up, then nodded. "Yes."

"Keep kissing the floor," Hawkins snarled, keeping his prisoner in line.

There was movement at the top of the steps and Hawkins traded his melee weapon for the suppressed SIG pro pistol. He waited off to one side at the bottom of the stairwell. Unlike the crowd that had rushed up from the basement, this group was taking its time. There was a grunt of pain from above, and Hawkins's understanding of French was enough to tell him that it was the man whose hips he'd cracked with the prep table.

The guard complained about it being hard to walk, and how the man didn't appear to have a firearm.

Suddenly the sentry who'd been speaking was hurled down the steps in a show of brazen ruthlessness. They wanted to make certain that Hawkins wouldn't greet them with the bark of gunfire, but luckily the Phoenix Force fighter had the presence of mind to keep his finger off the trigger. The wounded guard crashed to the bottom of the stairs and landed with a sickening crunch.

Hawkins did elicit a cry of dismay to make them think that they'd surprised him. It was a fake-out that brought a trio of men stomping down the stairs, handguns at the ready.

Hawkins snapped up the SIG and fired two parabellum rounds through the face of the first gunman on the steps. His face crumpled around the high-velocity bullets, his brains bursting out of the back of his skull. The point man collapsed in a boneless tumble, landing on the wounded sentry on the floor. The battered mercenary groaned in agony while the other two armed guards on the stairs wiped at the blood spattered into their faces.

One had enough presence of mind to keep his pistol aimed down at Hawkins, but the Southerner cut him off with three rapid rounds that chopped into his chest. The mercenary gurgled and staggered against the rail. Trying to make the most of his fading strength, he tried to lift his handgun, but Hawkins finished the job with a bullet that tore through his open, gasping mouth.

The last of the Second Sphere guards whirled and tried to get up the stairs, but Hawkins sent a pair of parabellum manglers chasing after him. The rounds stabbed into the man's back and he tumbled, smashing face-first into the steps. It was ruthless, gunning down the mercenary, but if Hawkins hadn't taken him down, he'd be a threat to Manning once the big Canadian arrived at the abandoned restaurant. The guard would also be able to grab more substantive firepower, even grenades, to retake the basement.

Alemeda whimpered at the carnage laid out around him. Two corpses and four wounded survivors groaning and bleeding puddles that stretched out to touch him.

"Grow some balls," Hawkins snarled. "You were going to send in remote-control weapons to destroy a nuclear reactor station and unleash a deadly cloud on a city of millions."

"I didn't… I've never seen anyone killed before," Alemeda stammered.

"If you're lucky, you won't ever see it happen again," Hawkins said. "How many guards did Second Sphere have here?"

Alemeda's eyes widened. First Hawkins had demonstrated knowledge of the infiltrator robots; now he knew the name of the organization they worked for. Hawkins restrained a grin of satisfaction over how on target the Farm's operatives had been in the course this investigation.

"Presley?" Manning's voice called from the top of the steps.

"Down here," Hawkins replied.

Manning came down the steps, pistol drawn. "I've got a prisoner up in the… What did you use on these people? It looks like Carl exploded on them!"

"My hooligan," Hawkins answered.

"Who is that?" Manning asked, noting Alemeda.

"The computer jockey working here on the relay

and preparing to coordinate the infiltrators," Hawkins explained.

"Where are the robots stored?" Manning asked.

"They're at the Nogent plant," Alemeda said. "They were smuggled past security in copy paper boxes."

"That'd make sense with the weight and the paper pads concealing compartments," Hawkins mused. "How many are on-site?"

"A dozen," Alemeda said. "I'm here to monitor the relay communications station until we release them."

Manning looked at the computer setup. "We could cripple it."

"There's a backup," Alemeda confessed.

"We have one, too," Hawkins told the programmer. "And he took out…"

"There's yet another relay station. Again, it's disguised as a box of computer paper," Alemeda told them. "Two is one and one is none. We decided to err on the fault of triple redundancy. The tertiary relay was also meant to take over after all personnel have evacuated the region."

Manning grimaced. "So if we destroy this setup, Second Sphere will know that we've compromised their operation and will release the robots with the third relay."

Hawkins got out his cell phone. "David?"

Manning saw Hawkins's face screw in frustration. "Voice mail?"

"Damn it," Hawkins cursed. "Hard to tell if he was taken down, or he's in the middle of a firefight."

Manning frowned. "Stay here and keep an eye on things."

Hawkins shook his head. "No way…"

"Listen, you secured this, keep it quiet and secure," Manning ordered. "I'm going to help my friend out."

Manning took off, hoping that he would be there in time to help McCarter if he needed it.

SHENCK LOOKED at the readout from Nogent and sighed. He snapped his fingers to draw Homm's attention, and the programmer came to his workstation.

"We've lost contact with the backup system," Homm said with a grim frown. "I'm going to check on radio traffic in Nogent."

"Bolfrey already alerted me to a shooting incident in the town," Shenck said. "That's why I looked at the setup."

"I thought that the enemy had gone south to track down the robot shipments," Homm growled.

"Well, we were fooled," Shenck said. "And maybe the enemy made a lot of noise about hitting the southern ports in order to get the French authorities to follow up the sheer number of leads that they didn't have the manpower to look into."

"If they know about Nogent, then that operation is compromised," Homm grumbled. "I liked that Alemeda kid…."

Shenck picked up the phone and got in touch with Stern. "Sir, the Nogent group has made hard contact with the enemy."

Stern's sigh on the other end was an exercise in anger management. The big Second Sphere commander spoke softly. "How much have we lost?"

"The secondary transmitter, and we believe that there was a gunfight with the team that went to respond to the breakdown," Shenck said.

Stern was quiet for a few moments. "Activate the

robots. Unlike the others who've the enemy captured, those men know too much for the security of our organization."

"Activating the infiltrators," Shenck announced.

"Homm, are you listening?" Stern asked.

The programmer spoke up. "He put you on speaker, sir."

"Keep a close eye on our other actions," Stern said. "The irradiation of Paris will put the world on alert."

"Release our video?" Homm asked.

"The message is go."

The programmer went back to his workstation. Shenck hung up and opened the observation screens for a half-dozen robots. As the deadly machines whirred to life, they were in absolute darkness. As part of their startup protocol, they activated their cutting saws. The sharp flexible blades slashed through cardboard easily—no surprise as they had been designed for slicing open metal ducting.

As light poured through the boxes they destroyed, Shenck caught movement in the security quarters where the Second Sphere had set themselves up. A slender, fox-faced man had grabbed a uniformed security guard and was smashing him face-first into a table with a brutal takedown move.

It was the man they had seen in Paris, the lone raider who had gone into the recreation center.

"Round two, mystery man," Shenck growled as he sent a digital command to his killer robots.

"Exterminate."

CHAPTER FOURTEEN

The hat, badge and dark jacket had carried the day for David McCarter, bringing him to the Second Sphere offices on the Nogent Nuclear Power Plant campus. The inobtrusive little building was nothing like the SWAT headquarters that had been set up for the proper French Department of Energy security team. Sure, Second Sphere had a good radio tower atop the building, but nothing like the nest of antennae that kept the government-appointed lawmen in contact with each other and with the main headquarters back in Paris. The office was nothing more than a prefab trailer with a few parking spaces off to the side, resting on the edge of the northwest parking lot.

Instead of squad cars and a single well-armored truck, Second Sphere was allowed a trio of unmarked sedans. McCarter slowed his approach, running scenarios in his head. He didn't have his machine pistol, only his handgun. That was something he didn't want to employ, however, simply due to the fact that gunplay would attract a swarm of lawmen with body-armor and assault rifles. The Briton knew that he'd be chopped to pieces by the overwhelming force of men who were dedicated to the safety of the two nuclear reactors.

There was also the possibility that some members of the Second Sphere agency were not part of the conspiracy. As far as McCarter knew, there was only one man, Kellion, who was directly involved. The other rent-a-cops would simply be men who were doing their job for a paycheck and would have no clue that they were working for a conspiracy that intended to bring death to thousands around the world.

McCarter would have to keep the pistol holstered. It would be too noisy, and would be too final a fate for security guards who probably had no idea of the global threat that their employer posed. That was all right with the Briton. He was a backstreet brawler who learned his arts in a rough childhood before he turned his youthful, reckless energy toward a career in the British army. McCarter couldn't escape the mental image of himself as a bank robber or a leg breaker had he not decided to serve his country and do his duty as a protector. The ease with which he could have slipped into the lifestyle of an adrenaline-hungry thug for hire was something that haunted him.

The Phoenix Force leader had had countless encounters where he hadn't been able to utilize a firearm due to the presence of bystanders or a weapons jam. McCarter was already a strong, rawboned fighting man who would even use his forehead as a blunt-impact weapon. Years of work alongside other martial artists had sharpened his bare-handed fighting skills until he was good enough to neutralize an opponent without resorting to lethal force. Any fool could break someone's neck or crush a windpipe with a knuckle punch. It took real talent to leave someone alive and incapacitated without permanently crippling or fatal injury.

"Hey, who the hell are you?" a security guard asked in French.

"I'm here from the offices in London," McCarter said quickly, explaining his accent. While he was fluent enough in French to pass as a native of the country, he had no doubt that the guard would know most of the other employees from the Paris branch office of Second Sphere. "Just a quick little checkup on you."

The suspicious guard raised an eyebrow. McCarter could see that while he didn't have a gun, he did have a collapsible baton, handcuffs and pepper spray. The lack of armament gave the Second Sphere man an air of innocence, but he still wasn't harmless if the sentry saw through his disguise. "A checkup? For what? Besides, we already have someone from Bonn on hand to do the checkup. Kellion…"

The guard's eyes flicked down to McCarter's badge.

McCarter sighed and grabbed the man by his wrist. With a swift pivot, he dragged the poor guy across his hip and slammed him into the ground with an impact that drove the breath from his lungs. McCarter followed up with a sharp jab to the stunned man's shoulder, rendering the hand that had started for the baton in his belt a limp, numb sack of misfiring nerves. "Kellion's rotten. I'm saving your bloody life."

"Help…" the guard softly rasped. McCarter sighed and jammed his thumb into the junction where his ear met his skull. The sudden sharp pressure on the carotid artery and the jumble of nerves there threw the security man into a quick slumber.

"Bloody idiots," McCarter sighed. He looked around, and luckily no one had seen the brief flurry of violence. Moving quickly, McCarter bound the guard with his own handcuffs, taking the backup key from its hiding space inside of his waistband. He hauled the man and tucked him underneath one of the parked sedans where the unconscious guard would be out of sight and protected by the chassis of the vehicle in case there was a gunfight, despite McCarter's best efforts.

"Carlo?" a voice called from the steps. "Where the hell did you go?"

McCarter stood after pulling off his hat and badge. The sudden movement left him looking rumpled, which would work in his favor for his next ploy. "He's chasing after some bloke who broke into my car!"

The second guard looked at him in momentary confusion. "Why didn't he get on the radio? Shit, why the hell didn't he call the real guards?"

McCarter shook his head. "I don't know, mate."

The second guard moved closer to him, and McCarter leaned against one of the Second Sphere cars. "Are you all right? Did he hurt you?"

"No," McCarter replied. "Carlo went down without a fuss."

The second guard's confusion deepened, but the Briton didn't give him a chance to figure out the cryptic statement. With a lash of his arm and tucking his fist against the guard's neck, McCarter snatched the private cop in a sleeper hold. There was a brief moment of thrashing resistance, but the sleeper hold sapped too much of his strength too quickly to make escape possible. The guard's legs sagged, and McCarter made certain to loosen his hold so that he could breathe and the blood reached his brain. Another bout of handcuffing his victim with his own restraints, and McCarter sent Carlo's friend under the body of the car to join him.

"Two down," McCarter whispered to himself. He jogged up the three steps that led into the trailer to see the man whose badge identified him as Kellion. The other man looked to be a ranking security guard simply because he had a pistol on his belt. The fact that both of them locked eyes on McCarter and displayed a surge of angry recognition meant that the Phoenix Force leader didn't have to worry about breaking something on either of them.

McCarter still couldn't engage in a gunfight, and the Second Sphere conspirators were reluctant to go for the weaponry on their belts, as well. McCarter scooped a portable shredder off the closest desk and whipped it at the uniformed Second Sphere guard. The six-pound hunk of plastic and motors tumbled through the air and smashed into the man's face, hurling him back over his chair in a tangle of limbs and upturned furniture.

Kellion flinched from the crash and grabbed up a letter opener. "You must be the prick that broke into my car."

"Guilty as charged, mate," McCarter answered. "So, are you going to just wag your chin, or do we do something interesting?"

"Putting this spike into your head won't be that interesting," Kellion growled.

"Oh, you're in for a surprise, then, aren't you?" McCarter taunted.

With a flash of motion, Kellion leaped over the desk, lashing out with the gleaming point of steel in an effort to tear McCarter's flesh. The letter opener wasn't razor-sharp, but the Briton knew that even a blunt metal object could cause severe tissue damage with enough force behind it. And with Kellion's deft hand movements, McCarter knew that catching the point's impact in the ribs would shatter bone and perforate his lungs. Luckily, McCarter had scooped up an in-box tray and the letter opener clanged off its metal shelf.

"You've got a skill or two," Kellion grunted.

"I bet that you say that to all the girls," McCarter said with a wink.

The letter opener lashed out again, but this time McCarter used the bottom of the tray to block the Second Sphere conspirator's forearm. There was a loud crack, and then the opener clattered on the tile floor. McCarter swung the tray again, this time intercepting a lashing fist before it could connect with his jaw. Metal clattered and the blow knocked the improvised shield from stunned fingers, but it gave the Briton a moment to stagger behind another desk.

"Running from an injured opponent?" Kellion snarled.

McCarter sighed. "Do I look like I'd fall for that?"

Kellion sighed and shook his head. "No."

McCarter waved Kellion forward. "It doesn't bother you that you're going to render a chunk of France uninhabitable?"

Kellion circled the desk, picking up a stapler with his good hand. "What should I care? It's not my family going homeless. Besides, someone has to stop the proliferation of nuclear energy."

McCarter nodded. "That's what this is all about?"

"We're poisoning the planet, meddling with forces that we weren't meant to," Kellion countered.

"So in order to save the planet, you're going to cause

environmental disasters in at least four locations on it?" McCarter asked.

Kellion chuckled. "Like I said, it's not my backyard. There's too many damn people anyway."

McCarter sneered. He picked up a pencil. "I can count too damn many people in this room."

"Me, too," Kellion replied. "Wonder who's right."

McCarter looked at the point of the pencil, then grinned at Kellion. "Want to see a magic trick?"

Kellion grimaced. He let the stapler drop and his hand plunged to the grip of the pistol in his belt. McCarter lunged swiftly, the point of the pencil spearing through Kellion's forearm muscles before the writing implement splintered under the pressure of McCarter's stab. The Second Sphere conspirator screamed and tumbled across a desk. Kellion had almost squirmed out of reach when McCarter grabbed a fistful of shirt and yanked back hard. His knee pumped into the mercenary's jaw, breaking it with an audible pop.

Stunned, Kellion was helpless as McCarter wrung him through a hip toss. The Second Sphere employee hit the floor, unconscious just as the whirr of cutting blades ripped through cardboard boxes at the other end of the room. McCarter spun to see the first of half a dozen heads poking out of the stack of copy paper boxes. It was an infiltrator, complete with a glowing LED eye and the black muzzle of a Glock poking from its "forehead."

"Bugger all," McCarter groaned. He hurled himself behind the cover of a desk as the first of the infiltrator robots opened fire. More guns crackled, bullets punching through the thin aluminum of the lightweight desks, prompting the Briton to scramble on all fours, seeking cover from a salvo of enemy gunfire.

Since the robots had gone loud, McCarter knew any pretense at stealth had been thrown out the window. He pulled the SIG from its holster and swung around the edge of the desk. He sighted on one of the slender, agile enemy mechanisms, but he only connected with one 9 mm bullet, and that didn't seem to do anything other than jolt the infiltrator momentarily.

Its brothers swung to face him and barked out their gunfire at McCarter. The lithe Briton whipped himself over a desk and scurried behind a filing cabinet as the serpentine automatons tried to plug him. It was a standoff right now. The Phoenix Force commander was secure behind sufficient cover, but it would only take a moment or two for the robots to flank him. He was armed, as well, but the steel serpents were too tough, or just filled with too many redundant systems for a mere 9 mm handgun to do anything to them.

Ideally, McCarter would have had his own copy of Manning's sawed-off shotgun, but he couldn't distract himself with what could have been. As he heard the hum of a half-dozen serpentine bodies slinking along the floor, the Briton grabbed the side of the filing cabinet and lifted it. Every muscle in his body screamed at the effort, but the sudden movement of the furniture froze the enemy robots in place. They couldn't slither and fire their head guns at the same time, something McCarter had noticed from his earlier encounter and reports relayed through the Farm. He just hoped all two hundred pounds of the filing cabinet had enough weight to do what he wanted it to.

McCarter shoved the clumsy, boxy missile through

the air and it hit the tile floor immediately. Momentum, however, turned the landing into a ponderous tumble. Metal smashed on metal with a loud thunk, and he spotted three serpentine shapes slither wildly in retreat. Hopefully, the Briton had taken out the other three with the bulk of the cabinet, but he noticed one of the automatons poking half out from under the fallen furniture. It was pinned, its hind section mashed from a four-inch diameter to a flattened mass of folded metal just under an inch tall.

The red eye glared at McCarter, as if in accusatory fury. Its head gun barked, but having been half-crushed, it couldn't get an angle on the Briton.

"Got you," McCarter said, allowing a moment of victory to flow through him. It faded with the jarring memory that the robots had self-destruct mechanisms. His instincts kicked in and he dashed out of the prefab office moments before the pinned robots detonated. Shrapnel and papers flew through the door, the cloud of debris barely missing McCarter as he crashed to the parking lot.

One of the robots squirmed through an open window, and McCarter heard other windows breaking around the trailer.

"Damn it," he cursed, thrusting his SIG at the robot that had squirmed into sight. He cut loose, firing the pistol as fast as he could pull the trigger. A flurry of 9 mm rounds sparked along the length of the infiltrator robot, but only a few hits made the automaton jerk in reaction to a telling bullet strike. The robot twisted and fired its weapon at McCarter. A bullet seared across his neck, slicing the muscle where it met the shoulder. Wincing at the impact, feeling a wash of hot blood flow down his chest and back, McCarter scurried to cover behind one of the Second Sphere cars.

Sirens wailed, and he could see that the Nogent security team had responded to the sudden storm of robotic gunfire. McCarter took a deep breath and knew that there was no way he could explain what was going on without appearing to be out of his mind. All he could do was reload the SIG and hope that he had enough time and ammunition to deal with the slithering snake-bots before they reached one of the massive cooling towers.

His right arm numbed by the bullet that cut through his shoulder, McCarter transitioned the handgun to his left hand after stuffing a fresh 15-round magazine into its butt. "I've had a bloody good run. Let's end this without a nuclear meltdown, though."

McCarter lurched into the open and locked the front sight onto the center segments of the serpent saboteur. A pull of the trigger, and he punched a single hot 9 mm round into the self-destruct module of the robot. The detonation slapped McCarter in the face hard, forcing him to tumble backward in shock. He crashed to the tarmac, feeling a dozen places on his face where shrapnel had sliced through his skin. The blast had knocked the gun from his hand, and he could barely concentrate with the chorus of bells and sirens rolling through the thunderstorm in his skull.

"Two more…" he grunted through gritted teeth. He rolled over and saw the shapes of a half-dozen booted feet stomping along the asphalt. The Nogent security team was here, but with his head seemingly stuffed full of cotton, he couldn't tell if they were barking orders at him.

It didn't matter—he'd committed himself to continuing. Somewhere through the audio fog clogging his ears, he heard the chatter of automatic weapons. He winced at the sound and scanned around for the fallen SIG. Something slammed hard into him, and McCarter felt as if one of his ribs had broken. Rough hands pushed his face to the asphalt, but through the cacophany of noise storming in his brain, he heard the unmistakable belch of a double-barreled shotgun go off.

"Gary?" McCarter asked.

No response, at least nothing that he could decipher through his ringing ears.

He craned his head up and saw the bulky mass of his Canadian friend standing amid a bunch of security men. Manning quickly ejected the empty shells from his shotgun and stuffed two more into the weapon. McCarter repeated his friend's first name, and the burly Phoenix warrior gave him a thumbs-up.

The security guard who'd tackled him hauled McCarter to his feet. Fingers were waved in front of his eyes, but the Briton pushed the hand away. It took two of the Nogent security team to push McCarter down onto his ass and hold him still. Finally, he could make out their voices as his hearing cleared.

"Sir, you need to sit still. You've got shrapnel injuries, and you may have a concussion," one of the men said.

"And a bloody broken rib, you sots," McCarter snarled. "And if I have a concussion, it's likely one of you caused it when you bounced my head off the tarmac!"

"Please, calm down, sir," the other guard said with German-accented French. McCarter blinked.

"I used to work with your friend Mr. Roy, when I was

in the GSG-9," the guard explained. "He alerted us to the problem."

"So I got my head screwed up for nothing?" McCarter asked.

"It took him a while to get hold of my cell phone number," the German said. "Who else is in the trailer?"

"Bloke named Kellion. He's definitely in on the scheme," McCarter replied. "And the head of the Second Sphere team here. I stuffed two other Second Sphere men under that car, but I don't think they're involved. What's going on?"

"Mr. Roy is leading the team after the last of the infiltrators," the German explained. "Please, sit still."

McCarter gritted his teeth. He hated being sidelined, but right now he was operating on only one cylinder. It was up to Manning and the Nogent crew.

CHAPTER FIFTEEN

Gary Manning hauled the prisoner out of the SUV for T. J. Hawkins to watch over and got behind the wheel again. He needed all the speed and horsepower he could get, and barring that, he was going to make as straight a line across country as possible. His friend and leader was possibly in trouble. He fired up the engine and tore out from behind the abandoned restaurant, revving the engine and laying a patch of rubber from the big off-road truck's knobby tires.

Manning flicked open his cell phone with one hand and put it on Speaker as he got a call from Stony Man Farm.

"Gary, you're going to hate us," Price said. "We were looking for French operatives you knew."

"You found one of my German friends instead?" Manning asked.

"We expanded our search parameters and found out that Alan Richter, a GSG-9 alumnus, has been living in France, and is the head of Nogent's primary security staff," Price said. "He's never been in the blacksuit program, so he wasn't on that list."

"Glad you went over my past associates," Manning returned. "Can you connect me with him?"

"I've already got him on the line," Price said. "He's on hold and is under the impression that I'm contacting him through Interpol."

"Wouldn't be the first time I used that cover," Manning replied. "Put him through."

"Can do," Price replied.

"So, you're called Roy now?" Richter began.

Manning grinned as he heard Richter's familiar voice. "That's what they tell me," Manning replied. "You're aware that there is a crisis situation in France."

"Yes. We've had alerts about Department of Energy infiltrations," Richter responded.

"We've got hard evidence that there is a group of remote drones that can be utilized for sabotage against nuclear reactors," Manning returned.

"I'd also heard rumors about that. Apparently some irate Briton made a stink that drew a lot of attention to the south coast," Richter responded. "You wouldn't know anything about that, would you?"

"Don't make me lie to you," Manning answered.

"Robotic saboteurs?" Richter asked. "Then again, with all the minidrones we've seen in use in law enforcement, I'm surprised they haven't miniaturized the bomb-squad units that have their mounted shotguns."

"They've done it, and they're designed for slipping through pipe systems," Manning answered. "My colleagues and I have encountered them several times over the past couple of days. And now we have irrevocable proof that they're on site."

"You snuck someone into the plant?" Richter asked.

"That I can tell you. Sure, he's trespassing now, but he's doing it with the best intentions," Manning promised.

"So I mobilize my men in order to help a trespasser against robotic infiltrators?" Richter asked.

"Who were brought in by your Second Sphere contractors," Manning added.

"Scheissen!" Richter spit. "The rent-a-cops brought in killer robots?"

"Hidden in boxes of copy paper," Manning explained.

Richter sighed. "Where are you?"

"About two minutes from the southwest gate," Manning said. "Maybe a little less. I'm doing around ninety miles per hour."

"Sure, why make it easy for me?" Richter complained. "I'll alert the gate and mobilize my men. I take it your friend is at the Second Sphere offices?"

"He's at least on his way. You'll hear it when he makes his move, if he's not lucky," Manning returned. "If he is lucky, then this will be over and all you'll have to do is pick up the pieces."

"Need gear? Armor?" Richter asked.

"I'm kitted," Manning said. "Just don't cut my SUV in half."

"What kind is it?" Richter asked.

"A dark blue Mercedes 550," Manning answered. "And it's pretty much flying."

"We'll be expecting you," Richter said, then signed off.

Manning had to chuckle. All the times he complained about David McCarter's driving, and here he was, launching the Mercedes SUV off berms and banks in the countryside, catching air with each slope. The suspension on the off-roader was good enough that Manning's spine wasn't hammered and jarred by the landings, but then, he was moving so fast that when the wheels touched the ground, it wasn't so much a downward plop as continual movement.

He had to swerve to avoid saplings and ridges that were too steep for even the high wheel base of his SUV, but finally Manning reached the road and hit the emergency brake to bleed off forward momentum and align his hurtling path with the pavement. He released the brake and tromped the gas, rocketing toward the nuclear power plant. He was off on his estimation, his frantic driving cutting thirty seconds off from his estimated time of arrival, but then, the Canadian was going to the rescue of a man he considered his best friend in the world.

The gates were open and a Jeep full of armored commandos was waiting. Manning cranked the emergency brake again, skidding to a halt until he was parallel with their vehicle.

"What kept you?" Richter asked as Manning snapped up his shotgun and his MP-5.

Manning smirked. "Where are the Second Sphere offices?"

"There's a set of trailers in the northwest lot," Richter responded as Manning grabbed on to the official Nogent security vehicle. The Phoenix Force veteran would be riding the running boards, and the driver took off once his grip was solidified on the top rails.

"They don't warrant their own spot in an existing structure?" Manning asked.

"They need their own parking places for official vehicles," Richter explained.

There was the krump of a distant explosion, and Manning, Richter and the Nogent security forces all looked toward the northwest lot.

"Your friend?" Richter asked.

Manning's brow furrowed. "He didn't bring explosives. Hurry!"

FIVE ROBOTS HAD SLITHERED out of the windows of the trailer. Manning and his allies immediately opened fire. The Canadian's sawed-off shotgun and the powerful Italian Benelli M-90 12-gauges roared heavily, pumping swarms of buckshot into three of the robots after McCarter had dealt with one of them.

Manning looked at his partner, but saw that Richter had taken care of him. There was still one robot left up and running, and the burly Phoenix warrior had been handed one of the Benelli shotguns.

"You'll want something you can hit a target with at more than a few feet," the Nogent security man said. "And you'll want some follow-up shots."

"Thanks," Manning replied, accepting the weapon. His cell phone chirped, and Manning tapped the side. The hands-free microphone on it came to life.

"Are the robots still in operation?" Hawkins asked.

"As far as I can tell," Manning returned. "What happened?"

"I put a magazine into the relay communicator here at the restaurant," Hawkins said. "They shouldn't be receiving a signal unless they still have something in their office."

Manning glanced at the trailer, pouring smoke into

the sky. It was unlikely that the tertiary transceiver had been damaged by the concussion of a single detonating robot, but the fire within must have been causing some damage. "We can't tell. The Nogent crew is doing something. Alemeda didn't have a means to jam the robots?"

"Failsafe lockout kicked in," Hawkins said. "Must have been from their central command."

"Damn." Manning grunted. "I see the robot. It's making a beeline toward one of the cooling towers."

There was a pause over the phone. The Canadian and his French allies were in a dead run toward the robot, but it moved just slightly faster than they could, staying ahead of them.

Hawkins spoke up again. "Alemeda says that the machine is on autopilot. The robots have artificial intelligence installed."

"How clever is that artificial intelligence?" Manning asked. He shouldered his Benelli and hammered off a quick round. Buckshot kicked up chips of concrete just to one side of the metallic serpent. The missed charge of shot at least gave the burly Canadian an idea of the point of aim in reference to the sights. He'd adjust with the next round as he pumped it into the chamber. The other Nogent men triggered their weapons in an attempt to catch the undulating, quick-moving machine snake.

"It's using opfor protocols from video games. A compact little program which has been tailored to work in concert with the control mechanisms of the robot," Hawkins said. "It'll evade if it senses danger, and it has the intelligence to fight like a son of a bitch."

Manning swung up the 12-gauge again, but the robot spun back on itself. Its head gun barked, a 9 mm bullet striking the helmet of one of the Nogent security force. The Kevlar helmet saved the man's life, but he'd been dropped onto his ass by the concussive impact. Another of the nuclear watchdogs grunted as a bullet hammered the joint of his shoulder into a mass of bone splinters and churned muscle tissue. Manning triggered his shotgun, but the swift little metal serpent twisted out of the way as the 12-gauge roared.

The Phoenix Force fighter lunged to one side as the infiltrator cut loose with its head gun. A round slashed across Manning's hip, slicing through the meat and only barely missing his pelvis. Another centimeter and the Canadian would have been on his back for months with a slow-healing fracture. Manning tumbled, rolling out of the way of the automaton's torrent of gunfire. As he did so, he cranked the slide of the Benelli and as he flopped prone, he fired another round.

The cloud of buckshot peppered the tail of the robot, flipping the robot serpent. Sparks sputtered between segments, but the front half still had enough motivator power to get it in motion. Manning pumped and fired again, the other Nogent security men cutting loose with their weapons. It was like trying to catch a cobra with bare hands. When the automaton wasn't firing, it squirmed on the open concrete. Manning thumbed fresh shells into the Benelli's tube magazine as his allies continued to pour on the heat.

Another of the sentries screamed as he clutched a bloody thigh. One of his partners leaped and clamped his hands on the sudden injury to apply direct pressure. Manning knew that the bullet had torn the femoral artery, just from the Frenchman's sudden reaction. Two badly injured, and another concussed, leaving Manning and one other to deal with the robot while the last of the healthy guards fought to keep one of his own from bleeding to death in under a minute.

The infiltrator whipped around and crawled as fast as its broken body could carry it, which was still quick. Manning ran as fast as his limp allowed him, blood soaking his pant leg, butt hurting from the bullet that cut through it. The Nogent guard fired his shotgun as fast as he could, divots of blasted concrete exploding in the wake of the metal serpent. The Frenchman's Benelli was empty within a moment, and the deadly automaton swung back and fired its head gun.

The guard screamed as his forearm was broken by a heavy weight 9 mm round. Manning took the small window of the robot's forward advance to fire his Benelli again. This time, the full weight of the 12-gauge payload was on target, heavy pellets tearing through metal skin. The infiltrator flinched under the wave of buck, then turned and fired at Manning. The Stony Man warrior grunted as he felt a rib break under his concealed Kevlar. He gritted his teeth, racked the shotgun and fired a second time. This blast connected with the self-destruct mechanism, and a wave of pressure and shrapnel knocked the big Canadian onto his back.

Had he been closer to the detonating robot, he'd have suffered more than a few scratches and ringing ears.

"Gary?" he heard Hawkins ask over the phone.

"I'm alive," Manning returned. "But the last robot shot us half to pieces…at least I hope that was the last robot."

"According to Alemeda, all six are down," Hawkins replied. "They only sent half a dozen."

Manning sat up, his head swimming from the aftereffects of the blast. "We'll know if there was one more that we missed…."

"Not a problem," Richter said, catching up with his group. "We have the reactors on quick shutdown protocol. Even if a robot gets through, the plant won't be producing enough energy to cause a dangerous meltdown."

Manning sighed. "How's the one shot in the thigh?"

"Tourniquet," Richter said. "He'll lose the leg. The one shot in the shoulder will have a paralyzed arm, most likely."

With a grimace, Manning rose to his feet. His hip hurt like hell, but the meat would heal. Two other men were going to live with disability for the rest of their lives because of the conspiracy. It was a price the Canadian hadn't wanted to pay for the safety of an entire city.

"Gary… Shit… Gary, we've got something here," Hawkins cut in over the phone.

Manning groaned. "What now?"

"All of France just got blanketed with a television and radio interruption," Hawkins said. "Regular programming was replaced with a message from a group calling itself the Fallen. They said that Paris is only the first to be threatened."

"They let out that the Nogent plant was attacked?" Manning asked.

Hawkins took a deep breath. "Yes."

Manning looked back at McCarter, who limped to catch up with the group. "You hear that, David?"

McCarter nodded, pointing to the wireless microphone and earbud on the side of his face. "The Fallen. What are the details of the broadcast?"

"I'm still listening to it now," Hawkins replied. "Hang on, I'm getting a call from home."

Manning knew that over the unsecured cell phone conversation, Hawkins couldn't even say the term "Farm" without violating operational security. The Canadian didn't need to listen in on the other call to know the mess produced by the sudden announcement of an attack on one of Europe's most powerful nuclear power plants. Only the details were unclear, but he was certain that Paris itself would be thrown into a panic.

McCarter's face told Manning all he needed to know about his friend's grim mood at the news of the Fallen releasing a nationwide announcement in regard to nuclear terrorism.

"Germany, Great Britain, Spain and Poland have had their airwaves hijacked, as well," Hawkins said. "We don't have the manpower to go and assist them if there truly is a pack of infiltrator robots operating in those countries."

"They don't have the manpower to deliver or release them, either," McCarter replied. "But they don't have to. They threw a bucket of chum into a swimming pool and shouted shark. There doesn't need to be a fin in sight for a panic."

"So even though we saved millions," Hawkins muttered, "thousands could be injured or killed in riots and looting spurred on by this news."

"Nogent was just the pin on the grenade," Manning concluded. "And you know how many times we've thrown grenades with the pins still in place to spook and flush opponents."

Manning and McCarter could feel Hawkins's wince of realization even without seeing his face.

The youngest Phoenix Force member sighed. "If it's going to be that bad here, how messed up will it be when they throw up the balloon in the States?"

Neither McCarter nor Manning was in a hurry to answer that question.

AS THE VIDEOTAPE BEGAN, a silhouette of a man sat in front of a fully illuminated red flag with a black-on-white circular emblem. The banner featured a five-spoked black intersection of lines. Each of the spokes was tipped in a sharp arrowhead, but bent at a ninety-degree angle.

The symbol of the Fallen was gut-churningly similar to the Nazi swastika; perhaps that was why it had been chosen. The human figure sitting in front of it was without notable identity, save that it wore a uniform-style cap that hid the dimensions of its head. It spoke in a deep, distorted rumble, electronically tweaked to be unrecognizable, yet clear enough to be clearly understood.

"They've released this in English, French, German, Spanish and Russian as far as we've seen," Price explained to Brognola and the President as they watched it on the screen. "The Polish edition was in English, but it was Warsaw specific."

The President glanced at Price. "Any other nations receive this?"

"Not that we could tell, but the Middle East has been under a television blackout for the past thirty minutes," Price answered.

The President nodded. "The symbol?"

"Unused by any modern or ancient agency," Price said. "It's completely anonymous, except for the imagery it evokes due to its similarity to the swastika."

"It's akin to the three-armed symbol that South African supremacist groups had adopted during the period of time at the end of apartheid," Brognola added. "It makes sense to go with more arms to give you that punch in the gut."

"This hasn't gotten into the U.S. markets, has it?" the President asked.

"Only through the BBC's American syndication," Price told them. "Even then, it's not a direct image, it's a repeat of the initial broadcast."

"They're still repeating it?" the President asked.

"Short of knocking out their own broadcast satellites, there's nothing that can be done, though standard antenna reception has been blocked and replaced with conventional broadcasting," Price said.

"Play it again," the President ordered.

"People of London, you are being addressed by the Fallen," the silhouette said. "We have been cast out of the ivory towers of power and influence because we have seen the horrors of your wrong-headed leadership. We have seen the way of the world, and we sought to speak of the wrongs wrought in the name of the status quo."

"Empty rhetoric," Brognola said as he paused the broadcast. "Its sole meaning is to spark the 'truths' of every conspiracy nut's musings. This is their evidence."

"Which is why you've got riots breaking out across Europe," Price added. "Every nuclear power plant and NATO weapons depot is beseiged by antinuclear protestors."

"While in the cities, immigrant groups and white supremacists are clashing," the President grumbled. "The immigrants see that flag and think neo-Nazis and the xenophobes are howling with joy that they have a new banner to wave."

"All of this is spreading police and military resources even thinner all across Europe," Price said.

The President nodded. "Keep playing," he directed.

"Nogent Nuclear Power Plant has been our first attack," the silhouette announced. "As we speak, our brave freedom fighters are striking a blow against the unnatural perversion of God's plan. We intend to do the same throughout the world. Even now, in the Middle East and in North America, we have forces gathered together to strike and destroy those who proliferate nuclear and chemical abominations."

Maps of the East Coast and the Middle East, centered on Syria, were superimposed in the corner of the video image. The silhouette waved its hand and the overlays disappeared. "For too long, scientists have pushed too far, thinking more of 'can we do it?' rather than 'should we do it?' As such, we have seen the horrors of Iraq's extermination of rebels or the devastation of Chernobyl. Radiation seeps into the soil, making our land and water unusable for human consumption. Chemical weapons slaughter thousands and provide excuses for international imperialism. AIDS and Ebola cull the populations of continents, keeping the masters high on their thrones and the rest of you poor sheep cowering and trembling as you beg for their protection."

The President gestured for Brognola to pause the video. "He's implying that one of the world governments manufactured the HIV virus or other diseases as population controls. But they weren't designed…were they?"

"Phoenix Force and the Russians had teamed up to contain a rogue bioweapon that utilized the immunity-destroying aspects of HIV and applied them to pneumonia," Brognola explained. "There had been a moment of debate about whether the bioweapon, dating from the seventies, was the inspiration of the less contagious AIDS virus or inspired by it. Since then, we've confirmed that the diseases the Fallen mentions are completely naturally evolved."

The President frowned. "Though, you've informed me that there was a recent case where a man-made strain of Ebola was utilized in a power grab in Africa."

Brognola nodded. "However, all strains have been contained and destroyed, save for inert samples kept under very tight control."

The President nodded, and the broadcast resumed.

"Now is the time. You know who your real enemies are. We have sliced through the reins that the bastards in their high towers have lashed around your throats. You know what you have to do—you are freed. Strike before they noose you again, and crush you for your rebellion!"

A montage of photographs played across the screen, images of dead Chernobyl citizens and the wasteland of the city, as well as piles of corpses in the wake of Iraqi chemical-weapon attacks on the Kurds. A wailing dirge played in the background.

"Be free, and tear down the false pillars of power that these monsters have erected."

The video ended. It had been looping for an hour, continuously. The President looked at Brognola and

Price. He didn't like suddenly being confined to the secure bunker hundreds of feet beneath the White House. However, the command center put him in touch with the whole planet and was NBC resistant. Here, he was as safe as any place on the planet. Few weapons could touch him in these depths, while above, millions of citizens were vulnerable.

"Phoenix Force prevented the Nogent sabotage, and there is still a wave of terror ripping through Europe," the President said. "I've notified our troops on NATO bases to assist with the civil disorder, but we're looking at a troubling situation that can only be worsened if one of those soldiers has to use lethal force to defend himself. And that's not counting the mayhem caused if they do the same transmissions here in the U.S."

"America is aware of the unrest," Price said. "A few survivalist groups have holed up in their compounds, and they're on lockdown. Law enforcement is trying to talk them out, but the militia groups are scared. They see Europe gone to hell, and they know we're next."

"And if I do anything to interrupt our regular broadcasts, I'll cause as much panic," the President growled.

"We have our cyberteam working overtime to ensure that nothing gets on to the U.S. airwaves, and Able Team is going full court press on the two situations we're certain the enemy is going to utilize," Price explained.

"And you're certain that these aren't distractions in themselves?" the President asked. "They only showed up once the Fallen were informed that there was an agency that was on them."

"My people have been running the probabilities," Brognola said. "With the Department of Energy and

FBI running their asses off looking into actual electronic and physical breaches, Indian Point and Calvert Cliffs are their biggest and best targets to cause hysteria, even if they fail in the attempt."

"But they pushed up their timetable now that Phoenix Force stopped them in France," the President countered. "And then there's Syria. And when Damascus suffers from their own chemical weapons, the response will be worse than riots. They'll hit everyone who knew about their facilities, which means our people in Iraq and Israel."

"And Israel won't pull any punches striking back," Price added. "But we have another Phoenix Force contingent slipping into Syria."

The President thought about the pictures of dead Kurds that had been used in the Fallen's video. "Europe's out of control, and America and the Middle East are under threat. If we ever needed a miracle, we need it now."

Price took a deep breath. "Luckily, that's Stony Man's job description. The impossible missions."

The President nodded in agreement. "Things don't get more impossible than this."

CHAPTER SIXTEEN

"I'm not quite sure what to make of your visit, Mr. Stone," Maximillian Edwards, the Second Sphere commander at Calvert Cliffs, said as Lyons stood in front of his desk.

Lyons declined to sit, merely folding one hand over the other, his eyes obscured by midnight-black sunglasses that made his craggy face even more inscrutable than usual.

"I want to check your facilities," Lyons said.

Edwards swallowed. Lyons knew that his sunglasses weren't fooling anyone who knew what he looked like, and judging from McCarter's experience in France, the Able Team leader knew full well that his cover as one of the conspiracy's enemies was blown sky-high.

What bought him time was the fact that Edwards didn't know exactly how to deal with the tiger who wandered into the wolf den.

It seemed almost a relief when Edwards's cell phone chirped and he picked it up.

"Sir?" Edwards asked.

Lyons held his ground, surrounded by Second Sphere men who were carrying illegally concealed weapons, given the specifics of the security company's contract. He could spot the bulges tucked into the guards' pockets, extra wallets where only one would suffice for their needs. In addition to the hardware tucked into their pockets, one of the men's lower pant legs betrayed the bulk of an ankle holster with another weapon.

Jacob Stern believed in equipping his henchmen with as much firepower as they could hide. Lyons had no doubt that other Second Sphere sentries had access to more than just handguns, as well. The earplug that Lyons had tucked into his ear crackled to life.

"Big man, this is the roost." Akira Tokaido's voice cut over the airwaves.

Lyons cleared his throat in a prearranged pattern to indicate that he couldn't speak freely.

"Yeah, figured you couldn't talk. Listen, the shit hit the fan in Nogent," Tokaido explained. "The conspiracy's attack was aborted when David and the boys landed squarely on their necks. Now the enemy, calling themselves the Fallen, have broadcast the news of the attack on Nogent. They've incited riots across half of Europe."

Lyons let out a low rumble of concern. He continued to watch Edwards, who looked nervously up from his conversation with the man on the other end of the phone.

"Whatever plan you have, the President wants you to use it. We've got the potential for international mayhem," Tokaido warned.

Lyons issued a nonverbal affirmative. He unclasped his hands and smiled at Edwards.

"Oh, Jesus," the Second Sphere commander swore.

"No, I'm not. And considering your group's name, the Fallen, I doubt you'll be meeting with Jesus when I send you all to Hell," Lyons said softly, his voice carrying a chilling bemusement.

The two Second Sphere guards flanking Lyons whirled, stepping away from him as their hands darted for pocketed handguns. The Able Team commander knew that the two men would make such a move. Professionals always attempted lateral movement in close quarters. A step to the side often could put the defender just out of reach of his attacker, or at least force a decision that would cause their opponent to hesitate.

The LAPD veteran known as the Ironman was far too experienced to fall for such a trick. Hesitation was something he'd burned from his nervous system with years of training. With a sudden flash of movement, he snared a fistful of one guard's uniform shirt and yanked the poor security man off balance. The other gunman nearly had his revolver freed from his trousers when his partner smashed into his face, driven by Lyons's powerful arm.

The meeting of minds was only momentary, but the second hired gun tumbled backward over an office chair. His revolver flew from numbed fingers as Lyons jerked his first opponent back toward him and pistoned an agonizing punch into the guard's kidney. The uniformed thug's legs gave out from under him, and he folded to the floor in pain.

Lyons turned and gave Edwards's desk a solid kick, driving the furniture hard against the man's stomach. With the wind knocked out of him, the Second Sphere leader's attempt to draw his pistol turned into a fumble. The gun clattered to the floor of the office and Lyons lunged, grabbing him by the shoulders and smashing him in the nose with his forehead. Edwards's nose exploded like a tomato blasted by a shotgun, and the security chief bounced violently off of Lyons's forehead and slammed into the wall.

The staggered conspirator limped away from the wall, eyes crossed by the concussive force and pain that smashed his face. Lyons reached out again, grabbed Edwards's shirt and hauled him across the desk, pressing the muzzle of his Smith & Wesson against the flattened nose, bringing new spikes of agony shooting from the mashed body part.

"You're going to tell me what the plan is with the hired guns and whether you have any robots on the campus here," Lyons snarled.

Edwards sputtered, incoherent from the hammering he'd just taken. Lyons eased off on the nose pressure and slapped him in the cheek. "Wake up, Edwards."

"Bashtuhd," Edwards murmured through numb, blood-soaked lips.

Lyons rolled his eyes and looked at the other two men curled up in the office. He doubted that the conspirators would have more than an inkling of what was going on. He spied Edwards's fallen cell phone and scooped it up and put it to his ear. Lyons heard that there was still a connection, but his amazement disappeared when he realized that his explosion of interpersonal violence had only lasted a few moments.

"Edwards?" said the voice at the other end of the call.

"Can I take a message?" Lyons asked.

There was a momentary pause of surprise. "So we

finally hear the voice of the caveman who shrugged off our robots' taser."

"And I hear the voice of the coward who murdered a good woman," Lyons countered. "You know that we've got your plans sewn up. Nogent's been blown, and you're not even going to come near Calvert Cliffs with that hired army of drug soldiers."

Lyons hoped that dropping a bombshell like advance information would throw his enemy off his game, but there was only a soft grumble of dismay at the news.

"Who's going to stop us?" the enemy asked.

Lyons snorted. "Calvert's SWAT team will be ready for it."

"Only if they can do it from the grave," came the reply.

Outside the office window, Lyons suddenly saw thick clouds of smoke and debris rising in a blossom of death. Lyons's gut dropped. The enemy had used some of their robots to infiltrate the security barracks. From the force of the blast, either it had been a good number of the deadly machines, or there were a few that had been packed with extra doses of high explosives. Either way, Lyons knew that the defenders of the nuclear plant had suffered a crippling blow. Any survivors would be dealing with the wounded, and any attacking force would simply overwhelm them.

"One man against an army." The conspirator chuckled. "Looks like you're going to have some trouble backing up your boast."

The madman on the other end hung up.

Lyons closed the cell phone, resisting the bestial urge to crush it into useless splinters. He had a nightmare to head off, and his only hope was a gun-toting outlaw and his young protégé.

STERN SET HIS PHONE DOWN and took a deep breath, glaring at the closed unit. Homm and Shenck were in his office to coordinate the Calvert Cliffs operation. Both of the head technicians had their laptops open, interfaces humming away to execute Stern's plan. Shenck had just detonated three of his extra-payload infiltrators in the command center of the security team, but he had others in reserve to penetrate into the depths of the power plant's vitals.

Each of the new automatons was loaded with a kilogram of C-4, the volatile putty also embedded with ball bearings. The steel pellets would release a cloud of death that shredded flesh and bone, destroy electronic panels and perforate sealed containment structures. The new model of infiltrators were not more technologically advanced, but Shenck had increased their lethality. Since the snakelike robots were easy to mass produce, being collections of simple electric motors and bodies formed from lengths of cut pipe, the kamikaze format would overwhelm any opposing force.

"So what now?" Homm asked. "Do we plop the rest of the robots into the coolant system and reactor core?"

"We need the world to know that we're taking action around the world," Stern said. "They stopped our operation in France. So far, we've salvaged that with your propaganda broadcast, but we need big and explosive results. Get me in touch with Anderson."

Homm nodded and tapped a few keys, engaging in a video conference through Anderson's phone. Anderson was a burly African-American man with a shaved head and a vicious scar across his forehead.

"What's up, boss?" Anderson asked.

Stern smirked. "How's your strike team?"

"Ready to storm hell armed with spoons," Anderson answered. "They going to get a good fight, or did you kidney punch the Calvert force already?"

"We took out their barracks, but there's another party on hand. The one we were concerned about," Stern explained.

Anderson's lips turned up in a cruel smile. "The three super-Feds?"

"At least one of them," Stern said.

Anderson nodded. "We'll move in."

"Don't be cocky, Anderson," Stern warned. "These super-Feds didn't become an urban legend by playing at half measures."

"And you didn't hire me because I folded in the face of a challenge," Anderson replied. "I'll take care of business."

"Just remember, you can't spend your money if you're dead," Stern pressed.

BIGGS LOOKED AT HIS CELL phone as he received a text message. It was Lyons.

"Bad news. Any assistance has been taken out. Last chance to back out."

Michael looked at the screen. Biggs glanced at the young man. "You might want to slip out the back when we reach the plant."

"You ain't in this for the job," Michael whispered.

Biggs shook his head.

"Then you gonna need all the trigger fingers you can get," Michael answered.

"You got a chance to be free of this life," Biggs warned. "If you throw in with us…well, look at the odds."

"Yeah. I get a clean slate, but only after the capital

eats enough radiation to make 'em think World War III was a true story," Michael returned. "No, thanks."

A man came up the center aisle, handing out assault weapons. Biggs accepted a pair of compact AKs with folded stocks. He looked at Michael. None of the rifles had ammunition. Presumably that would be handed out once they got off the bus, or maybe it would be distributed with the man's second trip up and down the aisle.

Michael took his weapon out of Biggs's hand. "They give us empty rifles?"

"At least on this bus," Biggs returned. "Safety measure, in case some of these fools touch the trigger A stray shot on a crowded bus could take out half the passengers."

Michael nodded. "There's that possibility."

"What's your suspicion?" Biggs asked.

Michael's eyes narrowed. "They need a distraction. In case you ain't noticed, there's some nice black SUVs been shadowing us."

"We're just cannon fodder," Biggs said. "Michael, my real name is Ramon. Ramon Biggs."

"The Face?" Michael asked.

Biggs nodded.

"And you're worried?" Michael inquired. "Damn, this is some heavy shit."

The man returned, handing out single magazines to each of the seated gunmen. Biggs took the pair for Michael and himself. He tested the top round by pushing down on it. There was very little slack in the spring. "Well, we've got at least thirty."

"So we'll look impressive pouring out of the bus," Michael said.

"When the bus stops, use the back exit," the driver

announced. "It's a larger hole, and whitey will be pouring lead into the front here."

"How you gonna make it, Slice?" a thug asked.

The driver punched the roof over his head, and an armored slat with a narrow viewport slammed down between him and the windshield. "I'm going to be behind an inch of steel, man."

The supply sergeant, as Biggs had taken to thinking of him, spoke up next. "You all only get one mag for now. Anyone who survives getting off this bus can hit our rally point where we've got belts of spare ammo. Some of you set your rifles to single shot already, and you might think you're smart. You're not."

"Step off, fool," someone else said. "An AK don't fire until you touch the trigger, or you smack it damn hard on the ground. And my stock ain't extended to set it up."

The supply sergeant's eyes narrowed. "Well, any one of you that levels a muzzle toward me is going to get a face full of .44 Magnum. Feel me?"

The assembled gunners nodded.

"We're closing in on the gate," the driver called. "Now you gonna see what them SUVs are packing."

Biggs glanced out the window to see one of the SUVs trailing them open its sunroof. A man poked out, hauling an RPG-7 rocket launcher.

Biggs repeated Michael's assessment. "This is some serious shit."

The young man with the two-tone face nodded in agreement. "If all else fails, we got our own chrome, right?"

Biggs nodded. "Handguns versus rifles aren't the best tactics."

"We just need enough shots to grab a new rifle, though."

Biggs smiled. "We might just have a chance."

"I ain't ready to see my brother alone in the world," Michael confessed.

Biggs flicked the selector on his rifle to single shot. It was time to do or die.

LYONS RETURNED to his car and popped the trunk. He'd need some firepower if he was going to be heavily outnumbered. As he stood in the parking lot, he was in position to see the first rocket-propelled grenade smash into the security gate. The small building was reduced to splinters. A second 77 mm warhead struck the gate's arms, blasting it into shards of yellow-and-black wood that hurtled like shrapnel.

There was a pair of Calvert Cliffs security officers visible, landing from where the destruction of their guard house had hurled them. Rage churned in Lyons's gut as he realized that the two sentries were dead, if not from the initial explosion, then from the jarring impact as they descended from twenty feet in the air. Two enemy SUVs burst through the churning cloud of smoke and splinters, followed by a yellow school bus.

Lyons popped the latches on his rifle case, pulling out a DSA arms OSW 58 carbine. The stubby rifle was no larger than an M-4 carbine, and was even shorter in overall length due to the fact that it had a true folding stock. Under the barrel was a forward grip that Lyons quickly detached and replaced with a stubby M-203 grenade launcher. He slung two bandoliers, one full of 7.62 mm ammo for the rifle and another laden with 40 mm shells for the grenade launcher. He left the holographic sight atop the receiver's rail, knowing that he'd need quick, close-quarters accuracy. The fighting carbine was select fire, and was the chopped-down version of the world-famous FN-FAL battle rifle. The choice of the heavy-caliber weapon over a chopped M-16 was a matter of pure stopping power. Alone and outnumbered, the stubby carbine would put an enemy down with far more authority than its 5.56 mm counterpart as its bullets weighed three times as much and moved at almost the same velocity as the smaller slugs.

Lyons snapped open the carbine's stock and shouldered the weapon, sighting on the lead SUV. With a flick of the selector switch, he triggered a quartet of 168-grain hammers that tore through the tinted windshield. The great weight and density of the bullets burst the glass, tearing through into the driver's seat and killing the man at the wheel. The black truck swerved violently as it was suddenly uncontrolled. The second SUV tried to avoid an impact with the other vehicle. It failed, the front right fender bouncing off the side of the other SUV. The collision was only glancing, but it stole velocity and momentum from the second attack vehicle.

The driverless vehicle screeched, brakes wailing as someone inside the shot-up SUV jammed on the pedal. Another gunman in the raider burst through the sunroof, triggering a stubby AK toward Lyons's position. The Able Team commander ducked behind his sedan, enemy rounds punching into the trunk. Lyons returned fire with his OSW, sweeping the rooftop gunner with a 3-round burst. The heavy slugs smashed the attacker's chest, shattering ribs and lacerating internal organs.

The second SUV backed up, and Lyons noted the arrival of two more school buses. He could see that the armored mercenary poking through the top of the first vehicle was a white man, informing Lyons that there were two groups, the hired guns from the streets of East Coast cities and paid professional mercenaries.

Three school buses could hold a lot of gunmen, and another four SUVs were entering the campus of the nuclear power plant. Rifles chopped at his sedan, bullets tearing into the sheet metal. Under that kind of heat, Lyons was glad for his concealed body armor. He also had to make certain that anyone between him and the invading mercenary army had gotten out of the way if he was to cut loose with the 40 mm grenade launcher. The high-explosive firepower added to his rifle was an indiscriminate force that would tear attackers and innocent bystanders apart with equal disregard for human life.

Lyons held his ground, letting the enemy weapons tear his car to ribbons. There must have been ten rifles locked on him, and most of them were firing on semi-auto. A quick glance over the fender showed him that it was the East Coast criminals, not the mercenaries, who were rushing to predefined positions that would give them control over this parking lot.

The enemy was setting up a beachhead at Calvert Cliffs, utilizing the street gang members as their back door, the buffer between external assault and their personal operations. He unknowingly came to the same conclusion that Biggs and Michael had assumed—that they were cannon fodder, extra bodies to serve as a cushion against emergency response by the Maryland State Police or National Guard.

Lyons knew that he didn't have much time for finesse, so he thumbed a high-explosive shell into the breech of his grenade launcher. A quick glance through the gap afforded by his car's undercarriage told him that the only feet visible for dozens of yards across the parking lot were in combat boots. He poked the OSW at a spot twenty yards away and fired. The short distance was barely enough time for the 40 mm warhead to arm, but when it struck the asphalt, it vomited up a volcanic cloud, in addition to a balance-jarring shock wave. The double effect of the vision-deadening storm of debris combined with the rolling pressure wall bought Lyons vital moments and enough cover to escape the parking lot.

He reloaded the grenade launcher on the run and paused as soon as he reached the cover of a building's corner. He sighted on the SUV with the dead driver and triggered the big-barreled blaster a second time, turning the vehicle into a mass of twisted metal and burning gasoline that held the gunmen at bay, reacting to the unexpected artillery fire that hammered their front line.

Lyons could only hope that his partners working undercover were still well out of the way, but he took an educated guess on the basis that the school buses were still well back from the front line of armored black trucks that had preceded them through the power plant's gates.

It was only a delaying tactic, and Lyons knew that if he stalled the enemy force, he opened Biggs and his young protégé up to brutal response. While the two men were outside of the law, and at least Ramon Biggs was someone who was fully aware that he would meet his end at the hands of the police, the two outlaws had given him allegiance.

As such, Lyons was obligated to give them every opportunity that he could. Biggs and Michael would have the chance to slip out the back or to link up with him so that he could use his super-Fed identification for something that was actually worthwhile, rather than as a mask to hide his movements while hunting murderers. He'd already told Price to arrange for credentials that would allow the two renegades to avoid prosecution if they were arrested.

Bullets hammered the corner that Lyons hid behind, but the brick and concrete shielded him. He snapped off a few short bursts against the raiders. It wasn't much of a resistance, but the longer the enemy wasted time in trying to flank him, the longer Lyons had to come up with a more definitive strategy than a delaying action. As it was, the OSW took down a couple of enemy gunmen.

"Come on, Ramon," Lyons growled. "Show me you've got something."

One of the school buses suddenly was rocked by a fireball, flipping the big yellow transport onto its side.

Suddenly the enemy was thrown into confusion, and Lyons could only hope that Biggs was the cause. If he wasn't, then Lyons was on his own against overwhelming odds.

CHAPTER SEVENTEEN

Barnabas Bolfrey checked his watch, noting the passage of the seconds. The timepiece was the one thing that he had to remind him of his twin brother, Leonard. To the outside world, Leonard Bolfrey was the man who ran the European branch of Second Sphere, a worldwide security agency tasked with jobs that just couldn't be trusted to the military or the police. Bolfrey looked at the irritation of the skin around the watch, a leftover symptom of the nerve gas that had killed Leonard on a cover operation in Russia. As often as Bolfrey had cleansed the timepiece, the chemicals still lingered, not strong enough to kill, but even mirograms of the contaminant were enough to irritate the skin.

Bolfrey couldn't get rid of the watch, however. It was his only remaining link to his lost brother. Leonard and Barnabas were part of the British military, veterans of the Special Air Service. Leonard knew Russian fluently, and could also communicate in other Slavic dialects. The Bolfrey twin had been on a deep penetration into the Chernobyl region. The irradiated zone was an ideal place for black marketeers to engage in clandestine trades with minimal chance of interference. Few intelligence agencies were willing to risk their lives entering such a hot wasteland, and it was years before the proliferation of sharp-eyed satellites and unmanned aerial vehicles that were immune to environmental hazards.

Leonard Bolfrey died because he chose to risk his life to stop the transfer of Syrian chemical weapons to a French communist terrorist group. There wasn't any guarantee that the SAS team would have survived, and Leonard had warned Barnabas off, then got close to the chemical weapons. A short burst of 9 mm rounds, and a tanker of chemicals vomited its contents in a deadly belch that killed dozens of men. Barnabas Bolfrey could only watch from the safety of a rooftop. He saw Leonard twist and writhe as nerve gas caused muscle spasms that shattered bones and ejected bloody vomit and mucus from his mouth and nose. Something broke inside of Barnabas. In the confusion of the chemical weapons release, Barnabas burned off his fingerprints and announced that he was Leonard.

The impulse to shed his original identity was wildly unformed, and he wandered through the rest of his days in the SAS, numbed and incoherent. As part of the initial thawing of the Cold War, the Russians had returned the dead Bolfrey's body to Britain with a quiet word of thanks for the young man's sacrifice. The surviving Bolfrey made a few noises about his discontent with the handling of the operation that claimed his twin's life, and the SAS cut a deal. With a handsome severance package and proper clearance paperwork, Barnabas Bolfrey was allowed to become a security contractor.

The organization was originally known as Globe Security, and Bolfrey picked up other men who were no longer enchanted with their duty to their country. It was all a blur as he worked seemingly on autopilot until he met an American named Jacob Morgan Stern who had Globe America Contracts, a U.S.-based private military contractor. Stern had avoided a dishonorable discharge after an operation, also in Chernobyl. The American was part of a United States Ranger contingent that had been tasked to a CIA operation. It was there that Stern's best friend had received a lethal dose of radiation poisoning while maintaining surveillance.

"Fucking nuclear bullshit," Stern had growled as he had drunk deeply, trying to deaden his loss. While Bolfrey suspected that there was more than just a friendship at work between Stern and the dead comrade, he never said anything about it. Bolfrey's suspicions were later confirmed as he investigated Stern's discharge papers, noting sealed conduct infractions.

"Nuclear energy and chemical weapons and diseases. This isn't any way to fight wars," Stern continued, voice slurred by alcohol. "You see a man, you shoot him. You don't annihilate his entire zip code with this NBC bullshit."

"My twin brother took out a nerve gas stockpile to keep it out of terrorist hands," Bolfrey confessed. "As I watched."

"Son of a bitch," Stern sighed. "And what happens to us? We sit on our thumbs, waiting for some psychopath to unleash that shit all over civilians. That's even if we're allowed to keep our jobs. You get too good at shooting and looting, they retire you."

Bolfrey nodded, only sipping his own drink. He was

still clear-headed, but the aimlessness that had ruled his life started to burn away. "We're not retired, Stern. We're still in the game. We even get paid better."

"Private military contractors," Stern spat. "Which is a fancy name for mercenaries. And it's not as if we can define policy…"

"Why not?" Bolfrey asked. "We've got connections. We've got the guns and muscle."

Stern's eyes narrowed. "What're you talking about?"

Bolfrey smirked. "Suppose we make the world too unsafe for nuclear power?"

"How? We work security on a power plant and blow it straight to hell?" Stern asked.

Bolfrey shrugged. "Why not?"

Stern took a drag off his liquor, then plopped the glass down. "You're fuckin' crazy."

Bolfrey nodded.

Stern's grim mood lightened. "But you've got some ideas."

That had been the start. The two Globe companies combined to name themselves Second Sphere.

And now, Bolfrey was on an airplane, ready to leap from thousands of feet above Damascus. Their goal was one of the Syrian military's primary chemical weapons production facilities not thirty miles south of the capital city.

"Five minutes until we jump," the jumpmaster said. "Plane's dark."

Bolfrey nodded. He stood, hating himself for the cowardice that had spurred him so long ago. It had taken a decade, but now he was in a position to unleash a nightmare against the damned Syrians, those monsters who had taken his brother from him. The phantom pain of his twin's loss was as real and solid as that of an amputee. The psychic trauma had been enough to make him surrender his own identity in a means of keeping Leonard alive.

But now, over five miles in the night above Damascus, there was a moment of clarity, an epiphany. He had chosen a new identity for himself because he hated himself for allowing his brother to do what he should have done. Had Barnabas Bolfrey been braver, been more willing to do what needed to be done, Leonard wouldn't have offered to sacrifice himself.

Bolfrey had hated himself for his cowardice. Only Stern knew that he still harbored an undying anger against Syria over the chemical weapons. This part of the plan, unleashing a similar holocaust to one that had slain Leonard Bolfrey, had been ready all along. It meant a few test runs on similar setups in Egypt, Israel and Libya, causing misdirection on the part of any investigators, as well as dry runs for the technological devices.

The first crates of mobile gun platforms were dumped out of the second air transport. Shenck had sent the Second Sphere Euro technicians the designs that would allow them to turn simple ATVs into armed robotic tanks. Bolfrey had brought enough not only to make a motorized squad of drone shooters, but to serve as steeds for his mercenaries after their skydrop. Two men per ATV would give them the speed necessary to reach the chemical weapons plant and overwhelm it. The mechanized cavalry also allowed them to carry sufficient firepower to outgun the Syrian defenders.

Was it really a suicide mission? Bolfrey asked himself. Sure, he'd written out a plan to hit the Syrian airport while the military was trying to deal with the release of thousands of cubic meters of chemical weapons, steal an aircraft and escape back to Israel. But he wasn't as certain of his extraction plan as he was of the infiltration. He watched the crates of four-wheeled steeds tumble into the darkness below. There was always a possibility, he confessed to himself. The ATVs carried light machine guns and grenade launchers, which would give his team the chance to shatter the corrupt Damascus government and expose its utilization of weapons of mass destruction. With the cloud of death unleashed, the backlash against such programs would be relentless.

Bolfrey could even see himself canonized as a hero, a savior of the world from the nightmare of nerve gas on innocents.

It was a pretty dream, he mused. His wrist itched. The reality was, he looked out into a five-mile jump from a perfectly good airplane, and a fight through the Syrian military with only the support of hijacked Israeli aerial drones and robotic remote-control ATVs as mobile gun platforms. The irritated skin of his wrist reminded him that once they released the stockpiles of deadly gases into the atmosphere, survival was an uncertain thing. Leonard Bolfrey had jammed a syringe of atropine into his heart before making the deadly run against the black marketeers in Chernobyl, but that hadn't been the counteragent for the lethal chemicals the Syrians had been trading. There was no guarantee that their antidote injections would save them from the life-destroying cocktail of weapons they cut loose.

Bolfrey saw the jumpmaster signal, then took the

first long step toward his appointment with vengeance. He tumbled into the cold blackness of the Syrian night.

TANYA KRISTOPOULOS and Ehan Farkas were impressed with how swiftly the desert sands whipped past the portal windows of Dragonslayer as the mighty stealth helicopter rocketed, nap of the earth, across the Syrian border after a short jog through Lebanese airspace.

"We're two minutes from Syrian airspace," Jack Grimaldi announced, his voice disguised by his helmet microphone. The Stony Man pilot felt a pang of regret for concealing his identity from allies who had thrown in with Rafael Encizo and Calvin James, risking their lives to head off an international catastrophe. Still, it was not his place to violate Stony Man Farm's operational security by letting his voice be known even to friends of Phoenix Force.

"How fast are we moving?" Farkas asked, looking at James and Encizo.

"On average, we can cruise at two hundred miles an hour," Encizo confessed. "We won't say much else, except that she's fast and she's hard to see."

"I understand," Farkas replied. "I'm glad that your people allowed me to tag along on this to the finish."

"We figured we'd need someone who could handle Syrian Arabic dialects," James explained. "Kristopoulos knows her fair share of Arabic, but the more linguists, the better. Just in case we have to talk with the local troops."

Farkas nodded. "Gosh, no need to get all weepy and sentimental."

Encizo chuckled. "You're our dog, Ehan. I'm glad our bosses cleared you to come with us, too."

"Besides, you represent an additional thirty-three

percent of ground forces should this helicopter need to drop us off," Kristopoulos added.

"I thought you and Assid were cool with each other," Farkas noted.

"We are. And you and I are cool, too," Kristopoulos said. "Thing is, every extra gun is one more point in our favor. This isn't going to be a picnic. We're going to have to kill some bad folks out in that desert."

"I'll do what I can to even the odds," Grimaldi said over the cockpit intercom. "Another bit of information we can let our allies know about is the sheer amount of firepower this bird has. We've got machine gun and air-to-ground missile pods installed in the streamlined blisters on the underside of the helicopter."

"So we might not even need to touch the dirt," James admitted.

Kristopoulos snorted. "We should be so lucky."

She put a pair of night-vision binoculars to her eyes with one hand while the other rested on the receiver of the FN MAG-58 7.62 mm machine gun propped between her knees. "They have a saying in the Israeli military. You can send all the flyboys you want over the battle, but it's not won until the infantry gets its boots dirty."

Grimaldi received a signal over his headset and switched the intercom frequency to pick up the message from Stony Man Farm.

"Two bits of news," Price said over the radio. "One is that Syrian military air control radar has been knocked out in a large perimeter around Damascus."

"How'd that happen?" Grimaldi asked.

"We're thinking that the Fallen have hacked into the air force's mainframe and crippled their communication network," Price said. "Though, there is also the possibility that someone fired a few antiradiation missiles to take out air defense sensors around the city. A few minutes before the blackout, Israel's unmanned aerial vehicle control reported that several of their Predator-style drones had gone off the reservation."

"You get that, gang?" Grimaldi asked.

"We hear," Kristopoulos said. "It could be hackers, or it could be traitors within the Israeli military complex who'd love nothing more than to see Damascus hoist by its own petard."

"I've got my cybernetics team working with the Mossad to tell the difference," Price told her. "The second bit of news that we have is that satellite radar has caught a glimpse of transport aircraft in the air approaching Damascus."

"Transport aircraft or bombers?" Encizo inquired.

"Transports. Infrared has detected warm bodies exiting the aircraft," Price noted. "Your pilot will have the coordinates of the jumpers' final location once they land."

"A high-altitude, low-opening insertion," Farkas noted.

"A HALO jump would allow them to get close to the city without being noticed," James agreed. "That kind of deployment will also give them access to vehicles, since it looks on the monitor as if there were two transports, but only one had heat sources leave it."

"They wouldn't send up an escort plane for no reason other than loneliness," Kristopoulos noted.

"How long until we approach their location?" Encizo asked.

"At Dragonslayer's currenty velocity, you'll be on

them in about twelve minutes," Price confessed. "You may have longer to catch up with them if their gear takes a while to assemble."

"They're working on a timetable that entails getting into a chemical weapons facility before dawn breaks," James said. "It shouldn't take them more than twenty minutes to be ready to roll. That gives us a cushion of eight minutes to make our move."

"And since we're looking at a plane full of raiders, and the potential for some form of robotic support, we have to make certain that they can't release any more of those infiltrator snakes," Farkas added. "From what you've said about the improved self-destructive abilities of the robots in France, if even one makes it through, we're looking at a nightmare."

Kristopoulos patted the medium machine gun propped between her knees, looking at James with a smirk. "And you said we wouldn't have a chance to use Maggie."

"Do I look like I'd be happy to deny you your fun?" James inquired.

The Greek woman grinned. "Of course, that means Dragonslayer is going to have to hang back before we make our strike."

"And if things go bad, he's going to have to unleash a load of scorched earth," Encizo said.

"Why not just sear the ground first and pick through the wreckage later?" Farkas asked.

"We may not have the luxury of investigating the site if the chopper cuts loose," James explained. "That much fire and thunder will be noticed by the Syrian military and they'll move in."

"A snoop and poop will give us the opportunity to

see if they let some of their infiltration drones loose in the wild," Encizo added. "And it will give us priority targets that will cut down on the noise when Dragon-slayer opens up."

"Fair enough," Farkas said. "So why didn't we bring along a few more Israelis?"

"Because we're not familiar with how they work in the field," Encizo said. "We're familiar with you. Besides, it's not as if we have extra room in here. That's why we've got Tanya lugging the big Maggie, and Cal's got that cannon under his rifle."

James did a count of the 40 mm grenades stuffed into his vest loops. The launcher under the barrel of his rifle was going to be their best form of ground artillery. With Kristopoulos working the MAG-58, the small team had plenty of force multiplier, leaving Encizo and Farkas to bat cleanup with their carbines.

"I'll be parked, but ready to swoop in and give you support or extraction," Grimaldi added. "We're going to cut it close on fuel as it is, so hovering while you guys make your stealth run is not going to be an option."

"Which means if we need air support, we'll have a solid forty-five-second wait," Kristopoulos said.

"No one said this'd be easy," Encizo said.

"Just marking how long we'll have to hold our own if we get in too deep," Kristopoulos replied. "Forty-five seconds at 800 RPM is six hundred rounds if I'm holding down the trigger. Of course, they only make belts that last two hundred rounds."

"Short bursts," James noted.

Kristopoulos rolled her eyes. "I know that. It's just easier to think in how long my ammo will last."

"Good math," James said.

Kristopoulos smirked. "Well, I can only pack six hundred rounds. But we're looking at seven seconds between belts."

"Intercept course has been received," Grimaldi announced. "We'll be touching down in ten minutes."

"Everyone has their optics?" James asked.

Farkas and Kristopoulos nodded in unison.

"The further we are from ground zero when we begin shooting, the better," James said.

The quartet remained silent as Dragonslayer slid closer to its goal. They were all going through their prefight rituals, whatever prayers or cleansing thoughts necessary to keep their minds as finely tuned as their weapons. It would be a quiet ten minutes as they put themselves into the proper frame to not only survive but also to win the upcoming conflict with the Fallen in the desert.

HERMANN SCHWARZ made certain that his Man-Machine Wearable Interface was secured around his torso. The MMWI vest felt heavier than he was used to. In addition to the protective trauma plates sewn into the body panels and the gear adorning his various pockets, there was a sandwiched layer of microcircuitry that served as a central artificial intelligence processor and also as a powerful signal relay. This would allow the men back at Stony Man Farm to operate the group of drones riding in the back of the Able Team van. Schwarz had added a helmet that streamlined and lightened the usual load of hands-free communications and enhanced optics.

The Able Team electronics genius had applied his usual advanced surveillance technology to the picatinny rails on his SIG 556 carbine, mounting both audio and video equipment on the weapon. The video was a compact, low-profile camera that was hooked to his helmet, allowing Schwarz to shoot around corners if necessary without exposing anything more than the muzzle of his assault rifle. The audio was an amplification microphone that served two functions. First he could record conversations by the enemy for later intelligence analysis and translation if necessary. Second he could focus his hearing on targets he wouldn't normally be able to locate by sound in a situation where vision, even electronically enhanced vision, was not a viable alternative.

Terrence Aspen raised an eyebrow at Schwarz's appearance, then looked at Blancanales. "I thought you said Ironman was working on a different squad."

Schwarz winked under his tinted goggles. "I don't have repulsor boot jets. Just armor and data gathering."

"Oh, okay. You're Robocop," Aspen said.

Schwarz grinned. "Dead or alive…"

Schwarz returned his attention to the wrist collar interface. The glove on his opposite hand had a small stylus point built into the pinky, allowing the out-of-the-way finger to activate the miniature controls on the panel without resorting to an easily lost toothpick. He tapped a few keys and the small LED display hummed to life. In the corner of the van, four little tank-treaded robots whirred to life, their camera images transmitted to the tiny screen so that he could see what they did. Schwarz tapped a button on the side of his helmet, and their video feed was input directly into his left eye lens, superimposing translucent images into his eyesight with minimal interference with his normal vision.

"How's it going?" Blancanales asked.

"It's overwhelming all of the data I have coming in through the helmet with the addition of the robot cameras," Schwarz said. "But I'm already adapting."

"Gadgets, are you sure you have to go EVA to work the robots?" Blancanales asked. "We're using unmanned drones in order to keep ourselves out of trouble and maintain the element of surprise."

"Unlike the infiltrator robots, these units are pretty much useless against personnel," Schwarz countered. "They're well-enough armed to take out an infiltrator robot, but with their tiny .22s, they won't be able to put down a man before he shoots them to shit."

"They're expendable," Blancanales noted.

"And worth their weight in gold in that they can pursue the automatons where we can't," Schwarz said. "I'm wearing enough metal to go jousting, Pol. Don't worry about me."

"I can watch out for him, sir," Aspen said.

"Don't call me sir," Blancanales told him. "He's my best friend. I'll watch out for him. You stay with the van."

Aspen nodded. He looked out the windshield and noticed a flicker of movement, the glint of metal in the evening shadows. "Sir…"

Blancanales caught the tone of worry in Aspen's voice, then lunged, tackling Aspen out of the driver's seat and onto the sidewalk beside the van. The instinctive leap had carried the two men out of the vehicle as a slithering mass of metal shot underneath Able Team's ride.

"Gadgets!" Blancanales shouted. "Gadgets! Get the—"

Blancanales was cut off as a thunderous explosion

erupted from the undercarriage of the van. The shock wave slammed him onto his back, stunning him as smoke poured through the broken windshield.

CHAPTER EIGHTEEN

Brognola was updating the President on the situation with Phoenix Force's Middle Eastern contingent and the two groups of Able Team operating in New York and Maryland. The President was watching the screen as Stony Man Farm transmitted real-time information from satellites that the cybernetics team had slaved to observation duty.

The sudden flurry of explosions in the Calvert Cliffs nuclear power plant parking lot was the first sign of trouble. Price, at the Farm, killed the transmission of that image, and spoke up, entering the camera.

"We do have good news. Phoenix Force has just crossed the Syrian border. They're seven minutes from interception of a force that has illegally penetrated the country," Price announced.

"As opposed to our invited visit?" the President asked.

"How did the State Department handle that?" Brognola tried to take the conversation in a different direction.

"It's all back-channel chatter, but the official gist is

that if our people get spotted, they'll be shot at," the President explained.

"So a standard day at the office for our boys," Brognola said.

The President squeezed his brow. "We have explosions at an American nuclear power plant. What about the other part of Able Team at Indian Point?"

"So far, they have been in contact via the MMWI," Price replied. "We're bringing it up right now."

The image on the laptop computer changed to an aerial view of a street. The President saw a van near a building that had the legend Indian Point Electronics Company identifying it. The President saw something wriggle in front of the van.

"What's that?" he asked.

"Generating the image analysis now," Price answered.

At that moment the camera picked up a blur of motion as the small object in front of the van darted beneath the vehicle. Two human bodies spilled out of the driver's-side door before the van was obscured by a cloud of smoke. The image suddenly shifted away.

"Another explosion?" the President asked.

"We're going to monitor this, but yes, things have gone hot inside of Indian Point," Price responded. "We're attempting to make contact with Able Team now."

The President looked at Brognola, who chewed on his unlit cigar. "Worried?"

Brognola nodded. "My people have been in this position before. It's where they shine."

"If they survive," the President noted.

Brognola took a deep breath. "I haven't given them permission to die yet."

HERMANN SCHWARZ blinked in the wake of the shock wave that had torn through the floor of the van. The helmet and body armor he'd worn had protected him from the shreds of peeled metal that had burst into the van's interior. Only the fact that he'd opened the rear doors of the van and shoved the robots out to protect them from the blast had kept his arms and legs from being covered in lacerations. The four remote drones had leaped forward at the commands of their operators hundreds of miles away. He heard Blancanales yell out his given name and thanked himself for having installed hearing protection into his helmet.

"Hermann!" Blancanales shouted as he ran around the side of the van. Schwarz didn't resist as his partner roughly turned him around, looking for shrapnel that had penetrated the vest or harmed his limbs.

"Will I play the violin again, Doc?" Schwarz teased.

"No, because I'm going to shove it three feet up your ass for scaring the shit out of me," Blancanales replied. "The outer layer of ballistic nylon's chewed up, but the lower layers and protective plating are holding the vest together."

Blancanales pried a length of metal off of the vest and plopped it in Schwarz's hand. "A souvenir of the 568th time you barely avoided death."

"Aw, you've been counting," Schwarz replied.

Blancanales leaned in the driver's-side door and slipped a pair of machine pistols from underneath the front seats of the ruined van. He tossed one to Aspen. "The bad guys know we're here, so we're weapons free. Anyone who looks hostile gets burned down."

Aspen nodded.

Blancanales turned back to Schwarz. "Time to go hunting for the local automated troublemakers."

"Got 'em," the Able Team electronics genius replied. "Want my rifle?"

"Nah, it's got too much crap on it," Blancanales returned. He patted the side of the Mini-Uzi machine pistol. "Sleek and clean. Unless it adds another barrel, then I don't care."

"And we call Carl the caveman," Schwarz replied.

Blancanales heard the chatter of an enemy assault rifle and looked for Aspen. The Texas cop was in the midst of charging the rifleman out in front of the IPEC building, his Mini-Uzi chattering as the Second Sphere guard returned the favor. Blancanales shouldered his compact buzz gun and caught the rifleman flat-footed, blasting him off his feet with a sustained burst of 9 mm slugs. Aspen paused, slinging his Uzi, and scooped up the dead man's rifle and spare ammunition.

Blancanales advanced quickly to Aspen's position as gunfire ripped through the doorway. The two Stony Man fighters were on either side of a gap that vomited lead and fire angrily. Suddenly a boxy little machine whirled into the opening between the two humans. The compact 5.7 mm pistol barked, lightweight rounds zipping into the open doorway and forcing the gunmen inside to keep their heads down.

Aspen and Blancanales swung through the door, both keeping low to the floor. They both triggered bursts of suppressive fire that forced heads down and enemy guns to remain quiet. The little boxy remote joined the Able Team commando and his recruit.

"I thought Gadgets said these things only had a .22,"

Aspen said, reloading his Mini-Uzi before attending to his captured rifle.

"Technically, yes," Blancanales said. "It's a spirited .22, though."

Aspen patted the compact M-4 he'd captured from the Fallen guard. "Then this is, too."

"You didn't fall down when he shot at you," Blancanales returned.

"Only took two hits, both in trauma plates," Aspen answered as he fired around a counter, catching a Fallen defender out in the open.

Blancanales picked up a mug and hurled it over the counter. The quick, sudden movement mimicked the flight of a grenade, causing another of the Fallen terrorists to bolt from behind his cover. Blancanales's Mini-Uzi cut the gullible defender off at the waist, 9 mm rounds slicing into his pelvis and shattering the bone.

Something groaned in a doorway off to the side. Blancanales looked up and noticed that there was an ATV pushing through a heavy fire door. He tilted his head to see if someone was riding the machine when there was the bark of an automatic weapon through the doorway. Blancanales hit the floor as heavy bullets chopped into the wall behind him.

"Shit! They've got a big robot!" Aspen snapped. "With a bigger gun."

"I've noticed," Blancanales replied dryly. "Put some heat on it."

Aspen popped around the side of his counter and cut loose with the M-4, sweeping the modified ATV with a half magazine of rifle rounds. The 5.56 mm bullets sparked, punching through the fiberglass frame of the offroad vehicle. Unfortunately, the mechanism that operated the automatic weapon was more heavily armored, and it swung. The mounted M-60 bellowed with thunderous authority and Aspen barely had time to leap back behind cover to avoid being torn to shreds.

However, the enemy robot was left wounded, smoke pouring from the engine undereath its fiberglass cowling. The gun swiveled, "looking" for targets through the camera lens implanted on a dome atop its machine gun. Blancanales took a chance and fired his Mini-Uzi at the electronic eye on the remote-controlled weapon. Bullets sparked off of it, and all Blancanales had accomplished was to draw a stream of 7.62 mm heavy fire that came so close, he could feel the heat of the passing bullets.

"Gadgets! We've got big trouble out here," Blancanales called over his hands-free communicator.

"I noticed it, too," Schwarz returned over the radio. "Luckily, they don't have tanks."

"Always looking on the bright side of life, ain't you?" Aspen asked.

Schwarz's voice sounded muffled, then he came through clearly. "Asked our boys back at the Farm to try a little precision work with their drone."

"Thank them for buying us some time to get into the building," Blancanales said.

The boxy little device leaped into the open like a miniature tank, its mounted 5.7 mm pistol swiveling as it advanced. The enemy robot attempted to lower its aim to hit the smaller counterpart, but the swivel mount its gun was attached to didn't have that kind of vertical movement at such close range. The Air Force robot opened fire, its armor-piercing 5.7 mm bullets smashing through the dome atop the machine gun.

Camera knocked out, the M-60 thrashed about, firing wildly. Aspen grunted as a 7.62 mm round struck him in his vest, the impact hurling him to the tile floor. Blancanales cut loose with his Mini-Uzi, raking the out-of-control enemy weapon in the hope of damaging the firing mechanism. Obviously the Fallen drone's operator was firing blindly, but Blancanales couldn't afford the time it would take for the M-60's belt to run dry. Not when the heavy-caliber slugs could tear through all of the protective cover in the flimsy lobby.

Blancanales scored a lucky shot that tore through the feed mechanism of the M-60, shattering the belt that passed through the machine gun. The deadly weapon fell silent, and the Able Team veteran reloaded his weapon before crossing over to Aspen.

"You all right, kid?" he asked.

Aspen sat up, wincing. "I'm pretty sure that thing broke one of my ribs."

"We weren't expecting to run into a heavy machine gun," Blancanales replied. "Can you walk?"

"Can you stop me?" Aspen asked, standing. He picked up the acquired M-4 and reloaded it. "I'm going to break a foot off into some of these—"

A series of explosions rumbled in the distance. Aspen glanced at Blancanales.

"Not again," Blancanales replied. "Gadgets?"

No response. The two Stony Man soldiers rushed to their partner's aid.

RAMON BIGGS was surprised at the violence of action on the part of the Fallen's elite corps. The sight of a rocket-propelled grenade launched at the Calvert Cliffs power plant was surreal, even after a life of fighting tooth and nail against some of the hardest drug dealers in Baltimore. He was even more impressed, however, with the return fire that could only come from the big man who he'd spoken with, the warrior he knew only as Ironman.

One of the Second Sphere SUVs had been reduced to crumpled metal as dozens of guns opened up on the blond man's position. He looked at Michael, whose eyes were on Biggs for any form of advice.

"We gotta do something fast—otherwise your buddy's going to catch a lot of lead," Michael said.

Biggs nodded, peeling the glasses off his face. He pinned the AK-47 against his hip and scanned around for a likely target. He spotted one of the Second Sphere lieutenants digging into a storage compartment at the side of a nearby bus.

"Get some grenades!" the lieutenant called out.

"Got it," Biggs said. He shouldered the AK and opened fire on the box that the Second Sphere conspirator was reaching into. "Duck!"

The AK's rounds tore through the wood of the grenade crate. It was a crapshoot, Biggs not certain that he could score a direct hit on any of the miniature bombs inside the bus's storage compartment, but if he was lucky enough, one good solid impact would set off the fuse. Just to make certain, Biggs laid on the trigger for all thirty rounds of the banana-shaped magazine in his rifle. He'd blown his cover as Ironman's ace in the hole, but if his desperate play worked, Biggs and Michael would have a great distraction to escape to safety.

Finally Biggs's rifle connected with something explosive in the bus. The lieutenant's arm and back had been shredded by heavy rounds, and he was a bloody, shambling wreck leaning into the storage compartment. The gunners who had poured out of that bus whirled their attention to the Baltimore outlaw only a moment before a lucky 7.62 mm bullet struck one of the Second Sphere grenades exactly where it had to.

One explosion became more as the grenade started a chain reaction that billowed out of the open compartment. Fire and shrapnel sprayed out in a billowing sheet, throwing hired guns off their feet and to the asphalt, heads and torsos chewed and scorched. Anyone with flesh not carbonized by ignited fuel was covered in bloody lacerations from flying metal. The school bus was lifted into the air by the force of the mighty detonation, flipped violently onto its side.

Panic broke out among the gang members as the world turned to fire and thunder all around them. Michael grabbed Biggs by the arm and hauled him away from the maelstrom that had just been unleashed.

"Anyone coming after us?" Biggs asked.

"I think they're preoccupied!" Michael responded. "Move!"

The Baltimore outlaw was hot on the younger man's heels, looking back over his shoulder to make certain that they were in the clear.

Of course, *clear* was a relative term. There was still an army of hired street toughs and trained mercenaries swarming around the Calvert Cliffs nuclear facility.

Biggs could only hope that the big blond warrior could follow up on the diversion he'd given him.

LYONS TOOK ADVANTAGE OF the fiery detonation of the enemy bus to target a group of Second Sphere troopers distracted by the light and noise. With the OSW on full-auto, he raked the trio of armored and heavily armed gunmen with a slashing burst. The high-caliber slugs ripped through Kevlar and meat with equal aplomb, tossing the power plant's invaders to the ground in a lifeless pile of twisted corpses. He followed the initial burst with a 40 mm grenade that speared into a second parked school bus. The fragmentation bomb struck the bus's fender and its explosion ripped through a squad of AK-toting marauders. Whatever wasn't crushed by high pressure was sliced asunder by hurtling bits of wire and broken shell that carved flesh as if it was on a serving tray.

The Fallen raiders, suffering under a series of explosions and concentrated autofire, were thrown into disarray. Lyons hated having to fall back and act as a sniper, but the odds simply were not in his favor at this time. There were too many attackers and it only took the force of killers a few seconds to recover from their dismay at death and destruction to pour thousands of slugs in his direction.

Lyons took off, running behind and between buildings as AK bullets chopped asphalt, brick and concrete in his wake. The series of explosions had cleared this part of the campus, people wisely taking to their own flight as World War III thundered only yards away. He saw two figures, one of them dressed in a pin-striped suit with a bow tie, the other a young man in a hoodie, and let loose a sharp whistle.

"Ramon!" Lyons bellowed.

Biggs halted, his face split by a wide smile. "Ironman?"

Lyons nodded as the newcomers drew closer. "That Two-Tone?"

"Michael's good enough," the youngster said.

"Call me Carl," Lyons offered. "I owe you a real name for risking your life."

"I'd prefer cash, but thanks," Michael returned.

Lyons grinned. "Nice trick with the bus."

"I saw one of them handing out grenades, and I saw somewhere about demolitions disposal," Biggs returned. "They detonate unexploded bombs with bullets, so…"

"Works for me," Lyons replied. "Any estimate of the kind of numbers we're still facing?"

"Not a damn clue," Biggs said.

Michael let his rifle hang on its sling as he checked the Glock stuffed in his waistband. "We won't have enough ammunition to deal with that kind of force, will we?"

"We can pick up some extra chrome off the dead," Biggs said.

Lyons nodded, pulling a couple of chains from his pocket. The two chains had badges attached to them, and Michael and Biggs put them on, identifying them as the good guys. "I want the two of you to head to the security barracks. The normal security crew is reeling from the initial sabotage. See what extra help you can get, but keep an eye out for robotic snakes."

"Robot snakes?" Michael asked. "It ain't enough that we're looking at every triggerman from New York to South Carolina, but you're throwing in sci-fi shit, too?"

"It ain't sci-fi," Biggs said. "Lemme guess, a variation on the shit the Army's using in Iraq?"

"Instead of backpack-size microtanks, we're looking at a more flexible version," Lyons returned. He popped open another pouch on his armor and withdrew a pair of compact radios with earphones attached. "The bots have firearms in their front section, as well as self-destruct mechanisms powerful enough to turn the barracks into a charnal pit."

Michael sneered at the thought of going up against machines. "If that's the case, let me go. I'm younger and faster than this old man here, and you need all the fire-power on your side that you can get."

Lyons frowned, but Michael shook his head. Lyons thrust one of the communicators into the kid's hand. "That's hands-free. If I need help, I can yell for you to come running."

"There should be two of you covering this spot. Then you can split up and catch those mugs in a cross fire," Michael pressed, putting the hands-free ear unit on. The boom microphone extended parallel with his jaw.

Biggs nodded, adjusting his own earpiece. "Boy has a point."

Lyons sneered, but gestured for the kid to take off. "Yell if you need some help yourself, okay?"

Michael nodded. "I got it."

"What else do you have?" Lyons asked, noting Biggs's rifle.

"I got my .357 and my shotgun," Biggs answered. He opened his jacket, revealing a double shoulder holster, a long-barreled revolver under one armpit, and a sawed-off shotgun balancing it out. "You need more?"

Lyons looked down at his own fighting harness. Aside from the rifle/grenade launcher combination, he had the Smith & Wesson MP-357 in a thigh holster and a .45-caliber Kimber Pro pistol tucked behind his kidney on his belt. "No. I'm good."

"How do you want to handle it?" Biggs asked.

Lyons scanned the scene around the corner with the help of a small pocket mirror. "Head about twenty-five yards that way, but hold your fire until I cut loose."

"Then shoot," Biggs said. "I thought you were some kind of strategic genius."

"Simplicity is genius," Lyons said. "We'll catch them at a ninety-degree angle, and when I pop my big gun, it'll sweep them right into your sights."

Biggs nodded. "Don't get dead."

"No, just make dead," Lyons replied. He thumbed a buckshot round into the grenade launcher and fed the OSW a full magazine.

The outlaw rushed off. It felt like a similar situation years ago when, as part of an organized-crime task force, Lyons had met the Executioner for the second time, not as a policeman seeking his arrest, but as a soldier on the same side, working against a common enemy. Lyons could see why Bolan would take the Baltimore robber as an ally. Lyons pushed the nostalgic urge aside and swung his rifle around the corner, triggering the powerful carbine. A full-auto swath of thunder lashed at the group of gunmen, no longer neatly segregated between trained mercenaries and hired drug soldiers. The groups had mixed, combining forces and reorganizing in the wake of the brutal punishment they'd received at the hands of Lyons and Biggs.

The 7.62 mm stream of bullets homed in on gunmen who were united with the intent of releasing mayhem on the nation's capital. Bodies writhed under a storm of hot lead, drawing the combined force's attention. Lyons pulled the trigger on the grenade launcher and the stubby 40 mm buckshot charge belched out a cloud of .25-caliber steel ball bearings. The tiny projectiles moved at a fraction over the speed of sound, somewhere around 1200 feet per second, and air resistance turned the compressed mass of pellets into a spreading cloud. By the time the buckshot reached the enemy gunmen, it had spread to be two meters wide and over a meter high. Five gunmen shrieked as the flesh was stripped from their bones by the devastating swarm. They died fast, but not so quick that they didn't scream and sputter their dying breaths.

The rest of the attacking throng jerked away from Lyons's brutal torrent of body-ripping lead. Now it was Biggs's turn to take action, and he held down the trigger of his AK, slicing the survivors to ribbons with his automatic fire. It had been a by-the-book ambush, brutal and quick, directing the enemy away from one source of death right into the path of another.

If they kept up this success rate, the Fallen marauders would be torn apart in no time, even if Michael didn't get assistance from the surviving Calvert security men.

That's when Lyons spotted the familiar puff of smoke of a launching RPG, the fat, teardrop-shaped warhead spiraling through the air toward him. The Able Team leader cursed, realizing that the enemy had their own carefully coordinated counterattack.

The 77 mm warhead's detonation lifted Lyons off his feet, hurling him bodily into a bone-jarring crash.

CHAPTER NINETEEN

Hermann Schwarz, with his trio of robotic escorts, had gone around to the loading dock under the assumption that he would have a better chance of finding the Fallen's automated minions deployed there. When he heard the sudden and intense chatter of a distant M-60 machine gun, he realized that the defenders either had a mixed weapons platoon, or the Second Sphere conspiracy had much larger mechanical drones with improved weapons systems.

He spotted the lurching hulk of two of the converted ATVs and ducked out of the way before the operators could trigger the heavy blasters mounted on the turrets Schwarz was relieved that the robotic opposition was nothing in comparison to the Ankylosaur series of drone tanks that he and the rest of Stony Man had engaged a while back. The weapons systems on those robots included grenade launchers and actual cannons that would reduce even the cinderblock wall he was crouched behind into a pile of dust. As it was, the M-60s on the two deadly ATV drones were steadily chewing through

Schwarz's cover. He poked the camera at the end of his rifle around the corner, scanning the weapons system. There was a team of Second Sphere security guards waiting in the wings, all of them armed with M-16s and handguns, and wearing armored vests and helmets.

"Gadgets! We've got big trouble out here," Blancanales's voice said into his helmet.

"I noticed it, too," Schwarz returned, putting the crosshairs at the center of his camera image on the face of one of the Fallen defenders. "I'm on it."

The Able Team electronics genius typed onto his wrist pad, muttering to himself in conjunction with the keys. It was a simple, fast text message. "Have the drones target camera domes on the enemy robots. Blind 'em," he texted.

"Asked our boys back at the Farm to try a little precision work with their drone," he announced.

The trio of backpack-portable robots zipped out into the center of the loading dock floor, training their integral 5.7 mm pistol barrels at the defending automatons. Two of them cranked off rapid shots that caused sparks to fly. Schwarz noted that an enemy rifleman reacted to the appearance of the compact observation robots and aimed his rifle at them.

Schwarz triggered his SIG rifle, punching a 5.56 mm round through his face. The man's features disappeared in a gory crater while the third drone that had held its fire punched a bullet through the armored vest of a second Fallen gunman. The ATV conversions, now blind, cut loose with their machine guns in wild panic. Schwarz had to throw himself flat as 7.62 mm NATO bullets cut through the cinderblock, nearly gaining revenge against the Able Team electronics genius.

Schwarz sneered angrily and continued to rake the Second Sphere mercenaries with his SIG, staying tightly behind the remnants of the dock entrance. His three drones whipped into the storehouse, losing themselves among stacks of crates as gunmen engaged in their own uncontrolled panic fire.

On one of his projected windows, Schwarz noticed an ATV robot lurch into the open. He was about to direct the miniature observers to nail its gun camera when he recognized that the weapon was a 40 mm grenade launcher. He pushed to his feet and launched himself down into the ramp below the loading dock. A moment later the last vestiges of the shattered dock entrance were blasted to powder by the thunderous punch of the robot's big cannon.

In his wild dive, Schwarz landed hard on the concrete ramp, his boom microphone snapping off as his helmet glanced off the ground. He grimaced in disgust at the clumsy landing that left him unable to speak to Blancanales and Aspen. At least behind a three-foot artificial cliff, Schwarz was safe from the miniature artillery cannon that the Fallen had rolled out.

His live video feed from the compact observer robots suddenly showed an all too familiar image—the serpentine form of an infiltrator automaton. With a tap of his wrist panel, Schwarz magnified the image and noticed that the enemy robot moved slower, as if heavily laden with extra bulk. That was all that Schwarz needed to know—he'd caught the news of the particularly powerful detonations McCarter and Lyons had encountered with the opening shots of their engagement.

Suddenly the camera image turned to snowy static, a thunderclap shaking the ground around the Able Team commando. Schwarz poked his rifle camera up and over the top of the dock, scanning. A thick plume of smoke twisted from a corner of the storeroom and Schwarz could see that the Second Sphere hired guns had been knocked off of their feet by the blast.

Schwarz also saw that the detonation had upended the drone ATV. He used his rifle camera to target the ammunition box for the robot's grenade launcher and pulled the trigger. The stream of 5.56 mm rounds smacked into the metal box, but he would need a full magazine to penetrate the rolled steel of the magazine, even with the heavy rounds he'd loaded into his SIG. The ATV struggled to right itself, but even as it did so, it returned fire against Schwarz, 40 mm shells sailing past the sleek rifle. Out in the parking lot, the grenades landed and erupted, tossing pebbles skyward. Schwarz hauled his rifle down, fed it another magazine, then poked the weapon up again.

"Come on…" Schwarz snarled. He spotted Blancanales and Aspen burst in behind the Second Sphere defenders and held his fire.

"Pol! Fall back!" Schwarz bellowed at the top of his lungs.

Like an angry puppy, the drone accompanying Blancanales and Aspen suddenly veered hard into the shins of the two men, tripping them up.

They looked down and saw the boxy little automaton high-tailing it back through the door they'd entered. It didn't take much to get the message through to Blancanales, who grabbed a handful of Aspen's shirt and hauled him into full retreat.

Schwarz tapped his wrist comm. "Thanks."

"No problem," came the text reply from home base.

Schwarz triggered the SIG one more time, focusing on the battered, chewed-up grenade launcher magazine. The ATV disappeared and the resultant shock wave pried the rifle and its camera out of Schwarz's hands. A wind of dust and debris hurled through the dock entrance, and only the heavy, reinforced concrete that Schwarz had hidden behind saved him from shrapnel and overpressure.

Rather than scramble after the fallen rifle, Schwarz transitioned to the Smith & Wesson .357 autoloader he carried in his thigh holster. Re-armed, he crawled up to the loading dock and saw the devastation wrought as the ATV had been blown to pieces. He looked for the surviving pair of robots. He couldn't see them directly, but according to the live feed projected onto his goggles, they were transmitting. The cameras could only see choking smoke, but they were relatively undamaged.

"Pol?" Schwarz called.

"Clear," Blancanales replied. "You healthy?"

"A little beat up, but I'll live," Schwarz answered.

"You had a rocket?" Aspen asked.

"No. I blew up their grenade launcher's ammunition," Schwarz explained. He looked around for a rifle that hadn't been mangled by the explosions.

Aspen saw the search and handed over his Mini-Uzi and its spare magazines. "Why trust their gear?"

"Thanks," Schwarz answered.

There were still the offices above and the workshop to clear in the headquarters, and Schwarz didn't want to rely on any handgun, even if it was the modern version of the venerable .357 Magnum. One of the remaining drones rolled into view as the dust and smoke settled.

Emerson sent through a message, audio and text for the Stony Man warriors on site.

"We lost one of the robots," Emerson explained. "But we sent the others to scout the other areas of the building. We've got a nest of inert infiltrator units in the workshop, and there is armed resistance in the second-floor offices."

"What kind of numbers are we looking at?" Blancanales asked as he observed Schwarz wrapping an earphone wire around a stick.

"Maybe a dozen men, and then there's an extra converted ATV on the workshop floor. It's packing the M-60 package as opposed to the grenade launchers from earlier," Emerson replied.

Schwarz plugged the improvised boom mike into his helmet and secured it with a swatch of duct tape. "Okay, the Gadgets network is back on the air."

"Glad to have you with us," Emerson responded. "Want us to use the minidrones to take care of that last ATV conversion?"

"Hold off. I want to coordinate with the aerial observation team," Schwarz said.

"They haven't seen anything surrounding the building," Emerson returned.

"Not here. Divert them toward the nuclear power station. This could all be a distraction," Schwarz explained. "If it is…"

"Right. I've got the team on it," Emerson said.

Blancanales took a deep breath. "So why waste time here?"

"Because this is where the main controls for the drones are," Schwarz said. "We've got a ton of encrypted traffic, so the only way to take care of a massed force of robotic opponents is to cut off the head."

"You can hack the system if we control it?" Aspen asked, feeding his M-4 a fresh magazine after refilling his partially depleted mags with loose ammo.

Schwarz handed Aspen a small thumb drive. He gave Blancanales a duplicate. "Universal Serial Bus drive. Loaded in is security-busting software that can crack any system within a few minutes."

"A few programs?" Aspen asked.

"Try a salvo of rootkits and logic worms," Schwarz corrected. "A gig of software designed to make sure those robots are under our control. It's been updated with sample encryptions from the Nogent operation, so this should lock out anyone on Second Sphere's side. All you have to do is find the USB port, plug it in, and the Farm will take control of the robots on the ground."

"Just in case any of us takes a bullet, there'll still be two others able to do what needs to be done," Blancanales said.

Schwarz called up an image on his wrist console. He showed Aspen and Blancanales. "This is what the Nogent control setup looked like, so keep an eye peeled for something similar."

"Good old Phoenix," Blancanales said.

Emerson cut in on the line. "Our Global Hawk picked up a group of robots cutting across the countryside. They're three minutes away from the Indian Point perimeter fence."

"What do you see?" Schwarz asked.

"Nine of the ATV rollers with a mix of firepower. We couldn't tell but the underbrush was fairly active, so we're also looking at a swarm of the infiltrators," Emerson replied.

"Nine… Odd number," Schwarz said.

"Global Hawk Three launched a Maverick missile and took down three of them," Emerson confessed. "Judging from the secondary explosions, we also nailed at least five of the infiltrators, and those little buggers are packed to the gills with plastic."

"Three minutes," Schwarz grumbled. "That gives us two minutes to clear the office and begin the takeover."

"Why just two?" Aspen asked as he took off after the racing Schwarz.

The Able Team genius sighed. "Because the M-60s give those ATVs a half click of lethal radius. They don't have to be on top of the fence to start causing mayhem at Indian Point. If they have units with grenade launchers, they'll be able to start shelling the campus once they're inside of three hundred yards."

"Civilian casualties if they can't secure a radiation release," Aspen mused.

"Movement in the workshop. Looks like the last of the ATVs is heading for you," Emerson announced.

"How'd they know—?" Blancanales began, then was cut off as Aspen slammed bodily into him. Gunfire chopped at the wall right behind where his head would have been. Schwarz whirled and cut loose with his Mini-Uzi, the infiltrator automaton having given away its position. The Mini-Uzi's load of armor-piercing full-metal-jacketed ammunition punched through the serpent's skin and connected with the self-destruct mechanism. The robot snake exploded with enough force to knock Schwarz off his feet, but luckily the machine was too far away to produce a lethal shock wave or sheet of shrapnel.

Blancanales coughed as Aspen helped him up. "Thanks."

"I'm just returning the favor, old man," Aspen replied.

Blancanales sneered at the comment on his age. "You like this kid?"

Schwarz nodded as he gathered himself to his feet. "Come on. We're running out of time."

Able Team and their ally raced up the stairs even as they heard the growl of the last ATV's engine reverberating down the hall.

RAMON BIGGS RACED to LYONS's side, trading his spent AK-47 for the double barreled sawed-off shotgun he favored when he was robbing drug dealers. The RPG blast had thrown the Able Team commander around like a rag doll, and while he was still moving, his senses must have been overloaded by the explosion. Biggs only had a few moments to reach Lyons's side and drag him to safety before the Fallen marauders fell upon him with the intent of getting revenge against the big ex-cop.

One armored mercenary came into view, the muzzle of his rifle aimed at the prone Lyons. Biggs's ally was still too dazed from a near miss by the RPG shell to reach for a weapon to defend himself, so the Baltimore outlaw extended the 12-gauge and shouted at the mercenary.

"Hey, asshole!" Biggs challenged, getting the raider's attention. As soon as the rifle's muzzle moved away from Lyons, Biggs triggered one of his shotgun's barrels, emptying a charge of 12-gauge buckshot into the would-be killer's face. The powerful blast knocked the man off his feet, facial bones caved in and skin flayed in the wake of a half-dozen pellets slamming into it.

Lyons grunted and rolled onto his side, clawing for his OSW carbine.

Biggs took that as a cue to pull his .357 Magnum revolver. As he got closer to Lyons, he saw that there were more enemy marauders around the corner, and they were alert for the presence of the downed Able Team leader's ally. What they didn't expect was Biggs to cut loose like a Hong Kong film star, the remaining barrel of his shotgun and the payload of his Magnum's cylinder unloading their contents into the assembly of Fallen gunmen.

The shotgun staggered two of the attackers as the charge's pattern spread to a meter wide. Biggs put a .357 Magnum slug through the upper chest of a third rifleman that missed his enemy's body armor through a combination of pure luck and years of practice with the thundering hogleg. The Fallen gunners went into retreat, the wave of firepower interrupted by Biggs pushing them so hard that they didn't take the time to aim their automatic rifles. Even so, a lucky bullet sliced across the outlaw's thigh and caused him to stumble.

Lyons sat up, OSW carbine in one fist, Smith & Wesson MP-357 in the other, and he took up the slack for the staggered Biggs. "Reload!"

Biggs let the shotgun drop to the ground and stuffed his revolver into his waistband on that command. It took a few seconds to rip out the empty AK mag and feed it a fresh one, but the Able Team commander had bought him enough time with both of his own guns blazing. Biggs triggered the assault rifle in short bursts, taking out the survivors of the attack wave with precision fire.

Lyons lurched, trying to regain his balance when Biggs hooked him under his armpit, helping him up.

"You still in the game?" Biggs asked.

Lyons dumped his OSW's empty magazine and reloaded. He thumbed a fresh grenade into the launcher's breech. "You bet."

Biggs grinned as they retreated toward cover. "My man!"

"We're still not going to hold hands and take long walks on the beach," Lyons grunted. He blinked away the cobwebs in his head. "Michael, you there?"

"I hear you, Carl," Michael returned. "Though next time, remember you have a radio microphone. I'm working on only one eardrum now."

"Sorry, kid," Lyons returned. "What's the situation with the surviving security?"

"They're pretty battered," Michael said. "Looks like you weren't kidding about those metal worms, either. Another came at us. A security guard hit it with a shotgun, and he's got a broken arm after the damn thing blew up."

Lyons grimaced. "Since they encountered unexpected resistance, they've moved up their backup plan."

"There's always some bastard trying to skate uphill," Biggs growled. "So what do we do to stop the robots if they go off like a thousand-pound bomb?"

Lyons grimaced. "No idea."

Price's voice cut across their radios. "Carl, Ramon, the engineers in the plant have shut down the intake and outlet valves on the cooling towers, but we're not sure how long that's going to last. We could be lucky and the shutters are heavy enough to withstand the kilogram of plastic we postulate is inside of the robots."

"But if they're not, one of those little buggers opens the door for another one and it kamikazes inside the reactor," Michael interjected.

Lyons's brow furrowed. "Michael, get back here."

"What you need?" the young man asked. From the sounds of his panting over the radio, the Baltimore kid was already on the run.

"Support," Lyons replied. "We're going to have to check out the Second Sphere offices. They have to have a command structure present."

"So why not have me shoot it up?" Michael asked.

"I've got a little USB flash drive that will turn over control of the enemy robots to the lady talking to us," Lyons replied. "We shoot it up, the Fallen have other systems to keep those infiltrators under their command."

"Carl!" Biggs called. "We've got an SUV tearing across the lot. That prick Anderson's hanging out the top like he's a tank commander."

The outlaw recoiled from the corner as a storm of bullets ripped through the air. Lyons grimaced and fired his grenade launcher as he caught sight of the vehicle, then retreated before the stream of 7.62 mm slugs sought him out.

"Anderson's the one in charge of this operation?" Lyons asked.

"Yeah," Biggs returned. The two men peered around the corner and saw that the Able Team commander's hastily shot grenade had discolored the front fender of the speeding SUV, but it was still tearing around in a circle. Anderson hung on to his M-60 machine gun, which was also cradled in an improvised mount on top of the truck.

"Heavy armor," Lyons noted. "That could work in our favor."

"How's that?" Michael asked, skidding to a halt

behind the pair. "Looks like Anderson's distracting you guys. I popped off a few rounds and sent the bastards slipping around your back door packing."

"Good man," Lyons returned. "Instead of hitting the Second Sphere office, we just have to get into that vehicle. This way we don't leave the invaders unmolested, and we can score some wheels for ourselves if we're lucky."

"That's a lot of ifs," Biggs said.

"Says the man who stuffs shotguns in the faces of heroin dealers," Lyons returned.

Biggs grinned. "Pretty and perceptive. This could be the start of a beautiful relationship. If your grenade launcher couldn't stop the SUV, what makes you think we could take it down?"

"Michael, Ramon, you two set up to keep any flanking units off my back. I'm going to draw Anderson in," Lyons ordered.

"He comes in for the kill on you, and you tackle that truck and take it over," Michael surmised. Lyons nodded. Michael gave Lyons's arm a squeeze. "You're ripped, but man, that's a ton of machine out there."

"Then it's a fair fight," Lyons said.

"Just hope that little drive works in Anderson's truck. Otherwise, we'd be wasting time," Biggs said.

"Keep the rest of these scum off my back," Lyons said. He tossed his rifle and bandoliers to Biggs. "I need to look like I'm on my last legs to draw them in close."

Lyons shifted the Kimber .45 to under his shirt, which he untucked. He handed Michael the Smith & Wesson autoloader. "If they shoot at me, then take care of them. If I'm dead, get the hell out, and tell Price to authorize a full evacuation."

"You ain't going out like that," Michael said, patting his AK.

"If it gets that bad, you'll only end up catching radiation poisoning," Lyons growled.

Lyons staggered into the open, unarmed, his suit in tatters. Blood spray from the Fallen that Biggs had shot made his injuries look real and crippling. He dropped to his knees and sagged on his arms. Anderson and his SUV roared from across the lot, but thankfully the M-60 machine gun remained silent. The Able Team leader hoped that his enemy's ego was strong enough that he'd want a good, close look at the lone man who had held off his army of hired guns. Rifles chattered on the flanks, but Lyons withheld a grin as he heard the 40 mm grenade launcher cut into a crew of hostile shooters.

The SUV squealed to a halt and Anderson, a six-and-a-half-foot man who looked as if he weighed three hundred pounds, leaped from his improvised cupola. Two brawny arms hauled the machine gun down with him, and he strode on long, stovepipe legs toward the "wounded" Lyons.

"Got any last words, punk?" Anderson asked.

Lyons collapsed, his arms giving out. Anderson walked closer and kicked the ex-cop onto his back.

"Super-Fed! I'm talking to you!" Anderson threatened. "Last words?"

Lyons gurgled, one hand reaching out weakly to tug at Anderson's trouser leg. He hated acting so weakened, but a light kick indicated that his role-playing was successful. "My wife…"

Anderson snorted. "What you want me to tell your bitch?"

He started to lower the M-60's muzzle toward

Lyons. Meanwhile, Lyons was watching out of the corner of his eye. Anderson's driver had opened the door on the SUV. The engine still rumbled, idle, but the Fallen driver had stepped away from the vehicle. On the other side of the huge mercenary leader, another gunman walked out into the open, gun held at low ready.

Lyons's labored breathing stopped and he flopped slack on the asphalt.

"Son of a bitch," Anderson snarled. "Pick this sack of shit up so I can put a bullet in him!"

The driver and the rifleman set their weapons aside and rushed over to the limp form of Lyons, hauling him up. Anderson tossed the M-60 onto the hood of the SUV and pulled a Desert Eagle from his holster. "Going to make this some damned anticlimactic…"

Anderson's attention was drawn by a sickening crunch, and he looked up from his mammoth pistol in time to see his driver falling away from Lyons with a twisted and mangled arm. The rifleman was grabbed in a headlock as a human shield, and the Able Team commander had the compact .45 auto from his waistband. Anderson rushed to bring up his cannon, but a hail of 230-grain hollowpoints slammed into the mercenary's face and chest, ending his disappointment.

"Move it, you two!" Lyons bellowed, tossing the surprised rifleman aside and lunging for the M-60 on the hood. Lyons swung the machine gun toward a knot of men who were trying to assail Michael's position, and he emptied the better part of a belt into the hapless gunners. They hadn't expected to be hosed down from behind by such a heavy weapon, and their corpses littered the ground in the wake of Lyons's withering fire.

Michael rushed out, racing to the big ex-cop's side as Biggs laid down a little more fire, a grenade and a magazine from the OSW, discouraging further pursuit by the mercenaries. Michael slid behind the driver's seat as Lyons climbed into the back.

A computer technician looked up at the Able Team commander as he crowded into the back of the SUV with him.

"You going to recall those infiltrators, or do I dump your headless corpse out of this thing?" Lyons snarled.

The technician swallowed noisily, then began tapping the keyboard on his laptop. "Robots are recalled, heading to this parking lot."

Lyons grinned. "Sit still and behave."

The minute Biggs joined Lyons and Michael, the young man gunned the engine and swung toward the blasted security barracks.

With the head of the assault force taken down and the robots neutralized, Lyons knew that the remaining hired guns wouldn't have the heart to stay and fight when the Maryland State Police showed up with their rapid-response SWAT.

There were lawmen who would need on-site assistance, and Lyons's first-aid skills could be put to use to help them. They were his brothers in arms, just like Biggs and his protégé. His rage had been spent in the destruction of the attack force on Calvert Cliffs, and for all intents and purposes, his partners and friends, Blancanales and Schwarz, were going to have to be front and center in taking out the men who had ordered Hirtenberg's murder only a few days before.

Lyons allowed his bloodlust to be sated. There were

lives that needed saving, even as the the nation's capital had been protected from mass murder.

He took a deep breath, offering a prayer for Pol and Gadgets. "It's up to you two now."

CHAPTER TWENTY

Terry Aspen held the stairwell, pouring magazine after magazine into the converted ATV drone that tried to crawl up the steps. Its knobby tires had been deflated after being shredded by 5.56 mm rounds, but the floppy rubber still had enough grip to haul its bulk up the spiral. Aspen's only saving grace was that he was so far above the elevation designed for the robot's machine gun that he was safe from harm.

That advantage wouldn't last long, as the ATV was one flight of steps below, and the minute it dragged itself onto the bottom step, its deadly M-60 would be tilted enough to allow it to chew him to ribbons. Aspen cursed the fact that they hadn't had the foresight to bring along hand grenades. All the while, he continued to count down the two minutes that Schwarz had announced earlier. The looming deadline would soon reach the point where the ATV drone's brethren would be in range to hammer the Indian Point nuclear power station with heavy machine gun and 40 mm grenade fire. Another few minutes, and the swift little infiltrator robots would make their assault on the cooling towers, ready to detonate the vital temperature control systems. When that happened, the reactors would burn out of control, and the resultant fires and breaches in the containment structures would vomit poisonous, radioactive smoke. The core reactors themselves would get so hot, it was conceivable that they would melt through the Earth's crust. With the kind of temperature they generated, it was fully possible that molten rock would turn into airborne fallout, increasing the potential for contamination.

The Russians had been incredibly lucky during the Chernobyl incident that the reactors were shut down before they reached critical temperature. When lucky was measured in terms of rendering thirty miles uninhabitable and thousands of miles being inundated with vaporized, radioactive ash resulting in millions of deaths, then Aspen felt a chilling dread that was even greater than the fear of the relentless, unstoppable machine struggling on flattened tires and a smoldering engine to crawl into position to open up on him with a belt of 7.62 mm NATO.

Aspen's ribs still hurt, and despite the fact that he'd destroyed the dome that made up the automaton's "eyes," the operator must have had some other means to guide deadly machine. A quick glance finally helped him locate the mirrored dome in the corner of the stairwell above him. He was about to fire on it and take out the tertiary set of eyes when a stream of lead cut the air close enough that he could feel the bullets pluck his sleeve. Aspen hit the dirt and triggered his rifle at the security camera. The plastic dome shattered, and the electronic eye behind it sparked and sputtered.

It was too late, though. The ATV drone would cut him apart if he stood. It fired single shots, probing for the Stony Man recruit.

"I couldn't stop it!" Aspen called over the radio. "It's still coming."

"Stay on the ground. It can't aim low enough to hurt you at close range," Blancanales reminded the blacksuit. "Maybe you can do something to slow it down some more when it passes you by."

Aspen gritted his teeth and rolled onto his stomach, crawling out of the stairwell. The Texas public safety officer looked around and found a desk. He threw all his muscle into lifting the piece of furniture and shoving it through the stairwell door.

"Terry?" Schwarz asked.

"Looking for a large enough weapon to knock this bastard out," Aspen grunted. Bullets chopped into the ceiling, one of them taking out a piece of the desktop as he pushed it to the top of the steps.

With a powerful shove, he sent 150 pounds of metal and corkboard sliding down the stairs. The ATV's engine revved as it fought against the sudden extra mass. The machine gun had been batted aside by the bulk of the desk, so that the weapon ripped divots out of the wall. Finally, the smoldering engine broke down. Too many bullets and now too much weight had knocked it out. The ATV slid back down the stairs and was overturned as the desk collapsed against it.

"Too bad we can't throw desks at all of those things," Aspen growled.

"Get back here and cover me," Schwarz commanded. "I'm throwing something more powerful against the enemy robots."

"Technology?" Aspen asked, staggering toward the Able Team pair. The offices were a mess, shot-up cabinets having vomited papers and the Second Sphere gunmen protecting the main server chewed mercilessly by the same bullets that had hacked them apart.

"Mess with their minds, I will," Schwarz said. "Okay, we're hooked up. Hopefully this will hijack the control mechanism."

"The team's getting counterattacks along our interface," Price announced. "Whoever this programmer is, he's damn good."

Schwarz looked at the corpse of a computer technician who had chosen to stand and fight rather than be tried for his part in the attempted mass murder of New York City and its environs. The syndrome was known as suicide by cop, though Schwarz had a problem seeing himself as a law enforcement officer. "Emerson?"

"We're down to one remaining UAV," the Air Force officer said. "We've been blindsided by an unmanned aerial vehicle of their own."

Aspen grimaced. "Where did they get the money to build all of these things?"

"Their airborne drone was a cheap knockoff, based off a radio-control aircraft," Emerson explained. "We live in an age of cheap digital cameras and disposable cell phones. A thousand dollars gives a hundred of these things eyes, and another thousand enables communication and remote control."

"It's not as if these are high-durability military models, either," Schwarz added as he typed on the keyboard of the hijacked control center. "They could be built to lower tolerances and still do their job."

"You're worried," Blancanales noted, reading his friend's features.

"I'm trying to figure out why the Farm doesn't see a backup transmission on these things," Schwarz replied. "The Fallen or Second Sphere or whatever these guys call themselves had all manner of backup systems in Nogent. I can't see anything here on the network… Wait. I see a ghost connection on this box."

"That's why we're having so much trouble," Price replied. "Someone is actively fighting us. Aaron says that it's in the building with you."

"The basement?" Blancanales asked.

"None was listed on the architectural plans," Schwarz replied. "Though considering the hackers we're up against, those plans could have been deleted from the main database."

Blancanales watched Schwarz zone out as he shut off the parts of his mind for speaking to concentrate all of his massive intellect on the task of emergency programming. "Gadgets has gone bye-bye. He's in cyberspace now."

"Keep an eye on him," Price said. "You're still not alone there, and right now he is the only advantage we have as the rest of the cybercrew is busy dealing with crisis points."

"The enemy is broadcasting like they did in Europe?" Blancanales asked.

"They're trying to," Price answered. "But we're fighting them on that front."

Movement registered in the corner of Aspen's eye and drew his attention. Blancanales caught the Stony Man recruit's head movement and subsequent quick draw of his SIG P-229 pistol. The Able Team veteran took a step toward the younger man. "We cleared this floor, didn't we?"

Blancanales nodded. "Of people. There could be infiltrators...but they're operated—"

"Move!" Aspen grunted. He shoved Blancanales aside and charged toward something on the floor.

"Terry!" Blancanales called out, struggling to maintain his footing.

The stocky young man had charged toward an infiltrator robot that had suddenly appeared around the corner of a cubicle. Aspen had restrained the urge to use his gun on the automaton, realizing that the self-destruct mechanism would have been triggered by a bullet piercing its skin. The new kamikaze-style robots seemed to be designed to detonate more easily. They had gone from having very little to damage with redundant systems to packed with high explosives.

Aspen reached down and scooped up the robot as if it was a football and ran with all the power in his legs. Blancanales tried to scramble to his feet, finally regaining his balance, and he took off instinctively after the blacksuit.

"Just throw it!" Blancanales shouted, charging after Aspen.

The warning came a moment too late. Aspen disappeared in a thunderous explosion. The shock wave hammered Blancanales to the floor. The blast had struck so quickly that Blancanales's head bounced on the tiles. Flattened, Blancanales felt as if his arms and legs were made of wood. As Able Team's combat medic, he knew immediately that he was suffering a concussion, but every instinct urged him to sit up and get to Aspen's side. A hand pressed against his shoulder, holding him down.

It was Schwarz, and the genius was moving his lips,

but no words made it to his ears. He tried to speak, and though he could form the words in his mind, his lips were unresponsive and the only noises he made were inarticulate grunts.

"Great, now you can speak fluent Ironman," Schwarz said, finally audible through the ringing haze in Blancanales's skull.

"Ears…work now," Blancanales blurted.

"Stay put. You took a nasty concussion," Schwarz ordered, his voice creaking with sadness.

"Terry?" Blancanales numbly asked.

Schwarz kept his lips pursed tightly for a moment. "Stay still. I have to get downstairs. We've managed to freeze up the robots sent to attack the Indian Point station, but there are conspirators on the premise that need to be stopped."

"Dead?" Blancanales asked.

Schwarz took a deep breath. "I liked that kid. Stay here."

The stunned Able Team veteran let out a groan in sympathy with Schwarz's pain. He could tell from his normally mellow partner's mood that Schwarz was on the warpath.

Blancanales felt bad for the men that his friend was going to hunt down. While Lyons was terrifying in his brutality, the kind of vengeance meted out by Schwarz would be chillingly cold and efficient. Blancanales sent his prayers after Schwarz, hoping to keep his partner from falling into a moral pit that he couldn't escape.

BROGNOLA LOOKED UP from his Stony Man laptop and regarded the President. "The threat to Calvert Cliffs has been averted, sir."

The President buried his face in his hands and sighed with relief. After sitting on edge, worrying about the fate of the city hundreds of feet above the protected White House bunker, the end of the menace was more than welcome.

"No word yet on Indian Point," Brognola continued. "But we have reports of explosions just outside of the campus in the countryside. It sounds like a full-blown battle."

"What about the threats by the Fallen?" the President asked. "Have they made it onto the air waves?"

"There have been posts on various conspiracy theory Web sites, a few snippets of secondhand video, but we've suppressed them in the major outlets," Brognola said. "The people with the tinfoil hats will be driven to distraction by what's gotten through, but Joe Average isn't going to be thrown into a tizzy."

The President nodded. "So there are rumors of panic and mayhem, but none apparent to the general public."

"The Justice Department is waiting for trouble. Riot police across the nation are on standby," Brognola said.

The President glowered. "That is one thing I didn't want to have happen. Riot police cracking down with martial law would be a terrible situation."

"We know, sir. We're not going to crack down and enforce curfews, but if violence does break out, we'll take action to minimize the damage," Brognola stated. "The police are no more interested in cracking citizen heads than you are."

The President nodded. The monitor on the wall flashed to life.

"Hal, we managed to stop the robots making their assault on Indian Point," Barbara Price advised. "We weren't able to get control of the devices, but we found the destruct codes. The Fallen's attackers were put down."

"New York is safe?" Brognola asked.

Price nodded. "As safe as possible. There's going to be a lot of news about the explosions at Calvert Cliffs and Indian Point, so people will be on edge, but as long as we keep the caps on the information released through the Internet and via hijacked satellite television signals, we won't have to worry about rioting in the streets."

Brognola looked at the President, who took a deep breath. "America's fine."

"That just leaves the Syrian situation," the President said.

"Anything from that corner?" Brognola asked Price.

"We know that Dragonslayer has just dropped off the team to intercept the Fallen's parachutists," Price answered. "They have to make sure that no one, or thing, escapes from the staging area."

"The infiltration robots in particular," the President concluded.

"Absolutely," Price replied. "And we can't have Dragonslayer do the work because an air-to-ground missile assault would attract too much attention from the Syrian military. We don't have permission to be there, remember?"

The President nodded, sighing. "I have my State Department head talking and begging for help, but we're not getting anywhere. They probably know we've got people in the region, though."

"We're lucky that they haven't taken action," Price said. "But then, Dragonslayer does have enough stealth technology modules to stay off the radar."

The President sighed and nodded. "The Syrians aren't going to take any action, because we're the ones who're between them and the terrorists, but they won't be happy about it. They'll take any opportunity to cut loose on Phoenix Force if they have the excuse. As it is, we've barely convinced them that their radar blackout was not started by us."

Price agreed. "We've caught images of unmanned aerial vehicles that had been in the air. They came via a circuitous route from Israel, but not from an official launch location."

"Renegades?" Brognola asked.

"Most likely. We're cooperating with the Mossad to investigate, and have given them the information necessary to move in," Price said. "Normally we wouldn't be so open with a foreign intelligence service, but like the Fallen operators in the south of France, we can't spare the manpower to resolve the situation otherwise. The Israelis also prefer to clean their own house."

"And the French and Syrians don't?" the President asked.

"The Israelis have a certain brutal efficiency," Brognola interjected. "And we have friends in their service. Almost family in some instances."

The President remembered that one of the founding members of Phoenix Force had been an Israeli intelligence veteran. "Syria's practically blind right now, and they have their own internal security problems to deal with. Even so, if they catch your people…"

The President didn't have the heart to say what came next. Should the warriors of Phoenix Force end up murdered by the Syrian military, they would be buried, unmourned and branded as terrorists who had invaded a sovereign nation, not as the champions who had risked their lives to prevent an apocalypse. "So even if they save the day, they're in danger of being killed."

The office, deep in the bunker, returned to an uncomfortable silence as the leader of the free world waited for the news from Syria.

BARNABAS BOLFREY felt lucky that the parachute drop had gone off without fatalities and only a few minor injuries. His group had one broken ankle, and there were other sprains and bruises from the landing. Bolfrey had the man with the broken ankle take up gunner duty on the back of the first of the uncrated ATVs, after his injury had been splinted tightly. A security perimeter surrounded the rally point, grim and ready men armed with rifles forming a circle of steel and muscle that allowed the rest of the commando strike force to uncrate their equipment.

It hadn't taken that long to assemble all of their gear into a central location and break the transport packaging on them. The ATVs were fired up first, and half of them had their control systems removed and a new gearbox and remote-control system installed. Hundreds of miles away, a team of technicians toiled to make certain the automated drones were in perfect working condition. The digital, encrypted data feed would be harder to intercept now that antiradiation missiles had been used to take out Syria's electronic surveillance systems. Not only did the military not have their normal air and ground defense radar systems, but communication networks were beseiged by a spotlight of garbage transmissions beamed down by satellites thousands of miles above Damascus. Homm's programming skills had enabled the hacker to cripple and blind the hated Syrians while allowing him a clear connection back to his partner, Stern.

Bolfrey's communicator chirped and he put it to his ear. "Jacob?"

Stern sounded grim on the other end of the line. "Our ambush didn't work."

Bolfrey's brow furrowed. "You were ready for their arrival, though."

"Neither of our operations succeeded. The enemy was too well organized, and now, they've overrun the upper floors," Stern replied. Bolfrey didn't like the fatalistic tone of his partner's voice. "All of our scare tactics have been squashed in the media, and there have only been token news reports about disturbances at two East Coast power plants."

"How many men do you have left?" Bolfrey asked.

"Homm and Shenck. Neither of them is going to be a match for a commando squad," Stern explained. "I don't think that you're alone in Syria."

"You mean, aside from their military?" Bolfrey asked.

Stern grunted in affirmation. "Get your people moving as soon as possible. The enemy is out for blood, and they've proved too good at getting it."

Bolfrey swallowed. "Do you think you can get away?"

There was a moment of silence. "That's not my goal right now."

Bolfrey winced.

"I'm going to kill as many of the fuckers as I can. Godspeed, my friend." Stern signed off.

Bolfrey turned off the comm link and sighed. "I don't

believe in God anymore, my friend. I hope you find a better life after this, though."

The Second Sphere mercenaries regarded their commander as he tucked the radio away. Bolfrey grimaced and steeled himself, knowing that he had to put on a strong appearance to keep his team from bolting or losing their morale.

"All right, we came here to change the world! Lock and load!" Bolfrey bellowed. He looked at the Heckler & Koch G-3 rifle in his hands. It was a beloved old friend from his days in the Special Air Service, a powerful and sturdy tool that had carried him through the dark nights in Chernobyl and in the deserts of Oman. As a professional, it was unseemly for someone to develop a bit of sentimentality about tools, but right now, the assault weapon in his hands felt as if it was a part of his body. He was comfortable and complete.

He'd spent too bloody long sitting behind a desk, doing nothing more than pushing papers and plotting, moving people as if they were chess pieces. Sure, he kept his skills from perishing by training hard every week, but it wasn't the same. It wasn't the fire that had forged him so long ago.

Barnabas Bolfrey took a deep, cleansing breath, his doubts calmed as he realized that he was back where he belonged.

He was a warrior, and he was on a march to make Damascus pay for the family it had cost him. Millions would inhale the deadly chemicals that the Syrian government manufactured to remain on an equal footing against the Israelis' nuclear weapons stockpile. They would die, most of them painfully, and their screams of agony would echo for years in the ruins of a slaughtered city.

"Let's do this," he whispered to himself. He cleared his throat and spoke louder to his subordinates. "Are those infiltrators loaded into the pull carts?"

"Yes, sir!" one of his mercenaries answered sharply. "Once we get to the stockpile's perimeter, we let them off the leash and they'll do their thing."

Bolfrey nodded. Each of the serpentine robots, packed with a kilogram of high explosives, would detonate at designated points, perfectly planned by GPS and reinforced by UAV surveillance. They had the power to cut through the tanks of chemicals to release their contents. Death would take to the wing on the night winds, and descend upon the very people whom it was designed to uplift.

He grinned. "Good."

That's when he heard the distant pop of a grenade launcher. Bolfrey turned toward the sound, but his knowledge overrode his instincts. "Hit the dirt!"

The 40 mm shell landed on one of the carts laden with the explosive-packed infiltrator robots. The resultant explosion shocked and deafened the ex-SAS man.

Phoenix Force had caught up with them, and their opening movement scattered the commando force with a single ground-shaking blast.

CHAPTER TWENTY-ONE

Rafael Encizo looked over the sights of his weapon at the assembled force below. The odds were ten to one, not counting the converted ATVs that were being assembled into mobile gun platforms. He glanced over at Calvin James, who was adjusting the sights on his grenade launcher.

"Looks like there are going to be twenty of those ATV drones," Encizo said.

"According to the Farm, those things are pretty lethal, but they're soft-skinned enough to be taken down by rifle fire," James answered. The CQ-311 that he had was note for note identical to the American-made M-16 that he'd favored across his career as a Navy SEAL, San Francisco SWAT team member and finally as one of Phoenix Force's cornerstones. Its familiar handling would serve him well, but the Chinese manufacture of the weapon meant that if the Syrians came across the discarded weapon, there would be no evidence linking it back to the United States. The MAG-58 was an Argentine-fabricated and unlicensed knockoff, and the CQ-311's brothers were represented in the hands of Encizo and Farkas. While James would have preferred a longer range weapon, they simply hadn't had the time to scour the Mossad's storehouse of sanitized weaponry to get the right tools for the job. It was a compromise, but at least they were well within the lethal range for both the 5.56 mm rounds and the 40 mm grenades that James had stuffed through loops on his load-bearing vest.

"They seem to be attaching carts to the back of some of the ATVs," Farkas noted.

"Yeah. And they unloaded the crates from specially padded packages," Encizo added.

"Then those have to be the infiltrator robots," Kristopoulos said. "The impact of even a parachute landing would have set them off if they weren't cushioned."

"Why not leave the detonators out?" Farkas asked.

"Because they don't want to spend too long dicking around with installing trigger mechanisms in twenty or thirty robots," James answered. "They don't look like they're going to stick around as it is."

"I think I see Bolfrey," Kristopoulos said, looking through her pocket scope. "He's talking on a radio."

The other members of the group focused on him. Encizo didn't have to reference the photograph slid into a see-through panel on his wrist, but since he had his spotting scope ready and an excellent reference image to work from, the confirmation of Bolfrey's identity was rock-solid. "Confirmed identification. Anyone get a good look at those crates?"

Encizo suddenly heard Bolfrey shout. He had been skeptical of Hermann Schwarz's insistence on having at least one member of each team utilize his improvised rifle microphone in the field. The technology itself weighed only ounces, but it seemed like something else to run out of batteries and malfunction at a critical time.

Over his earphone, however, the microphone produced a very clear phrase.

"Are those infiltrators loaded into the pull carts?"

James looked at the odd grin that crossed the Cuban veteran's face. "What did you hear?"

"Gadgets's magic ear confirmed the infiltrator robots are in the pull carts," Encizo replied. "And since they're no longer cushioned…"

James nodded. He thumbed a 40 mm round into the M-203 knockoff that hung under the rifle's barrel. "One opening statement, ready to fire."

"Tanya, set your Maggy on another of the carts," Encizo ordered. "We want shock and awe to carry the day, and by carry the day, that means not letting a single damn robot get away."

"There's four down there, one for each of us?" Farkas asked.

"We're using M-4 knockoffs," Encizo replied. "The grenade launchers have the reach to destroy matériel, but not our rifles. We're on antipersonnel duty."

"Ready?" James asked.

"Do it," Kristopoulos answered.

The Phoenix Force grenadier and the Israeli agent fired in unison, launching a hail of 7.62 mm slugs and a packet of high explosives. The kamikaze-robot-laden carts erupted, rocking the Fallen maruaders between almost seismic level events.

Encizo lost sight of Bolfrey, but for now, his purpose was plain and simple. He had to deliver precision fire against any mercenary who still had a gun in his hand

and the strength to regain his feet. Utilizing the iron sights, the flat-shooting 5.56 mm rounds made sniping the opposition easy. Neither he nor Farkas was utilizing autofire, choosing instead to maximize their accuracy on semi-automatic. To compensate for the range and the slightly shorter barrels, Encizo triggered the weapon twice for each silhouette that he saw. The pair of 69-grain bullets proved sufficient to anchor an enemy gunman.

It was butcher's work, firing from the top of a sand dune, flash hiders lowering their profile even without the blinding and deafening effects of their bomb drones destroying their senses. Encizo didn't worry too much about the moral implications that he was effectively shooting fish in a barrel. The men down in the sands were on a mission of mass murder, preparing to kill a million Syrians unrelated to their government except to be the oppressed of a terrorism-supporting regime. There were many things that Encizo would have traded to take out the corrupt government in Damascus, but the lives of countless everyday people were not on that list. The thought of a city dying to avenge an old wrong, or to promote some form of twisted idealism, made the Cuban's stomach turn.

It was easy to say violence was the answer, and indeed, Encizo had often been part of that violent, brutal solution. The difference between the actions of Phoenix Force and their enemies, however, was the focus of their killing skills. The Fallen were looking for a maximum body count, and they didn't care who died, as long as the world was appalled at the carnage committed. Encizo and his brothers in arms, on the other hand, focused their cleansing fire against those who committed such indiscriminate violence. Instead of dropping a thousand-pound bomb to take out one man in a building with hundreds of bystanders, Phoenix Force was willing to go in and risk their personal safety to take out the target and those who would commit violence in his cause.

Bodies tumbled as the third and fourth carts were destroyed by James's and Kristopoulos's streams of explosives and heavy 7.62 mm belt-fed slugs. The only problem with their weapons and the destruction of the enemy's robots was that now, instead of an open killing field, Encizo had to struggle to find opponents in the midst of a choking smoke screen.

By now, the surviving Fallen commandos knew which direction the slaughtering sheets of lead and thunder were coming from, and they had moved behind the thick dust cloud. Encizo grimaced and looked at James.

"I'm going in close. Cover me," he told his partner.

"Let the smoke settle," James said. "We have the high ground and Jack can scope out any survivors if—"

An RPG sliced out of the cloud like a thunderbolt. Farkas leaped and dragged Kristopoulos out of the way before the warhead slammed into the dune that they were on top of. James fed his grenade launcher and returned the favor, even if his 40 mm shell was only half the size of the 77 mm rocket that had landed far too close for comfort. There was a rumbling blast on the other side of the cloud, the flash visible and lighting the night sky. Encizo's rifle microphone picked up the sound of a man screaming in pain, but he couldn't tell if the man was newly injured or still suffering from the initial torrent of death dropped onto the Fallen's invasion force.

"Dragonslayer's good, but those RPGs can knock Jack out of the sky," Encizo replied.

James cursed. "You've got a point."

ATVs snarled to life below them, and Encizo could see that they were the mobile gun platforms. He targeted one of them, bullets sparking off its frame, but the CQ-311's chambering wasn't enough for robot elimination at over two hundred yards. James reloaded the grenade launcher and speared another high-explosive package into the converted vehicle. It went to pieces on impact, the blast flipping another of the ATV drones onto its side.

Unfortunately, the rest of the robots, ten of them at Encizo's count, had homed in on the Phoenix Force pair and the armed units cut loose with a combination of M-60s and grenade launchers of their own. James and Encizo retreated as the top of their dune disappeared under the churning storm of 7.62 mm and 40 mm slugs. The irony of the robots' counterattack being the same kind of weaponry that had taken out the infiltrator units was not lost on Encizo.

"They're hitting us as hard as we hit them," Encizo replied.

James shrugged as they reached the bottom of the hill. "At least it looks like we took out half their number."

"Just because we only saw ten doesn't mean that there aren't others holding back with the human survivors," Encizo returned.

James sighed. "You always take the silver lining out of the cloud."

Encizo winked. "It doesn't do any good up there anyhow. Tanya? Ehan?"

Farkas helped Kristopoulos to her feet. To her credit, the Israeli machine gunner hadn't lost her MAG-58 knockoff. "What the hell did you two do?"

"We woke up their gun platforms," James answered. "And they're moving in on us."

"Too much suppressive fire for us to find another position to shoot from," Farkas noted.

"Jack?" Encizo asked over the radio.

"I thought you said that the enemy's RPGs would make it too dangerous for Dragonslayer to take to the air," James stated.

"That was before we had the march of the big-gun-toting robots," Encizo countered.

"I'm all fired up," Grimaldi answered over the radio. "Looks like we've thrown the low-profile approach out the window."

"To be fair, they're a lot noisier than we are," Encizo said. "You'll have to keep your distance. The enemy has at least one RPG-7 down there, not to mention the danger you'll run into from their M-60s."

"I'll hang back and let them have it from outside of their range," Grimaldi answered. "I'm approaching contact distance in a few moments."

Encizo spotted the shadowy form of one of the converted ATV gun platforms as it rounded the dune, fifty yards away. The machine's turret swiveled toward the Phoenix pair and their allies, and the Cuban grabbed a handful of James's sleeve.

The enemy machine disappeared as a burst of .50-caliber fire tore into it. Massive 750-grain slugs turned the sturdy chassis into a pile of mangled metal and fractured fiberglass. The buzz of the tribarreled .50 on Dragonslayer finally reached Encizo's ears, moving at only a third of the velocity of the deadly bullets. More divots of sand exploded skyward.

"Optically guided sighting helmet. Accept no substitutes," Grimaldi said over the radio.

Encizo turned to Kristopoulos. "You okay to fight?"

"I took some shrapnel, so I'm not going to be running and jumping with this thing," Kristopoulos said, holding out her machine gun. "Trade you for that little plastic rifle, though."

"Deal," Encizo replied. The stocky Cuban was only five-nine, but his upper-body strength was impressive. He was able to wield the MAG-58 like a rifle. "Jack, what's the movement look like on the other side of that smoke?"

"I've got three ATVs cutting across the dunes. They're running for the Lebanese border," Grimaldi said. A smoke trail sliced into the sky, and Encizo heard the Stony Man pilot curse from the proximity of the RPG shell. "Everyone else looks grounded."

"Can you save us an ATV?" James asked.

"Don't ask for a particular color," Grimaldi said. "I'm working off of infrared here."

"Thanks, smart-ass," James returned.

"Don't mention it." Grimaldi laughed.

James and Encizo rushed around the dunes, unafraid to take action now that they didn't have a swarm of enemy gun platforms to deal with. There were a few Fallen soldiers who still had the stomach to fight and who hadn't hopped on the closest ATV to escape. Unfortunately for them, they ran straight into two of the most highly trained combatants on the planet. M-16 and MAG-58 knockoffs chattered as the shell-shocked defenders made their presence known.

The mercenary force had been reduced to five active shooters who opened fire at the first sign of movement, but disoriented by the swirling sand and smoke from the explosive opening round of this final engagement, one of the men triggered his rifle at a swirling column of darkness and not a human.

Once the muzzle-flash betrayed him, Encizo shouldered the MAG-58 and ripped off a dozen rounds from the general-purpose machine gun. A storm of 7.62 mm slugs tore into the area around the gunman, a long exchange, but Encizo didn't have an exact target to hit. It didn't matter, as the extended burst found flesh and the enemy's G-3 fell silent. Encizo moved laterally, avoiding the fate of his opponent by not staying where his weapon had placed him in the smoke. Two more of the Fallen riflemen fired at where Encizo had been a moment ago, not where he was now, and James took the opportunity to nail both of them with his own weapon.

James's muzzle-flash betrayed his position to the last of the gunmen who'd stood their ground, and they fired, as well. Encizo didn't give the would-be killers time to move, cutting loose against them with the machine gun once more. The weapon's belt had been burned down to only a few rounds, but right now, there were only five men on three ATVs left to go.

"Grab a rifle," James said, throwing himself into one of the off-road vehicles left behind by the fleeing conspirators.

Encizo picked up one of their G-3s and a bandolier of magazines. "You're driving?"

"No, I thought I'd sit here and—" James began. Encizo cut him off by jumping onto the back of the ATV.

"Move it. Bolfrey's not getting away," Encizo snarled.

The four-wheel-drive quad-bike belched to life and shot out, tearing off after the enemy.

"Jack, you picked up Tanya and Ehan yet?" Encizo asked over his radio as the ATV zipped over the dunes. He held on to the frame of the vehicle with every fiber of muscle in his legs as James attempted his best David McCarter impersonation by moving at full speed and turning every raised undulation of the Syrian desert into a stunt ramp that hurled them into the air.

"Picking them up now. You need help?" Grimaldi asked.

"Only if you can toss me a parachute," Encizo answered.

"You want to catch up with these pricks, or do you want a comfortable ride?" James snapped.

"If I didn't know any better, I'd swear you two were married," Grimaldi remarked.

"You know, I hear jokes, but I don't see the escaping Fallen," Encizo snarled.

James gunned the throttle as they reached the top of a dune, and the quad-bike took to flight, arcing high enough for Encizo to catch sight of the fleeing enemy in the distance. The Cuban gritted his teeth in anticipation of their landing, but James had timed his leap perfectly so that forward momentum carried them down the opposite slope of a dune. "How about fast and gentle?"

Encizo didn't bother to fight off a laugh. "That'll do, Cal. That'll do."

"Looks like Bolfrey's by himself on one of the four-wheelers," James noted.

Gunfire crackled in the distance, and Encizo restrained the urge to bring his own rifle up. At the speeds that the off-road vehicles were moving, any attempt at accuracy at farther than arm's length would only be a waste of ammunition. It would take skill for James to get them that close, and Encizo was surprised to see his friend cutting down the distance with each launch into the night sky.

"Why didn't they take one of the fast ones?" Encizo asked.

"This isn't a fast one. My ass is skinny and you're short," James replied. "We're just a lighter strain on our ATV than they are on theirs. Throw in that we're airborne half the time, and we're making up their lead."

Encizo grimaced as the quad-bike jolted on the sand at the end of another of James's hops. "You have been hanging around with David far too much, Cal."

James swerved around a dune rather than go over it. They had gotten to within twenty yards of the enemy. The terrain was still too lumpy for Encizo to attempt any form of decent shot, but that worked in his favor, as well. The gunners on the back of the enemy escort quad-bikes were wasting ammo as they hammered off long bursts. Bullets zipped into the sand and cracked through the air around them. One of the enemy drivers opted to take a small hillock that was too steep and soft for his vehicle and its weight. His speed bled off, and James aimed their ATV toward them.

Encizo extended the G-3, not for use as a firearm, but stock first to catch the driver and his gunner with it. James took a more oblique approach to the slope, his diagonal path allowing him to maintain momentum as they climbed to intercept the enemy vehicle. Encizo's rifle crashed across the heads of both Fallen riders as the Phoenix ATV whipped past it. The quad-bike tumbled back down the dune as the two men were hurled into the sand. The conspirators wouldn't be getting up anytime soon, and James swung their ride down to the riderless vehicle.

"Happy birthday, Rafe," James said.

"You're a sweetheart," Encizo replied, transferring to the new vehicle. The driver had an MP-5 jammed into a scabbard between the handlebars. It made sense, especially since he'd need both hands to navigate this treacherous terrain. "Lets hope the others don't get a clue, drop their last gunner and throttle for the border."

James leaned back in his saddle and popped off a 40 mm grenade from his CQ-311. "Go for Bolfrey. He seems like his bike is too heavily loaded to reach optimal speed. I'll handle his security team."

"Just make sure I'm not the only one riding back to America," Encizo admonished, taking off across the dunes. A parachute flare, launched by James, sizzled in the night sky like a miniature sun. He could see Bolfrey and his quad-bike in the distance. The SAS washout had stopped the vehicle and was tearing saddlebags off it in an effort to lighten his load. Encizo knew he didn't have long, especially since the other ATV orbited the stopped off-roader, looking for enemies. James appeared over the top of a sand dune in a jump that carried him twenty feet into the air. The Chicagoan cut loose with a war whoop that drew the attention of the enemy riders, distracting them from Encizo as he gunned his own engine.

Bolfrey glanced up from his task of lightening his

quad-bike and saw the Cuban Phoenix Force veteran charging him down. He reached for the .357 Magnum on his hip and got it up in time to trigger a single shot. Fortunately for Encizo it was such a rushed quick draw that the bullet flew high and wide. As it was, Encizo ducked off his saddle, and his machine collided with Bolfrey's. Both vehicles tumbled wildly in a mangled wreckage of fused chassis and twisted suspension. Bolfrey snarled angrily and triggered a second powerful revolver bullet toward Encizo.

"You realize that these animals would kill you for being in this country to save their own citizens!" Bolfrey snapped.

Encizo rolled in the sand. He reached for his pistol, but it was gone, torn from his body somewhere in the mayhem of the past few minutes. Most likely, the holster had torn open when he leaped off of his ATV. A third .357 slug speared into the sand dangerously close to Encizo's head and he scrambled sideways. "That still doesn't mean you're free and clear to murder those people, Bolfrey!"

"Why not?" the Fallen leader asked. "The world didn't judge my country when we firebombed Dresden and murdered thousands of stinking Germans. They worked under Hitler. Is Damascus somehow more sacred because they're Islamic?"

Encizo pulled his Cold Steel Tanto from its sheath. Springing on his steel-coiled limbs, he dived aside as Bolfrey pumped out two more shots from the big revolver he carried. The trouble was, with the new breed of .357 Magnum revolvers, the British conspirator could have been one trigger pull from empty, or had as many as three more rounds to end the Cuban's counterterrorism career. Still, Encizo's load-bearing vest was armored and would provide some protection from a handgun, even one as powerful as the one that Bolfrey wielded, and he'd gotten within ten yards of the renegade SAS veteran.

"They're not combatants. You are. You're a sick, weak coward who can't do battle with someone who can actually defend himself," Encizo challenged, hoping to knock Bolfrey off his game. "Even now, all I've got is a knife and you're packing that pistol."

"Oh, so you want this to become some dramatic knife fight?" Bolfrey asked. He fired two more shots, one of them striking Encizo in the chest. The trauma plate stopped the powerful round cold, but it knocked the breath out of him.

Bolfrey snapped open the cylinder on his revolver, dumping seven empty casings out of it. He fumbled for a speed loader as he advanced toward the staggered Encizo. "Sorry. This isn't some action movie where the hero gives up his advantage to take the villain in a fair—"

Encizo gathered up the last of his strength and launched himself like a human missile at Bolfrey. "Shut the fuck up!"

Bolfrey tumbled backward as the knife in Encizo's fist plunged viciously through the man's armored vest. Muscles that had been developed by years of swimming and fighting oppression around the globe had given the razor-sharp blade enough force to cut through Kevlar, deflect off ceramic plate and spear deep through muscle and bone to the vulnerable organs underneath.

"You're no hero," Encizo snarled. "You're a sniveling weakling. You wanted to kill with nerve gas and radiation. You wanted to kill ordinary citizens, not soldiers. You are a failure, and you're dead now!"

Bolfrey clawed at Encizo's face as if to dispute the reports of his demise, but the Cuban, seized with wrath, wrenched his chisel-pointed knife through his opponent's rib cage. The six-inch cutting edge carved through Bolfrey's lungs and heart, ribs dislocating and popping loose from the breastbone as Encizo's anger-filled might worked the knife in his chest. Blood poured from Bolfrey's lips, and his eyes bulged in horror as he was eviscerated.

"So do the world a damn favor and lay down," Encizo growled.

Bolfrey's arms went limp, his fingers no longer gouging at Encizo's eyes and nose. The corpse slipped off of the blade and toppled back into the sand.

"Rafe!" James shouted.

Encizo looked up from the sack of worthless meat flopped on the ground in front of him. James rushed up to him, and took hold of the Cuban as his legs gave out. "Got to call the Farm. Bolfrey's done. Syria is safe."

"We'll do that, man," James said. "You're bleeding all over."

Encizo looked down and noticed that Bolfrey's .357 Magnum slug must have been more powerful than he thought. Blood glistened on his vest, burbling through. He could breathe, though now in the postadrenaline crash, his right lung ached like hell. "Bolfrey pissed me off."

James nodded. "I know, brother. Let me take care of that wound. Jack's on the way to pick us up."

Encizo smiled, sitting in the sand. "I'm going to need a vacation after this."

"We've all earned it," James agreed. He tore open Encizo's vest and shirt, and found the bullet just under the skin. A rib had broken to stop it from entering Encizo's vital organs, no doubt the cause of his friend's weakness. James plucked the bullet out and applied direct pressure to the wound.

A roar of wind announced Dragonslayer's arrival to take them back to friendly soil, where all of their lacerations and bruises could be tended to.

CHAPTER TWENTY-TWO

Jacob Morgan Stern looked at his lieutenants, Darrin Homm and Mischa Shenck. Homm, the talented hacker, had been in the military, and he looked ready for battle, holding on to a compact machine pistol, his face cast in a grim war mask. Shenck, the robot designer, was not so fearsome. His hand trembled as it gripped the Colt .45 auto that Stern had lent him.

"Mischa, I think you'd better go to ground," Stern offered.

"You mean run out and leave you two to fight to the end?" Shenck asked.

"You're not a soldier. You don't need to keep on fighting," Homm added. "We'll do what we can against the enemy."

"I'd consider that, but you intend to fight to the death," Shenck replied. "You raised me, Jacob. And, Darrin, you're the closest thing to a brother that a man could ever hope for. I can't abandon you. We're family."

"Damn it, Mischa," Stern complained.

"Enough. I'm staying and fighting with you. That's all!" Shenck said.

Stern nodded solemnly. "It's been an honor, Mischa, Darrin."

The two lieutenants gave him brave smiles.

"Same here, sir," they said in unison.

Stern smiled back. "All right, let's do some damage. Mischa, you hang back and cover us."

Stern threw his strength into pushing aside a joist that had fallen across the stairwell and blocked it after the infiltrator robots had detonated on the main floor. The basement ceiling hadn't caved in, but one of the serpentine robots must have been too close to the basement entrance, and when it had been destroyed, the power of its blast had been enough to weaken the stairwell's structural integrity.

After hauling the heavy beam out of the way, Stern unslung his M-16. He intended to throw as much firepower at the enemy, and while he'd have preferred something bigger and more powerful, the autorifle was still a handful of devastation. Homm, equipped with an MP-5, wasn't as well equipped, but the little buzz gun could fill the air with a lot of lead. Homm pushed ahead, reaching the top of the steps easily since the length of his weapon didn't snarl him in the stairwell.

"Darrin!" Stern urged.

"Move up," Homm called down. "I've got you cov… Wait."

Stern tensed, knowing that the hacker had spotted movement. He fought the urge to storm up the steps and back the Army vet's play when the MP-5 stuttered out its lethal message.

"He's down!" Homm said, vacating the doorway. "Move up!"

Stern looked back at Shenck. "Stay put."

"But…" Shenck began. A handgun barked up above, drawing Stern's attention away from the robot engineer.

"Stay down!" Stern snarled. He charged up the stairs, M-16 ready. He paused, using the top step as cover, scanning the shattered floor outside of the doorway.

"Darrin?" Stern called, hoping to flush out the man with the handgun. Whoever it was, he was disciplined enough not to indiscriminately fire and give away his position. Luckily, Homm was also savvy enough not to give himself away. A cartridge, stripped from Homm's submachine gun, bounced in front of him as a sign that he was all right. It was a waste of ammunition, but it was better than speaking and bringing down enemy fire.

What Stern couldn't figure out was that the enemy only had a handgun. From the racket and the damage caused by the raid, Stern would have expected a half-dozen men with assault rifles and grenade launchers in action. Maybe Shenck had done considerable damage to the attackers with the last of the infiltrator robots.

Stern got up and raced through the doorway. A quick pivot and he dived out of enemy sight behind an over-turned table. He caught a glimpse of Homm, who gestured toward a target. Stern peered around the upturned table and saw a figure in body armor and a helmet, both hands wrapped around a single handgun. Stern frowned at the sight. He looked back at Homm with a questioning glance. The words didn't need to be spoken.

"Anyone else?"

Homm shook his head. Stern smirked. He stood and fired the M-16 at the lone gunman, a stream of 5.56 mm rounds filling the air. The armored figure dived for cover, his pistol barking in counterattack.

"All by yourself?" Stern taunted, walking into the open. The .357 SIG rounds had missed him, and he felt pretty cocky now. "We take out the rest of your team?"

"Yeah," Schwarz answered grimly. "I'm taking it out of your skin."

"What makes a little ol' ant like you think he can move me?" Stern asked. "And where's the SWAT team backup?"

Schwarz retreated from sight. Stern sent a stream of autofire chasing after him.

"Oh, you come after us, but now you don't have the stomach for it?" Stern asked. Homm moved in the shadows, maneuvering himself to flank Schwarz. "What? That big blond ape you work with was too scared to come after us? Or did we blow him up real good?"

"You really want to talk about that now?" Schwarz asked, his voice echoing in the wrecked workshop. "You really want to remind me what you did to a good man?"

"Nailed him, huh?" Stern returned.

A pistol cracked loudly off to one side and Stern spun in time to see Homm jerk under bullet impacts. "Darrin!"

Stern shouldered his rifle and cut loose. His M-16 chattered, filling the area where the muzzle-flash had originated with a storm of 5.56 mm bullets. Electronics sparked and sputtered under the punishing hail, and in the end, Stern had wasted his ammunition on a boxy little remote observation drone with a 5.7 mm pistol attached to it. He rushed to Homm's side, but the man had bled out, his thighs and groin perforated by the 20-round magazine of the miniature robot.

"Damn you!" Stern cursed.

"You don't have room to talk," Schwarz growled from the shadows. "I don't care if that punk was your son. You murdered a good kid today. I'm just sorry he died so quick. He deserved to suffer. But you'll hurt enough for twenty of your punks."

Stern opened fire with the M-16 again, the magazine emptied in the space of a second. "Big talk, coward. Show yourself!"

"Stern! Look out!" Shenck cried from the stairwell. The robotic engineer lifted his Colt .45 and aimed it at the shadowy form that had flanked around behind Stern. The big mercenary whirled and threw his rifle like a spear, hoping to distract Schwarz from the young Russian. The weapon clattered against the wall, and Schwarz, with the swiftness of a snake, had wrapped his arm under Shenck's chin. The pistol clattered to the tile, and Shenck's face reddened as pressure was applied to his throat.

"Let him go!" Stern bellowed. "Let him go!"

Schwarz looked down at his prisoner. "Who is he? Your dad?"

"Fuck off," Shenck barked.

Stern raised his hand. "He's not a soldier! He's no one!"

"I built the robots, asshole," Shenck hissed to Schwarz. "If anyone died because of them, I'm fucking glad, you murd—"

Schwarz didn't let the engineer finish his taunt. With

a powerful shrug, he broke Shenck's neck, twisting his head until the bones between his shoulders and skull were ground into powder. Disdainfully, he tossed the corpse to the ground. Schwarz hadn't been expecting the kind of rage he inspired in Stern, but at this moment, he didn't care. One restless ghost had been avenged, and now he had the mastermind who wanted to irradiate nearly thirty million Americans.

Stern lunged, hands outstretched. There was no hint of martial arts discipline in the Second Sphere founder's movements. Only primal, animalistic fury, and against any other man, the sheer intimidation factor of a six-foot-two-inch muscular monster like himself would have caused a flinch. Schwarz whipped his arm out, grabbed Stern's wrist and, in a display of supreme leverage, hurled the big mercenary to the floor with the sickening crackle of twisted forearm bones. Red-eyed with fury, Stern rolled over, struggling to his feet.

Schwarz caught Stern in the jaw with a scything heel kick, the mandible bone shattering under the lashing impact. Stern spit teeth and blood, and staggered. The Able Team electronics genius was a master martial artist, his movements were fluid but scarcely predictable. Schwarz somersaulted forward and brought his heel down hard on Stern's shoulder in an ax kick that, assisted by the momentum of his entire body tumbling, broke the man's collarbone.

A ham-size fist slammed into Schwarz's gut, expelling the breath from his lungs. Schwarz grabbed the heavily muscled forearm that drove that blow, but Stern pulled harder, yanking Schwarz off the floor. Schwarz used Stern's lifting power and the strength of his own legs to turn the pull into a head-butt that smashed

Stern's nose into a flattened mess of blood and mucus. Stern wrenched his fist free and clocked Schwarz with his broken forearm. The mercenary was so furious that he ignored the agony caused to his shattered limb, and Schwarz was knocked to his knees.

Schwarz slipped his arms between Stern's knees, hooked them and stood, toppling the conspirator off of his feet. As Stern landed, Schwarz brought down his heel into the Second Sphere leader's crotch. The angle of the stomp meant that it not only crushed Stern's testicles into paste, but it broke his pelvis. Stern's legs flopped limply to the floor.

"He was my lover's son, you bastard!" Stern growled through a wave of nauseated agony. Schwarz could hear the bile bubbling in the man's throat as he bellowed. "You didn't have to kill him!"

"He's a murderer. So are you," Schwarz said, walking around Stern as he lay crippled and helpless on the floor.

"Fucker," Stern gurgled. "What gives you the right?"

Schwarz closed his eyes. He remembered the crime-scene photos of Mare Hirtenberg's murder. He thought of Terry Aspen, clutching a bomb to his side and running it away from Able Team. Two faces that he could concentrate on that made the evils of Stern's plot all too real.

"If you have to ask, I'll never be able to explain it," Schwarz said. He brought his foot down hard on Stern's throat, crushing his windpipe under his heel. "Just go to hell."

Stern's eyes bulged, blood pouring over his lips. Schwarz stood on the man's throat for five minutes, keeping the pressure on until every last twitch of the corpse faded away.

Surrounded by the dead, the Able Team electronics genius started up the stairs, alone and quiet.

Rosario Blancanales, his best friend in the world, needed medical attention. Millions saved, hundreds avenged, Schwarz had his priorities.

The guilty and and dead could rot for all he cared.

FROM BEHIND HIS DESK in the bunker, the President smiled weakly at Hal Brognola. The big Fed had just confirmed the resolution of the latest nuclear crisis.

"Barb received word that the mastermind of the attacks on Indian Point and Calvert Cliffs has been neutralized," Bronola said. "We won't be hearing from him or his associates anymore."

"Thanks, once again, to Able Team," the President said. "Any update on the situation in Syria?"

"Situation likewise resolved. Phoenix Force is safe and sound, and on its way home," Brognola answered.

The President's sigh of relief was audible. He knew how close the free world had come to a nuclear incident that would have involved millions of people, just as he knew that the safety and security of those very people had once again been protected by Stony Man Farm and its allies both at home and abroad.

Brognola closed his laptop and stood, ready to accompany the President out of the bunker. He could hardly wait for the fresh air and sunshine.